THE CHIEF'S MAIDEN

BORDER SERIES BOOK THREE

CECELIA MECCA

To Border Ambassadors and early Border Series readers. Thank you for helping make my dreams a reality.

1

Brockburg Castle, Scotland, 1271

"I refuse to kill an unarmed man."

Toren stood with such force, the heavy wooden chair toppled behind him. He began to pace between his guest and the fire, which had been stoked by a servant moments earlier.

"This is not my request," his companion said.

Toren stopped and stared at the man sitting casually in his hall. He'd sent everyone else away to allow for a private conversation. He'd known James Douglas for many years, well before the older man had been appointed Lord Warden of the Marches. His even tone was typical of the battle-hardened baron. Douglas's appointment had not come as a surprise to anyone. Fierce enough to confront the unruly border clans, he had earned his place and Toren's respect. Which was all the more reason the request surprised him.

"Bloody hell." Toren stood before the hearth looking at the elaborate carvings inscribed in the overmantel. It had likely been commissioned when the fireplace was moved from the center of the hall to its current location. Generations of Kerrs had lived here, eaten here, and fought to keep this hall their own. And he would be the one to destroy his clan.

If he dabbled in border politics a second time, Toren was sure it would be the end of them.

But if the request was not from Douglas, that could only mean one thing.

He turned and watched the man's face, torn between sinking back into the high-backed chair, though it needed to be set straight, and tossing it across the room. He did neither.

"One does not refuse an order from his king," Douglas reminded him.

"A royal decree," Toren spat. "Why me?" He continued without waiting for an answer, "I can understand his wish to dispense with the English warden. But Clan Kerr stands on its own. You know that. *He* knows that."

Every month, the criminals from either side of the border were brought to justice in a peaceable meeting overseen by the English and Scottish wardens. The thirty-year tradition allowed for some modicum of peace along the otherwise tumultuous border. But recent events had threatened that tradition.

"I suggested Graeme deSowlis." Douglas shifted in his chair. "Sit back down, Toren. You're towering above me."

At over six feet tall, Toren Kerr, Chief of Clan Kerr, was the largest of his brothers. Indeed, the largest man in his entire clan.

He righted the heavy chair as if it were a feather and sat on the ruby red cushion, grateful he'd ordered his people to leave the hall. It wouldn't do well for his demise to be witnessed.

"Mark me, Douglas. This will not go well. If I am successful," he amended, "*when* I am successful, it will cause as much turmoil as defeat would. How do you hope to attain peace by murdering the English warden? It may calm the clans, but what good will that do if the English refuse to treat?"

"We have no other choice. You saw what happened last month. Unrest continues to spread among the border clans. If the warden can be bought, so too can his sheriffs. And if they can't be trusted, the Day of Truce unravels."

And chaos along the border would once again prevail. Toren knew it well.

"The English king refuses to consider a replacement?"

Toren raked his hand through brown, shoulder-length hair, knowing where this discussion would lead. He began thinking ahead to the preparations that would need to be made for his absence.

"Aye. The king will not hear a bad word against the man and vehemently refuses to even entertain the idea of deposing him from his position. As long as he's alive, Stewart Hallington will remain English Lord Warden of the Middle Marches. A man increasingly distrusted, and one who will be the downfall of any modicum of peace along the border. Because if the truce falls apart here, the east and west marches will not be far behind."

"Dammit, Douglas. Why me?"

His friend was avoiding the question. Shifting in his seat, the Scottish warlord looked decidedly uncomfortable.

"Hallington is traveling to the tournament—"

"Ah, Christ, Douglas."

"The king understands this to be a perfect opportunity. He sends his most renowned warrior, an undefeated tournament champion who has never lost a battle. And he expressly forbade me to attend. But none would be suspicious of your late entry to the tourney."

The Tournament of the North. The only other time Scottish and English border families and clans came together under the flag of peace. Toren had not participated since the death of his father. As chief, he had no use for games and role-play. His family and clan needed him too much for him to participate in the decades-old tournament.

And why was Douglas forbidden to attend? As warden, he'd be expected there. Douglas was not telling him something. "You're full of shite, Douglas. He has plenty of other men, and why would the king—"

"There is the bit about Bristol. And deSowlis is a mite aggrieved with you as well."

"Ah, finally some truth, old man."

He held Douglas's gaze. The man's white, clipped beard and hair reminded him that his friend was getting along in age.

So the king was still upset.

Five years earlier, despite a tenuous peace along the border, the King of the Scots had ordered Toren to take Bristol Manor, an English demesne just south of the border. At the time, their countries had not agreed on the border line, and the king had assured him that pushing south would help him secure his own holding. In truth, Toren had been given no choice.

The invasion had been doomed from the start. The lord and his wife had been killed in the upheaval, and while other casualties had been kept to a minimum, holding such a property had proven difficult. It had been a never-ending battle to prove himself to the Englishmen and women who were accustomed to the leadership of the family he'd ousted.

Toren had resented Bristol for keeping him from his home. His clan.

And then there was the situation with Catrina.

The Waryns had eventually returned to claim their rightful property. Unfortunately, they'd also discovered Toren's injured sister along the creek and taken her captive. How Catrina had fallen from her horse unnoticed, Toren would never understand. But the tenure of her captivity in Bristol had been the longest of Toren's life.

To this day, he wasn't sure what was worse—that they had held her captive or that she had married the Englishman who'd taken her. She'd fallen in love with her captor.

An English lord.

"So he still blames me for Catrina breaking off the engagement to deSowlis?"

Douglas lifted a grey brow. "And mayhap losing Bristol."

Toren scowled at the man.

"His message was clear, Toren. Kill Hallington, and the unfortunate situation at Bristol will be forgotten."

"You mean the situation that I advised against? The one I attempted to dissuade our stubborn sovereign from in the first place?"

Douglas shrugged.

"He is the king."

And had been wrong before. But Toren left that bit unsaid. It would do him no good to disagree with the messenger. And though he had no great desire to enter into the tournament, and even less to kill a man who was not his enemy, Toren would do both. For his king. And for peace. With any luck, it would be accomplished quickly and a new English warden would be chosen. One less inclined to take bribes that allowed criminals their freedom.

And then he could return to Brockburg and concern himself with the only things that mattered to him. His family and his clan.

"It appears I have no choice, old man. But tell the king I will find a way to challenge the Englishman. I am no murderer."

Douglas smiled. "He expected nothing less. And he's confident the man will not be a problem much longer."

Toren nodded in agreement. Douglas was right on one account. He was undefeated in battle, in tournaments, and in single combat. The warden's days were coming to an end.

"Father, please," Juliette Hallington pleaded. "I've been looking forward to this for months. Surely the earl can wait until after the tournament?"

Why did she even bother?

Her father was as stubborn a man as any. And he disliked disagreements, especially when it was she or her mother—or any other female—who offered an opinion counter to his own. She loved her father dearly, but he would never be dissuaded. At least not by her.

Stewart Hallington, the second Baron Chauncy, took his duties as Lord Warden of the Middle Marches very seriously. Juliette hardly saw him, which was why she had looked forward to the tournament. Well, mayhap that was not the only reason, but it was the only reason he need know.

"Please," she tried again, lowering her voice. They sat on the raised dais for their midday meal, in full display of their entire household. Which was precisely why he had chosen this moment to tell her they would not be attending the Tournament of the North. Instead, she would rot inside this hall, only allowed to escape if she wed her father's choice of husband—another border lord who would order her about and insist it was unsafe to travel beyond their walls.

"Mayhap we can attend the opening ceremony, and you can—"

"*You* are still going."

"What did you say?

Juliette leaned forward to catch the slow smile on her mother's face. At two and forty, twice Juliette's age, Lady Elizabeth Hallington was still lovely. Mother and daughter shared the same long blonde hair, although Juliette's was streaked with light brown.

"Your mother has convinced me to allow you to travel with Lady Christina." Her father rushed to clarify, "And her husband, of course."

Juliette thought it best to appear calm at this bit of news. She would attend her first tournament with her very best friend! With Christina's lands bordering her own, they'd grown up more like sisters than friends. It had always been a welcome respite to the harsh and dangerous land in which they lived this far north. She tasted the soup in front of her as regally as a queen. Or what she imagined the queen would look like. Juliette had never met the queen, of course. Or anyone, for that matter. With the exception of Christina, the nuns, and the few noblewomen who traveled this far north, she'd met few ladies in her lifetime. Her life often felt too small compared to the many worlds she'd traveled in books.

She chanced a look at her father.

"I see you're no longer upset with me, dear?"

He was too observant by far. She set the metal spoon down very slowly, raising the corners of her mouth in a careful smile. Grateful, but not exuberant. Her father grew suspicious easily.

"I am disappointed, of course, that I will not spend time with the most magnificent, handsome, fierce—"

"That's enough," her father said without conviction.

"Strong knight and lord in all of Christendom," she finished.

And it was all true. Aside from his antiquated views on her marriage, her father was quite a man. Of course, many might argue that his views were as they should be, that he was right to want to arrange his daughter's marriage. That, indeed, the neighboring lord's son, Lord Wytham, was a splendid match.

But Juliette knew better. The abbess taught her as much. She wanted more from marriage than a man who readily admitted he looked forward to life with a subservient wife, one who had been appalled by her penchant for reading.

"Juliette," her mother interjected. "Your father knows you will be well taken care of. I only wish I could join you."

The reason her mother would need to stay behind—Juliette's carefree young brother—came bounding through the hall and only stopped running when he saw the baron's stern glance.

"Kelvin," Juliette admonished before her father could do so. "Walk, please."

Her brother immediately obeyed when he saw the quick wink she gave him. That should stave off the inevitable rebuke from their father.

At only nine, her brother was full of energy. It was hard to imagine someday he'd be fostered by their overlord, a great honor, and one her father continually fretted about since the boy had difficulty attending to any one task at a time. He was bright, though, and had inherited the comely Hallington looks. And was overly coddled by her mother.

She would miss her brother, but this was her only chance to fall in love before she was properly 'wedded and bedded,' as the sometimes saucy abbess liked to say.

Sister Heloise was quite unconventional in that way.

"Yes, Jules."

He skirted the dais to sit next to her. Before her father could begin the lecture on punctuality that was undoubtedly on his lips, Juliette addressed her mother.

"I wish you could come as well, Mother. But as you say, I will be well cared for by Lord Hedford and his wife."

Juliette clasped her hands together. Attending the tournament with her dearest friend would be the most exciting thing she'd ever done. Though she'd barely eaten a bite, she had no appetite to finish. This was going to be the greatest adventure of her life. And she was determined—absolutely determined—to find a husband of *her* choosing. One her father would approve of, certainly, but also one she could love.

She didn't care who thought her ideas silly. Juliette would not repeat her parents' mistake. She would *not* settle for a life of polite conversation. She would find a Lancelot at this tournament.

And she would even embrace her reputation as the "jewel of the north," which normally embarrassed her to no end. Indeed, she would take advantage of it to change her own fate.

Her father need not know that she would not be marrying Lord Wytham. First, she must find an alternative husband.

How difficult could that be at an event that was sure to attract the finest men in all of Northumbria and beyond?

2

Condren Castle, Northumbria 1271

"You know I can't allow you to roam the castle unescorted."

Juliette made what she imagined to be an unladylike sound at that absurd proclamation. Her friend was taking this chaperone assignment much too seriously.

"Christina, you are being—"

"Responsible."

Alone in Juliette's small private chamber, the women squared off, opposites in every way. Looking at the two, a stranger might notice their outward differences—Christina's dark hair to Juliette's lighter locks—but that was such a small thing, really. Where they differed the most was inside. While both knew their place in the world, only one of them accepted it, a fact that maddened Juliette even now.

"So you say." Juliette placed her delicate hands firmly on the hips of her new crimson gown. "But tell me, when exactly did being responsible work in your favor?"

Christina rolled her brown eyes and perched on the end of the beautifully appointed bed. The earl had clearly spared no expense in his furnishings. Of course, a man who could afford to sponsor such an elaborate affair as the Tournament of the North could purchase many such beds. The cost of the opening ceremony alone would bankrupt lesser lords. In the morn, the ten-day event would begin in earnest, and Juliette could only imagine the spectacle that was to come.

"My marriage, to start."

It was Juliette's turn to roll her eyes. "You were lucky, 'tis all. And you yourself have said you don't love the man. Yet. What kind of marriage is that, exactly?"

Rather than take offense, Christina laughed. Though only two years her senior, her friend sometimes acted as though she were the same age as Juliette's mother. No wonder her father hadn't balked at the prospect of Christina and her husband serving as her chaperones. On the eve of their departure to Condren Castle, Juliette's handmaiden had taken ill. Her mother had thought to send her own maid, but Juliette had insisted there was no need. That she was properly chaperoned.

It would seem her assessment had been sadly accurate.

"A fine one, to be sure."

Juliette rushed over to her friend, beset by guilt, and took both of Christina's hands in her own. "I meant nothing more than—"

"I know what you meant. But I am truly happy with Matthew. He's kind and treats me well. And with time—"

"You may learn to love each other."

It was a refrain she knew well. One her mother reiterated every time the subject of her marriage arose. Noblewomen didn't marry for love. Marriages were made for political gain. And if she were lucky, she would learn to love her husband.

If she were unlucky, he would mistreat her, and she would have no recourse. And while her father thought Wytham to be right and honorable, she disliked the look in his eyes. The man made her wary.

Of course, finding love had not happened for her parents. It also did not seem to have happened for the few married nobles who came to visit at Chauncy Castle. Or, as yet, with Christina, though she and her husband seemed to rather enjoy each other considering it was an arranged marriage.

But would *she* be the lucky one?

It was a chance she wasn't willing to take.

"My dear Christina, the fairest lady in all of England—"

"Go," Christina said with a sigh. "But as you say, only where others are present. Please return in time to prepare for the evening meal."

That would be plenty of opportunity to explore.

"Thank you. I will, you have my word. Though the castle is brimming with people, I'm sure the earl would not house unsavory characters."

"Which shows how little you know about the ways of men, Juliette."

"So you've told me, now that you are a maid no longer."

Christina's head whipped to the door as if she expected her husband to materialize any moment. "Shhhh."

She couldn't help but have a bit of fun at her friend's expense. "And to think, all those times we wondered if the servants' wagging tongues were exaggerated. Now we know the truth. That the marriage bed—"

"Juliette!"

"You really are too proper. If you didn't want me to know—"

As if on cue, a knock at the door startled them both. They stared at each other wide-eyed.

"Yes?" Juliette creaked.

"Is my wife inside, my lady?" a male voice asked.

Juliette tried to control the flush creeping onto her cheeks as she ran to the large oak door and tugged it open. It was easy to be bold with Christina, less so with her husband.

"Lord Hedford," she exclaimed. At thirty and one, the dark-haired man only had a few streaks of gray at his temples. He was good-looking in a very proper, 'I'm an important knight of the realm' sort of way.

His raised eyebrows, normally quite straight, told Juliette she had not been as successful in controlling her pink cheeks as she'd hoped.

Peering around her to search for his wife, Lord Hedford smiled ever so slightly. "I thought to find you here. Your maid is searching for you. Shall I send her?"

"Tis not necessary, my lord." Christina took her husband's arm, and they made their way into the stone-lined corridor.

The lack of windows in this part of the castle gave no clue as to the time of day, though she knew it was late in the afternoon.

"Do get some rest, Juliette. My lord has warned me the meal will be overly long with so many in attendance."

Juliette bowed her head as demurely as an attendant addressing her queen.

"I shall," she responded as the couple walked out of sight.

But first, she would take in the sights and sounds of one of the greatest castles in England on the eve of the grandest event of the year.

She waited a few moments, smoothed her hair as best she could with her hands, and pinched her cheeks as her maid had done so many times. Juliette had lost count of the potential suitors who'd traveled to Chauncy Manor attempting to claim her hand in marriage—and also of the number of times her cheeks had endured her maid's pinches. Still, she was desperate enough to willingly subject herself to such mistreatment now.

Her father would be put off no longer. Which was exactly why she could not spare a moment idly waiting for her fate to be sealed. Mayhap she should not have put off so many suitors, forcing her father to choose one she cared for the least. But she'd felt nothing for any of them, and she wanted more than suitability. Juliette would find an honorable and trustworthy man who loved her above all else.

And if she did *not*, Juliette had begun to form a plan. One that would save her from Lord Wytham and a life of complacency. She would simply join Sister Heloise in the convent. Her father would have no way of stopping her after she'd taken the vows.

Juliette closed the door behind her and made her way toward the great hall.

"'Tis thievery!" Toren cried when the blacksmith's apprentice named his inflated price.

"You want yer shoe repaired or nay?" The boy yelled over the striker's constant hammering. "Go see the village smithy if you prefer."

Toren had already done so. That man had named an even more exorbitant fee, which was precisely why he'd made the visit to Condren's inner bailey. The space was brimming with knights and their servants, and lord and ladies from across the land—exactly the sort of crush he would have typically avoided. Especially at an English holding. But then, a visit to the castle gave him the perfect excuse to look for Hallington.

Most Scots, with the exception of a few nobles, avoided any public spaces other than the lists during this particular tournament, even though all were invited to attend meals and celebrations. They were there to fight, not to dance and dine, unlike most of these English fops.

The Tournament of the North limited the field to one hundred men on each side, chosen by their respective wardens. Most were personally invited, including the Waryn men, who thankfully would not be attending. A small number of men vied for a limited number of spots granted "super faciem," but those knight errants were not invited into the castle until after they were formally accepted.

"Fine." Toren shoved coins into the boy's hand. No point in

attempting to haggle with the boy's master. The blacksmith, his face black from coal soot, had never once acknowledged him.

"Come back in the morn," the lad said. "It'll be waitin' on you then." With that, he quickly looked away, as if not wanting to meet the gaze of the man he'd cheated. Or mayhap he simply didn't wish to lock eyes with a Scot.

"Damn Englishmen," he muttered, turning away from the forge.

A woman slammed into him so hard, Toren had to step back to regain his footing. "What in the devil—"

"Oh! My apologies—"

He steadied the lass and disengaged himself from her. And thank St. Andrew she gave him no time to respond—he'd need a moment before he could form words again. By God, she was lovely.

"Please—" she began, but her missive was abruptly cut off.

"My lady, there you are!" A young knight, no older than twenty and one, bounded toward them.

Toren looked back and forth between pursuer and pursued, reading the situation at a glance. Without speaking, he took her arm and placed it in the crook of his own.

The boy stopped and stared. His surcoat proclaimed him of the earl's household, so Toren held back the disparagement on his tongue.

"I'm grateful for your service to my lady." He inclined his head ever so slightly. "Toren Kerr, Chief Kerr of Brockburg."

Thankfully, it took the boy but a moment before he began to back away. "You are the Kerr."

Toren simply nodded.

"The. . . the. . . no offense. I meant no offense." And with that, the boy turned and ran away.

"The English," Toren muttered for the second time that day, shaking his head.

"Begging your pardon," the lady pulled her arm away and raised her chin.

A perfectly formed one to match every other perfectly formed feature on her face. She was small but well proportioned, with long blonde hair that fell in waves around her shoulders, a pert nose, and light blue eyes

A lady? Her speech and dress hinted as much, but most of the English women he knew were not inclined to run around unescorted, fleeing from amorous young knights.

"I'm sorry to have disturbed you." She turned to leave.

"Wait," Toren stopped her. Unaccountably, he wanted to know more.

"What is your name? Why were you running from that boy?"

"Boy?" The sound she made was anything but ladylike. Her dress and behavior were at odds. Perhaps she'd stolen the bright crimson gown? Silver thread decorated both the loose sleeves and the neckline, which plunged into an ample bosom for a woman her size.

His damsel in distress stared back at him, brown arched eyebrows framing a defiant expression that was entirely unexpected.

Frankly, she should be afraid of him.

Most women were. Men too, on account of his size.

"Were you not running from him?"

She looked around the courtyard as if ensuring they wouldn't be overheard. Not likely. Wagons creaked along the well-worn path to and from the castle, and children shouted as they ran through a courtyard as expansive as Brockburg's entire village. The king of England granted his lords only five licenses to hold large tournaments such as this one, and Condren Castle had been chosen for the tournament for a reason. The castle and its grounds were as grand as any in this godforsaken country.

"Aye, but he was no boy," she said, her voice deep and melodic.

"His suggestion was highly improper. One of a man, and a dangerous one at that."

Toren leaned against the stone wall of the forge, studying her as he listened to the sounds of metal on metal drifting out from the windows.

"What's your name?"

"You're Scottish." She avoided his question and tossed out the accusation as if it were an epithet.

"You're English." He tried to keep his voice neutral, remembering belatedly he'd cursed her countrymen at least twice within her hearing.

"Well, at least I don't judge a person by his loyalty to the wrong king."

He flattened his lips, fighting the impulse to smile. It was the kind of comment his sister would have made.

"I don't judge you, my lady."

"I heard what you said. 'Tis clear you have no love for my countrymen." She crossed her arms and waited for his answer.

"Your words and actions contradict each other. You accuse me of being Scottish but then preach tolerance. Which is it?"

Her narrowed eyes told him she would not back down so easily. "'Twas not an accusation, but a fact. You'll meet none more tolerant of your people than my family. In fact—"

She stopped.

"In fact?" he prodded.

Something had caught her attention near the entrance to the old wooden tower that had once likely served as Condren's main keep.

"Good day to you."

With that, she abruptly walked away.

So be it.

There was only one English who interested him, and it was time for Toren to find the man and form a plan. For the sooner he did that, the sooner he could return home to his clan.

3

Juliette ran to the other side of the building, darting out of sight of Christina's watchful eyes. Never before had she felt so alive, or so terrified. And not from the unwanted attentions of the overly amorous young knight who'd followed her from the hall.

The Scotsman was huge!

Bigger than anyone she knew, nearly a head taller than her father, who was not a small man. Running into him had been akin to slamming into the side of a stone wall, and she'd been fleeing from her pursuer at full tilt. Though she'd wanted to scream when the young man had started pursuing her from the castle, Juliette had made a vow to Christina en route to Condren.

She'd promised to stay out of trouble.

She would be like Pope Joan, Juliette had assured her friend—so inconspicuous that some might even question her existence. A feat that would be a tad easier when she was *not* being chased by a strange man.

And then the Scots chief had saved her.

She'd known the Scots would be in attendance, of course, since the purpose of the tournament was akin to the Day of Truce

—a temporary halt to hostilities. Although some past tournaments, not unlike the truce days her father mitigated, did end in bloodshed. But she hadn't expected to land in the arms of a Scotsman on her first day here.

An extremely attractive Scotsman. With deep brown hair that fell to his shoulders and a slightly square jaw, he could have passed for an Englishman until he spoke. Though no coat of arms identified him, the quality of his clothing, the deep blue of his surcoat, identified him as noble.

And yet, there was an unfamiliar wildness to the man. His words were not as measured as the language used by the lords who had come to call on her. Juliette's first instinct had been to walk away—he was too big, too much of a presence not to intimidate—but he'd fascinated her enough to keep her feet rooted to the ground for their brief conversation.

"There you are!"

Juliette turned to find Christina rushing toward her.

"I thought you were exploring the keep?" Christina held out her arm and Juliette took it, grateful for the familiar company.

Ignoring the question, she asked one of her own. "I don't believe your husband would have let you out of his sight. Where is your Galahad?"

They walked arm in arm toward the stairs that led to Condren's great keep, skirting errant geese and puddles of mud.

"There." Christina nodded ahead, and Juliette spotted Lord Hedford speaking with another man.

"I am in trouble then?" She was not overly concerned. She had no doubt that her friend had given Lord Hedford a good explanation for her absence.

Christina's sharp glance was mitigated by the dimples that appeared at the corners of her turned-up mouth. "Nay, I'll explain later." She lowered her voice. "I saw you talking to a man?"

Juliette laughed at her friend's hushed tone. "Aye, you did."

"Well?"

"He's a Scotsman." And one not too keen on the English—he'd made that much clear. Juliette had no real opinion of his countrymen. She knew many of her own people blamed them for the frequent unrest at the border, but her father often cautioned that the men on both sides were equally at fault.

Christina strained her neck as if looking for the man who was nowhere to be seen.

"What did he say to you?"

"He asked my name, which I declined to mention. And made his dislike of our countrymen clear."

They'd reached Lord Hedford, whose nod confirmed that her friend had indeed excused her solitary jaunt. *Bless her.* Even though Christina did not fully agree with her designs, she was a good enough friend to help her.

Continuing past the guards, they walked through the massive entrance and climbed the steps that led to the great hall and their own quarters.

Juliette stopped and looked at her friend, allowing Hedford ahead of them.

"What have you been saying to me about this tournament? About my idea of finding a husband here?" This was not the place for such a conversation, but Juliette had to make her friend understand fully. She needed her.

Christina moved against the side of the wall as two servants scurried past them up the narrow, winding staircase. "That Sister Heloise should not have allowed you to read so many books that filled your head with flights of fancy."

Indeed, Christina was not the only person miffed at Juliette's tutor. While there was no denying Sister Heloise's success in teaching Juliette how to read and write in three languages, she'd also encouraged her to pursue some more questionable studies. The baron had threatened to forbid Juliette from returning to the convent if she wouldn't stop reading the books given to her by her tutor.

"Which is extremely unfair. Orpheus is a beautiful story of love—"

"And Eurydice is a nymph. You, my dear Juliette, are not."

She ignored that.

"Let me see if I can remember your words correctly," Juliette continued as if Christina had not spoken. "You said one does not simply fall in love at command. That there's a greater likelihood the king himself will attend this tournament than that I'll meet a man, fall in love, and gain my father's acceptance of him."

Again they stepped aside as two armored knights made their way down the stairs.

"Come, we can't stand—"

"Wait," Juliette whispered. "This is important."

She looked into her friend's eyes, imploring her to understand.

"I know you think me silly."

"I do not—"

"Nay, 'tis fine. *Everyone* thinks me silly. Even Sister, who allows me to read every book in their library for the sake of learning, thinks me silly. And mayhap you are all right. I've not explored the world, or even my own country. I've never even kissed a man, so what do I know about love?"

She lowered her voice.

"But what choice do I have, Christina? Accept the inevitable? I cannot. I will not endure a life of loneliness, like my mother."

At least her friend could not argue there. Although Juliette's mother was kind and gentle, and she seemed at peace with her life, no one could accuse her of being in love with Juliette's father. Theirs was an alliance, and anyone who spent any time with the couple knew it well.

"My father has already threatened to invite Lord Wytham to Chauncy Manor after this tournament. If I must choose a life married to that cold fish or a solitary one in the convent, I promise it will not be a difficult decision."

"Juliette, you can't be serious."

She had never been more so in her life.

Christina frowned. But at least she finally understood how important this week was for Juliette.

"And you're saying that Scotsman—"

"Heavens, no. That man is a brute." Her stomach lurched at the thought of marrying such a man. Granted, he was extremely good-looking. And his voice. . .

"So," Christina conceded. "We have ten days to find you a husband."

She hugged her friend, grateful to have an ally—and even more grateful that Christina would do something counter to her nature to help her.

"Which is why I can't spare a moment. Come, let's prepare for the meal."

It had been quite a day so far and had not started very well, but Juliette knew in her heart it would only get better.

Toren's day could not have been worse.

After arriving at Condren and setting up his tent, he'd spent longer than anticipated finding a squire to hire for the tournament. Though not armored as heavily as his English counterparts, he would still need assistance.

No one other than Douglas and his brothers knew of this mission, and he had ordered Alex and Reid to remain behind at Brockburg, not wanting to risk their safety should his intentions be discovered. He had the Gods to thank that his sister was safely installed with her new husband, her English husband. If Catrina had known he was here, and why, the devil himself would shy from her wrath.

Having finally secured the assistance he needed, both in the form of a squire and the necessary repairs to his horse's shoe, Toren's next task had been to seek out Hallington. The English warden would not miss this event, which was so thoroughly tied in to his position as warden. After all, the Tournament of the North had been devised to celebrate the success of more than thirty years of monthly truce days.

Successful until recently, that was.

But nowhere could he find the baron's blue and black banner with its distinctive fire-breathing black stag. Washing now in the stream that ran behind the field of tents marking the Scottish encampment, Toren resigned himself to the inevitable: he would need to attend the nightly celebrations to learn where Hallington was. . . and when he was coming.

Returning to his tent, more modest than most but with enough room to fully stand, Toren grabbed his only surcoat, fitted it atop his fresh tunic, and began to harness his sword. He dreaded attending the festivities, something he'd hoped to avoid. He had already begun to regret his stubborn decision not to take one of his men with him, a feeling that pressed in on him more and more as he left his tent and made his way toward the great keep. This experience would have been far more bearable with their company.

"You're a damn fool," Alex had admonished in response to his insistence on attending the tournament alone. "There are more than a dozen men I'd trust with the knowledge. And yet you risk yourself by telling no one aside from us."

"Risk myself? Dear brother," he'd said, "I risk even more if the wrong person learns of this plan."

"Then take one of us. At my age, you had already been chief of Clan Kerr for six years. I am a child no longer, Toren. And I'm capable of keeping Brockburg secured in your absence. Take Reid with you."

His brother's request hadn't failed to move him, but he'd denied it. Maybe even shouted a bit—Toren had always found it difficult to rein in his temper when provoked. They had lost their father and mother in the same year. If this mission was unsuccessful, his purpose discovered, he didn't want his siblings to have to endure a dual loss a second time.

Keeping his family safe was the only thing that truly mattered.

But it was also damned inconvenient.

He stopped, not realizing his thoughts had carried him so far, and stared at the sight in front of him. There was no denying Condren Castle, built on a great hill, was mighty impressive. A sprawling estate, the seat of the Earl of Condren, it was known in Scotland as "the gateway to the south." With the exception of Kenshire Castle, which was now held by the late Earl of Kenshire's daughter and her husband—brother to Toren's new brother-in-law—Condren was grander than any other Northumbrian holding.

Torches flickered proudly from every tower, lighting the night sky in a spectacular display of opulence. The drawbridge had been lowered in welcome.

Leave it to the English.

Normally, the castle grounds would have been quiet by this time of day, but this was no ordinary night. It was the eve before the twenty-second Tournament of the North, and there were people everywhere.

Had Toren been back home, in his own hall, surrounded by his clansmen, he would have been content to join in the celebration. Here, he was an outsider, much like he'd felt during his forced occupation of Bristol. A rare Scotsman in a sea of English.

He sat at the trestle table closest to the door and looked around.

The earl sat with his wife and daughter, along with their honored guests, on a raised dais at the back of the hall. Few keeps could accommodate such a large number of guests—more than three hundred, most likely. Servants made their way to each table, filling mugs and scurrying to and from the buffet tables scattered around the sides of the room. Back home, feasts were not uncommon, but he'd never attended one quite so large. The staff's efficiency was impressive.

And then he saw her.

She still wore the same crimson gown, which was quite unusual—most ladies made a point of changing for dinner. But her hair had been arranged atop her head, and a ruby necklace now adorned her neck. He watched as she stood from the table and made her way to the edge of the hall. Alone. *That* was even more unusual, particularly after her brush with the lascivious knight earlier.

Toren stood, intending to follow her, when a hand grabbed at his tunic.

"Leavin' so soon?"

He'd nearly reached for his sword on instinct. Luckily he stayed his hand. The man who had clearly been drinking for some time had already released his sleeve.

Every man at the table had stopped talking to witness the exchange. Most appeared his age, but two were young enough to be squires. All English.

Not wanting to draw any more attention, he played a part that would not cause suspicion, slipping easily into an accent that would avoid any questions.

"What use do I have of food when the comely wench I'm keen to bed just made herself available?"

Toren did not give the man a chance to respond. With a tight smile to his dinner companions, he strode through the festivities. Ladies' jewels sparkled and serving wenches' hips swayed to the music floating in the air. The bright colors of the troubadours' costumes competed with a dazzling display of wealth, but the fabrics became richer and the jewels brighter as he ventured toward the back of the hall. As chief of his clan, by rights he could have sat much closer to the hosts, but he'd preferred to avoid notice at the back of the great room.

As he passed through the hall, he looked for Hallington. There was no sign of him.

Or the girl.

He'd assessed the buildings earlier that day while wandering the grounds. If he was correct, this particular passage led to the East Tower. Why? It appeared he would have a chance to ask her. She must have gone to the privy or some such, because she was already coming back toward him.

"Oh!"

She stopped in her tracks, eyes wide.

"My lady," he said, taking in the sight before him.

Torches lit the passageway, casting a glow that made the rubies on her neck sparkle. But it was the smooth, creamy skin beneath that held Toren's attention. And the swell of a bosom that he itched to touch.

The woman was perfection. Head held high, she was clearly every inch a noble. How could he have questioned as much earlier?

"I saw you leaving."

What else could he say? That he had not been able to stop thinking of her all day? That he'd worried for her safety enough to leave his meal? The whole thing was absurd. He didn't even know her name.

"I—"

She stopped.

His mysterious lady was hiding something.

"Where is your escort? What is your name?"

To question her thus was impolite, but Toren didn't care about decorum. He wanted to know who she was. What she was doing.

"Will you kiss me?" she asked, her voice husky.

It was the most outrageous, unexpected thing she could possibly have said.

So a lady, aye, but not a maid. And yet. . . she looked too young to be a widow. Could he have misheard the question?

"I asked if you will kiss me," she repeated, her voice more hesitant this time.

Her escort, whomever he or she was, would surely question her whereabouts if they weren't doing so already. But he would accept her offer. He'd be a fool to deny her the very thing he wanted.

Grabbing her hand, Toren pulled the most unusual—and alluring—woman he'd ever met in the direction from which she'd come. If his assessment was correct, there was a small bastion nearby.

There.

He led her to the stairwell that opened to the outside. The dark sky above them was punctuated with stars in every direction. A warm summer night. The only noise was a distant murmur from the hall filled with music and guests. Much more pleasant, to his mind, than being down below. In front of them was a short wall, and a taller semicircle of exposed steps loomed behind them, which they could climb to a parapet that would offer a better view of the bailey below. But that view came at the cost of exposure, which would not be welcome at this particular moment.

Her hand was small. Soft. Perfectly fitted to his own.

He spun the Englishwoman around to face him. She looked up at him with eyes so wide he nearly changed his mind. What game did she play?

"Will you be gentle, please? This is my very first time."

Like hell it was. No gentle miss would have made such an offer to a stranger.

"Aye, I will be gentle."

Toren pulled her toward him, savoring her sweet scent. Roses. She smelled like roses. Usually, he did not have much time for gentle things. Being chief was both a blessing and a curse—he did not lack for female company, but usually it was only inside his bedchamber. This woman was. . . different.

His arm muscles flinched as she placed her hands on his arms. Tentative. Unsure.

"Do I keep my eyes open?" she asked.

Damn, was she serious? Had she truly never been kissed? It made no sense. Toren's instincts had saved his life on more than one occasion, but they failed him now, for he knew not what to think.

Though it was dark, a nearby torch lit her face enough for him to get a good view of every perfect feature. Lips waiting to be kissed. Long lashes that blinked now, revealing her nervousness. The lass should be nervous. She stood in relative seclusion with a stranger, one who could easily do her harm.

He would not, of course. But someone must counsel her on the ways of men, as she either was truly so innocent that she didn't recognize the dangers, or so wily she knew them well but did not care. And this after she found herself in need of rescue from an ardent suitor just earlier in the day.

But *that* lesson would not be from him. Toren had other plans.

"Nay, close your eyes."

Sure enough, she listened.

Blood rushed to every part of his body.

He lowered his head to hers and placed the softest of kisses on her lips. Roses and warmth assaulted him. His body told him to crush her against his chest, press her to the evidence of his need, open her mouth with his own, and show her what a proper kiss felt like. But he could not. Would not. Because one thing was abundantly clear.

She was an innocent.

And Toren did not take advantage of young virgins.

He tore himself away from her and took a deep breath.

Her eyes fluttered open. Her lips turned up in a sensual smile, or at least one that appeared sensual to him. A hint of what lay underneath the brazen but innocent exterior.

"Thank you."

He was at a loss for words.

"I really must be going. My friend will be looking for me."

"Your friend? Who is your chaperone? What is your name? And what the hell are you doing out here with a strange man who could have easily taken advantage of you?"

He hadn't meant to raise his voice, but bloody hell, someone needed to talk sense into her—even if it was him.

Frowning, she turned and walked away.

Damned if that wasn't the strangest encounter he'd ever had. This one woman kept surprising him and catching him off guard, as if he were a laddie and not a grown man.

In a daze, Toren walked up the stone stairs that led to the top of the bastion. As he'd suspected, it afforded him a perfect view of the inner courtyard. He found himself staring at the forge, where he had met the maiden earlier that day. Thinking about how startled she'd been at his rescue. The alarm with which she'd glanced up at her pursuer.

When he'd watched her walk into the corridor alone, the urge to protect her had been instantaneous. He'd gotten to his feet without really thinking about it. Then she'd asked him that question, and he hadn't had time to think about that either. . .

And now he was left with more questions, ones he should not care to have answered.

But he did.

Toren shook his head and descended the steps. He was finished holding court with the enemy for the evening. Tomorrow was soon enough to find the man he came here for. Soon enough to learn the identity of his hesitant lass.

4

"I still can't believe how incredibly foolish you were," Christina whispered.

Juliette squinted. The sun beamed down on them in the wooden galleries. As the warden's daughter, she had been invited to sit with the earl's family, but she'd wanted to stay with Christina. It was a decision she was questioning at the moment.

"I suppose you—"

"Suppose?" her friend shrieked.

Christina's husband sat on her other side, and he glanced over in surprise. Juliette ignored them both, pretending to listen to the proceedings below as heralds shouted rules that everyone knew, and few followed, to the two hundred knights and many spectators.

She had never seen anything like it.

Juliette had been allowed to attend one mock tournament years ago, before they were as heavily regulated. But that event could not be compared with this grand affair. Even mass that morn had been an event to remember. Lords, ladies, knights, and their squires and grooms had stood outside Condren's chapel with heads bowed as the priest blessed all in attendance. Though the church officially forbade these events, no priest would pass up the opportunity to bless so many potentially damned souls.

She'd needed to tell someone what had happened on her way back from the privy last night, so she'd spilled the truth as soon as she and Christina were alone together. It was an openness she'd had reason to regret. Christina would not stop lecturing her about the recklessness that could have seen her "raped or killed." Granted, it *had* been foolish. Not to mention quite brazen.

Juliette had tried to explain her reasoning. Most ladies her age had stolen kisses before, and since she had never done so, how was she supposed to distinguish between a normal kiss and true love's kiss?

And for some inexplicable reason, she trusted the Scot. Knew he would not harm her. When the request had flown from her lips, they had both been taken aback—she hadn't intended to make such a request.

For the briefest moment, Juliette had panicked. What madness had made her say those words? But then he led her out onto the bastion and leaned down to kiss her, and Juliette found she was quite glad for her temporary lapse in judgment. It was the most glorious feeling in the world. For such a large man, he was surprisingly gentle. His lips were warm and soft, although she had expected it to last a bit longer...

In truth, she'd *wanted* it to last longer.

"Christina, look!" She attempted to avoid more of her friend's whispered lecture by pointing out that the first match was about to begin.

After days of jousts, one man would be deemed the individual champion while the melee on the final day would determine which country was this year's winner, the "armed defenders of Scotland or England's honor." Last night, all the guests had been whispering about Sir Bryce Waryn. Apparently he had been proclaimed jousting champion so many years in a row that there had been talk of banning him from the event. Sir Bryce would not be in attendance this year—rumor had it that his hands were full with a new wife and his reclaimed lands—and without him present, it was an open playing field.

She said as much to Christina, hoping it would be enough of a prompt to end this talk about the kiss.

"Aye, 'tis said that only the youngest Waryn brother still competes in the tournaments. But apparently he is building quite a reputation for himself in the south. One to rival his elder brothers. I'm unsure if he is in attendance."

"Where do you get your information?" Juliette was glad her friend was more exposed to the outside world, but it was another poignant reminder of just how sheltered she was at Chauncy Manor.

Christina tilted her head to the side. "Surely you've heard whispers of Neill Waryn. They say the youngest Waryn hasn't lost a single match yet."

"Nay, I hear nothing of importance at Chauncy."

Her friend offered a conciliatory glance before turning her attention to the field.

As the herald introduced each knight by their coats of arms, Juliette searched the field below. Spectators sat on the ground surrounding the wooden fence, marking the lists as the participants walked the length of the area, each flanked by his horse and squire. Or squires, in some cases, though a recent law forbade any knight from bringing more than three.

Christina adjusted her pale yellow gown, a pretty contrast to Juliette's own deep blue one, and pointed to the men still waiting to be announced. "If you're looking for the Waryn brothers, perhaps you should turn your attention toward the English knights."

A flush crept up Juliette's cheeks. She had indeed been watching the Scots. They were being introduced first as a courtesy from the host country. Great care was taken to ensure the Tournament of the North was a peaceful event. And while injuries and sometimes deaths could not be avoided, most who were present wanted a peaceful gathering between the two countries. For ten days, at least.

"I'm curious is all."

"Curious. Is that why you're leaning so far forward Lady Hemsworth can feel your breath on her neck?"

Juliette laughed, eliciting a glance from Lord Hedford.

"I'm pleased you ladies are enjoying yourselves," he said. Though he seemed sincere, Juliette was nevertheless suspicious. He was too kind. Too thoughtful. No man was so perfect. She overheard him silence his squire on their journey to Condren, and though she attempted to listen to more of the conversation, only the word "France" had been discernible.

Or perhaps. . . could he truly be that nice? "Your wife has always had the ability to make me laugh," she responded. "She's the kindest and most amusing woman of my acquaintance. And she has a beautiful singing voice too."

Christina reached over to squeeze her hand.

"What are you doing?" Her voice was low but insistent.

"Ensuring your husband knows what a fine woman you are."

Hedford looked fondly at his wife. "Aye, I'm learning as much and shall not disagree with you, Lady Juliette."

Christina's cheeks colored, and she squeezed Juliette's hand again before releasing it.

As if she had no control over them, Juliette's eyes shifted back to the field. Every color one could imagine was on display. She jumped as the horn sounded again, louder than it had been for the previous contestants.

There he was.

He was taller than every other man. Held his head higher. Was easily the most handsome.

"That's him, is it not?"

Juliette tried to sound unconcerned. "Him?"

Christina tsked as the man's name was announced.

"You said he was a brute," her friend reminded her in an undertone.

Juliette shrugged. "Mayhap I was quick to judge."

As the Chief of Clan Kerr of Brockburg walked across the lists, he looked up at the galleries. Could he be looking for her? She snapped her head away.

"Is he looking here?" she whispered to Christina.

"For heaven's sake, see for yourself."

Juliette forced herself to turn back toward him. The Scot had circled around to join his countrymen behind the galleries where Juliette and the others sat. But before he disappeared from view, he stopped. . .

And looked right at her.

Juliette's heart pounded as their gazes met and held. A small squire accompanied him, she noticed, and her Scot, the chief, held the reins of a black charger that resembled the stag on his coat of arms. The silver lining of his surcoat glistened in the sunlight, but otherwise there was no pageantry, no excess about him. Just pure, unbridled. . . manhood.

He finally looked away.

"Oh my. Juliette, did you—"

"Aye."

She attempted to steady her breathing. What was happening to her? Juliette felt as if she'd run across the lists herself, only she had not moved at all. Shock wore off as reality set in.

"My father will not like this."

"You can't be thinking—"

"In fact, he will likely forbid it."

"Juliette, please tell me—"

"And I'm not even sure such a man is capable of falling in love."

Christina grabbed her hand.

"Aren't you being hasty, my dear? 'Tis only the first day of the tourney. Look. . . there are so many handsome, well-placed

Englishmen in attendance, and every unmarried man here has made their interest in you known. Why, even this morn Lord—"

"And I intend to find out."

"Find out what?"

Juliette had turned to look at her dear friend, so she saw Christina's face crease into a frown the moment she interpreted her meaning.

"Juliette, no."

She smiled in response.

Toren had not competed in a tournament since his father died. His brother Alex had been grievously injured in the melee during the last one he'd entered. It had served as a lesson: why risk his life in a mock battle when he could, at any moment, be called to participate in a real one? His family and clan needed him alive, and it wasn't worth the risk.

When his name and title were announced, Toren walked quickly across the muddy field. He pulled his horse's reins, understanding the beast's apprehension. They belonged back in Brockburg, not in the midst of this elaborate ceremony, on display alongside these English border lords and knights.

Where the hell is Hallington?

The warden was nowhere to be seen in the galleries, and he'd been looking—was looking even now. Douglas had insisted the warden would be in attendance, but he hadn't seen...

The Englishwoman. *His* Englishwoman.

He stopped, about to walk behind the pavilions to hang his shield alongside the others and await his turn for the individual joust. He'd been looking for Hallington, aye, but for her too. By God, the girl was comely. Was that her chaperone next to her? The other woman was married, or so he assumed from the way the Englishman sitting next to her was leaning in—it was closer than would be proper for an unwed couple. Toren didn't recognize him.

Forgetting the girl, or pretending to, he finally handed his horse off to his squire, who was out of breath and clearly in a panic.

"Did you not see?"

He had seen quite well. The serene expression on her face. The slight lift to her chin proclaiming her a noblewoman in truth. Her golden blonde hair, which was pulled away from her face, revealing an extraordinarily—

"You're to compete straightaway," his squire interrupted. "You aren't likely to. . . well. . . maybe your size. . ."

Toren tore his gaze away from the Englishwoman.

"Who is it?" The poor boy wrung his hands so tightly he was likely to injure himself. He was obviously concerned about his competition.

"Lord Blackburn," he replied.

Blackburn was one of the men involved in the fight that had seen two dead and more injured at last month's truce.

Interesting. He looked forward to besting the bastard.

"I've asked Ferguson's groom to prepare your mount," the squire said.

"And that cranky old goat allowed it?

Though Toren's senior by only a few years, Ferguson MacDuff had not aged well. He'd not yet seen the other man, even though his tent was the only one near his own. Toren had purposefully chosen a spot away from the others. If his purpose were ever discovered, he'd not see any of his countrymen implicated.

He looked at the lad, who seemed to always keep his head down. "Alfred, is it?"

The boy's hand stayed, and Toren's chain hauberk dangled in mid-air.

"You know my name?"

Toren's mouth lifted at the corner. "You've had such poor masters they haven't even bothered to learn your name?"

He nodded toward the mail, and Alfred resumed his ministrations.

"Aye," he answered. The lad's honesty took Toren aback.

"How do you come to be here?" he asked, genuinely curious.

"My master, a knight errant, was killed when I was ten and six. Since then, I've no true master but follow the tourney. . . "

Attempting to feed himself. Toren understood better than he wanted to. But it was too soon to make any decisions about the lad. The boy seemed competent enough. . . and yet there was something odd about him, something Toren couldn't yet place. It could be the unusual cap he wore. The worn and dirty cloth that covered his entire head was unlike anything Toren had ever seen.

He'd get to know the lad a bit more first, although he seemed reluctant to answer questions about his past. And though Alex always welcomed opportunities to train new men, it was too soon to offer him a position just yet.

Alfred helped him arrange his well-worn mail over the padded gambeson that had protected him in more than one tournament. If his opponent fought cleanly, it would be an easy match. However, most of the men who were present likely knew Toren's reputation. . . even though this squire clearly did not. And even though the weapons had been inspected this morning, and everyone had been reminded of the rules, some men were not willing to go up against a seasoned fighter without some advantage. Even so, he was more worried about his target's absence than he was about the joust.

With two hundred knights, this would likely be his only contest today, which would leave the remainder of his afternoon free for inquiries regarding the man's whereabouts. He couldn't kill the man if he failed to make an appearance. The thought of hunting him down in this godforsaken country did not sit well.

"You're all ready then," the lad said.

Indeed, he was. Best get this finished quickly.

As he and his squire made their way toward the front of the list, Toren put thoughts of the English warden from his mind. The woman he'd kissed, if it could be called as such. . . she was harder to forget.

"Over there, if you please."

They were ordered to wait alongside a makeshift wooden fence as two armed combatants circled each other near the center of the lists. Toren didn't plan to let it come to hand-to-hand combat. He would fell his opponent quickly and be done with it.

Finally, one of the men fell, the signal sounded—the wail of a trumpet, and Toren mounted his horse and took his helmet from his squire. It had been specifically made for this tournament by Brockburg's armorer, an Englishman who'd found his way north thirty years ago, after reivers from his own country had burned his village. Even at the man's advanced age, Toren would match his skills with anyone's.

Before he put it on, he stole a quick glance at the galleries. It was something he'd avoided doing earlier, but he had to know if she was still watching.

And she was.

An unexpected and unwelcome warmth that had nothing to do with his armor forced him to tear his gaze away and concentrate on the task at hand.

He swept his gaze across the lists to his opponent and moved his mount into position. Determined to end it on the first pass, he readjusted his wooden lance, painted bright red to match the Kerr coat of arms, and relaxed every other muscle in his body save his inner thighs and lance arm. Only avoiding a hit and delivering a direct one to the center of his opponent's shield would fell the other man with enough force to keep him on the ground. He had one chance to end this quickly.

As he waited for the sound of the horn, Toren attempted to slow his rapidly beating heart. He breathed deeply, ignoring the heat, and focused on the mounted Englishman preparing to charge at him.

The trumpet blared, and Toren spurred his mount forward and lowered his lance. He ignored the shouts and concentrated on the pounding of his destrier's hooves, waiting for the perfect moment to thrust his lance at his opponent. The charging knight and his horse loomed closer. Every time he met such a force, Toren marveled at the power behind the two acting as one for this brief, violent moment.

Now!

Splintered wood shattered everywhere, and before he could slow to look back at Blackburn, he already knew the outcome. There would be no need to dismount. His squire's incredulous face confirmed as much. He did turn then, to be sure, and took off his helmet.

"Here," he said to Alfred. "Tell him I have no need of his money or his armor." These were the usual gifts made to the victor, but he had no wish for them. He was here for one purpose, and this wasn't it, despite the man's involvement at the last Day of Truce. Vengeance led down a dangerous path, one he had no interest in exploring.

Alfred reached up—the boy was quite small—and took the steel helmet from him.

"You. . . you felled him with one pass."

If Toren had been the type of man to brag, he'd have quite enjoyed the look on his hired squire's face.

But he was not.

Toren dismounted and handed the reins to the squire. "Aye, laddie. Now go. The poor man is likely preparing his forfeit already. Get him fed and meet me at the tent."

Alfred looked as if he wanted to say something, but he must have decided otherwise, for he closed his gaping mouth instead and began to walk away.

When he turned back, the boy who so reluctantly looked into

his face did so now. Before he could speak, Toren realized his error. As his squire, the boy would have benefited from the other man's forfeit. Alfred needed the coin. Desperately.

As was his custom, Toren made a quick decision relying on his instinct.

"You've no need of the spoils, lad, if you'll come to Brockburg with me."

His reaction was not what Toren expected. If he was right, the first look that ran across his features was one of fear. But just as quickly, it was replaced by another. Alfred swallowed noticeably and finally spoke.

He bowed. "I would be honored."

It was not the bow of a low-born servant, but one of a well-trained noble. Toren nearly commented on it but held his tongue.

Alfred turned and ran as if afraid he would call him back.

Toren made his way to the wall of shields behind the pavilion. The makeshift wooden wall served as a notice to spectators who wished to view the field of participants. It was a true spectacle, with nearly two hundred shields of every shape and size hanging on it. A tournament official indicated where he should place his shield, and Toren did so without glancing at any of the others. It hardly mattered who he would be matched against next. What mattered was finding Hallington.

"I've never seen anything like it."

The voice that had spoken the soft words was already familiar to him. He turned and watched her eyes widen as he resisted the impulse to reach out and touch the woman he'd too briefly encountered the night before.

"How did you come to be here so quickly?" he asked.

"How do you know from whence I came to be here?"

Bloody hell.

"You sat there," he pointed to the back of the stands, where he'd spied her before the joust. "Just moments ago."

"You looked for me."

He had no reason to lie.

"I did."

He was vaguely aware of the chaos around them. Shouts and screams from the galleries as new contenders took to the field. Merchants who were given leave by the earl to sell their wares called to passersby, turning the wide-open field into a makeshift marketplace.

"Why?"

Asked innocently enough, her question sent blood flowing to various parts of his body. The answer was simple—the chaste kiss had left him wanting much more. But whether or not he took it depended on her answers to some important questions.

"You never told me your name." Or your marital status. But he left that unsaid. He was fairly certain she was no man's widow, unless her husband had done a piss-poor job of instructing her. Neither was she a woman of loose morals, judging by that same kiss. Which meant his unmarried lass was either well-positioned, in which case he would not take his pleasure with her, despite her beauty and apparent willingness, or a well-dressed but low-born noble, allowing for the slightest chance of a dalliance, one that would leave her virginity intact.

Cocking her head to the side, his lass opened her mouth but then promptly shut it. And whether on purpose or innocently, she licked her bottom lip. Toren spied the tip of her pink tongue and imagined capturing it with his own.

"I think, perhaps, it may serve me well not to tell you my name."

She may not be experienced, but the lass knew how to flirt.

"Then I shall ask someone else to tell me."

He moved as if to stop two ladies walking past them, but she grabbed his arm.

Though he couldn't feel her hand beneath the padding and mail that covered it, Toren stilled. His reaction to her was instantaneous.

"Nay, do not!"

Her panic was evident. So there was a reason she wished to remain anonymous?

"If you meet me this eve after supper in the same spot as we. . . well. . ."

"Kissed?" She was an innocent, indeed.

As if on cue, her cheeks pinkened under his gaze. How did she manage to appear both deliciously enticing and unquestionably innocent all at once? Who the devil was this woman?

"Aye, that. If you promise not to make inquiries, I will tell you my name this eve."

Though it was almost certainly a bad idea, Toren found himself agreeing nonetheless.

"Very well. When?"

She looked over his shoulder toward the galleries.

"If you're attempting to appear inconspicuous, searching for your companions thusly won't help your cause."

Though he only teased, she did not appear to be amused. Just the opposite.

"Meet me there when the play begins."

"The play?"

"Aye, there will be a play honoring the countess, 'tis the highlight of tonight's entertainment. I will find a way to meet you."

And as quickly as she had appeared, his English maiden was gone.

It was the strangest wooing of his life. Toren watched as she walked back toward the spectators. He really had no time for assignations, even with such a lovely maid.

And yet. . . she intrigued him—the mixture of boldness and innocence, inexperience and wit. What was he to make of it?

5

It was the most spectacular sight Juliette had ever witnessed.

Granted, she had only been to a few holdings besides Chauncy Manor. She'd begged on more than one occasion to travel with her father to London, but he always insisted it was too dangerous, his answer to most anything.

"They are all looking at you," Christina whispered.

"Pardon, my lady."

A handsome gentleman, a noble by the look of him, bumped her arm as he walked past them into the great hall. He looked back and smiled, the message in his eyes unmistakable.

"Juliette, can you not see for yourself? Everywhere we go, men's heads turn to gaze at you. Nice, *English* men. Ones your father would be happy to accept as his son-in-law over Lord Wytham."

Juliette wished she had not been so forthcoming about the unusual arrangement she'd made with the chief earlier that day. But though she was certainly a dreamer, as her father was fond of saying, she was not without brains. Juliette had wanted to ensure someone knew in case anything went awry. Though she trusted the Scot, the man was also a stranger, and one could not be too careful.

Christina had originally insisted on coming to find her after the play. But Juliette had talked her down, and she'd ultimately consented to meet Juliette later in her bedchamber.

"Just look at all these flowers!" Christina marveled. "Do you suppose they've imported every single one in all of England?"

They walked over fresh rushes toward the table where they'd sat the previous evening. The slight crunch beneath her leather-soled feet gave evidence that they were, indeed, new.

"I don't know where to look first," she continued.

"Mayhap at the earl and his wife," Lord Hedford answered. "The splendor of their dress is a sight to behold."

Oh. Juliette had intended only to speak for Christina's ears. She took his advice and glanced at their hosts. Hedford was right, but how would he know of their splendor? He was gazing not at the 'sight' of the noble couple but at his wife.

She would have to rein in her excitement in the future and speak in a lower voice. If Lord Hedford discovered her plan to be alone with the Scottish chief, she had no doubt she would be escorted quickly up to her chamber.

While her father brokered for peace along the border, her friend's husband was not inclined to look beyond the wrongs of their northern neighbors. His brother had been killed by a Scottish reiver in a raid on their village when he was just a boy.

"My, that is a most magnificent gown," she said, gasping as she did indeed look up at the dais. "But that head covering..."

"It's quite appalling," Christina said.

Her husband didn't seem to mind her bluntness. "'Tis a gorget," he replied.

"Another of my husband's hidden talents? Discerning women's fashions?"

Lord Hedford didn't flinch. "Lest you forget, I spent some time in France, where such was a favored pastime," he replied.

"Quite right, and you were injured there?" Juliette asked, attempting to keep suspicion from her tone. Though his limp was evidence to the affirmative—the reason he was not participating in the tournament—she had never been able to ascertain much information from her friend about the incident.

She suspected it was because he had not explained the circumstances to her.

Lord Hedford ignored her observation.

"My lord, do introduce this most magnificent creature you're chaperoning this evening."

Juliette hadn't noticed the man who sat directly across from them, but being called a "creature" did not impress her. He had not sat at their table the previous evening, though perhaps that was because tonight's dinner was the official start to the tournament celebrations. After a full day of preliminary jousts, all the participants had been introduced, and some of the guests were already discussing favorites for the individual tournament champion. Of course, the last day's melee was the culmination of the tourney, but the jousts, once only a warm-up to the main event, were beginning to rise in popularity.

And much of the talk was about a certain Scottish clan chief.

"Lord Blake," Christina's husband replied, "I'm pleased to introduce my wife, Lady Christina, and her friend, Lady Juliette, daughter of Lord Hallington, the second Baron Chauncy."

Though the man was not unattractive, Lord Blake's predatory gaze made Juliette wish he were sitting across the room rather than across the table. Admittedly, the man dressed in high fashion, but unlike the muted tones favored by another man she couldn't seem to stop thinking about, Lord Blake wore nearly every color in existence. The bright yellow of his surcoat made her dizzy.

He finally tore his gaze from her bosom to address Christina's husband.

"I understand you were in France recently?"

An interesting question.

"Aye, and returned to accept this fine woman as my wife. Christina, tell Lord Blake of the magnificent ceremony you planned."

Lord Blake allowed the conversation to meander away from France. She wondered whether he ever talked about the time he'd spent overseas with Christina. Perhaps her friend would be willing to tell her. Juliette had once read a story, *Livre des Merveilles du Monde,* which Sister had insisted was so fantastical it could not possibly be true. She often imagined Lord Hedford similarly traveling the world and meeting adventures, though he was much more mysterious about it than the subject of the story.

"Lady Juliette?"

Lord save her.

"My apologies," she murmured.

They all turned to her as if awaiting a response.

"Lady Juliette prefers French wine, do you not?" Christina prodded.

"Aye, very much. But I will admit 'tis the only variety Father allows, so I'm not exposed to many others."

Lord Blake shoved a morsel of meat into his mouth. Unfortunately, he didn't bother to finish it before speaking.

"Where is the warden? I would have expected him to attend as an extension of his duties."

Lord Blake was not the first to inquire about her father's whereabouts. "Regrettably, he was forced to attend to matters that kept him away from this fine event. He sends his deepest regrets for his absence."

Seemingly satisfied, Lord Blake devoted his hearty attention to the meal in front of him.

As the pre-course was served, Juliette washed her hands and dried them on the linen towel, but she did not touch the bread and cheese.

"You must eat something," Christina whispered.

She glanced at Lord Blake, who was in deep conversation with the man sitting next to him. "I'm too nervous," she replied.

"And rightly so. This idea of yours is foolish. You hardly know the man." Christina looked toward her husband, who paid them no attention.

"I know Lord Wytham even less. Yet my father insists I should accept his hand in marriage simply because he's inherited Providence Manor from his great-uncle. I care not that his land will border ours. Or that "twill be a fine match.' He's not spent any time in England—"

"But at least he's English."

"Cares for nothing save my father's title—"

"Juliette."

"Smile, they're looking at us."

Indeed, the conversation around them had come to a stop. A troupe as large as Juliette had ever seen had gathered in the corner of the hall closest to the hosts. The earl and his wife raised their goblets, and all at once the lutist and harpist began to play. Another man, dressed similarly to his companions, in an array of colors only Lord Blake could rival, waited with his horn raised. When he finally joined in, the soft tunes echoed on the stone walls of the great hall despite the fact that it was filled with people.

"He's not here," her friend whispered.

Indeed, Christina was right. The Scotsman was absent from the meal. She had thought to find him, perhaps catch his eye and get silent confirmation of their pre-arranged meeting.

"'Tis well enough. I'm of a mind to tell Matthew of your assignation."

She stared into Christina's eyes, begging her to do otherwise.

"I will be fine. If the man wanted to harm me, he'd have done so last eve. In fact, his rebuke for putting myself in danger was as vigorous as your own. Besides, I can't very well meet someone who is not present."

But before Christina could reply, the very object of their discussion entered the hall.

She spotted him immediately.

His size alone made him stand out, but it was not the only reason he demanded attention. At least, he demanded hers. She had not known his name last eve, but it seemed she'd heard little else throughout the day, whispers and comments about his match seemed to follow her all afternoon.

"Knocked him from his mount with one blow."

"Has been champion more than any other Scotsman."

"And he's only seven and twenty."

"Keeps to himself, even with his own clansmen."

"None will best him."

And he was here. The clan chief entered the hall alone, paused at the entrance, and looked around the room. A serving maid immediately sidled up to him on the pretense of offering a mug of ale. But even at this distance, Juliette could tell she wanted to offer something more. She let out a breath when he did not appear to reciprocate her offer.

Clad in the same surcoat as the evening before, the only difference now was that his hair was wet and smoothed back, giving him a nobler appearance. But no less fierce.

She was unable. . . unwilling. . . to look away.

His gaze found her.

He took the mug offered to him and, without hesitation, began to walk toward their table. An initial burst of pleasure—he was coming for *her,* and he'd ignored the comely serving girl—gave way to panic. *What is he doing? We didn't plan to meet until after the play began.*

"Juliette—"

"Yes, it is," she answered her friend. If Christina sounded alarmed, it was with good reason. There could be no doubt now. He headed toward them.

Juliette reached for her wine but changed her mind when her

hands began to tremble. She traced the outline of the rose pattern on the copper goblet, concentrating on the leaves. If he told Lord Hedford what she had asked him to do. . .

"Greetings," his voice boomed. "May I join you?"

She looked up and watched in horror as Lord Hedford nodded to the empty seat next to Lord Blake.

"Your clansmen—" Lord Blake started pointing to a nearby table, presumably one which he believed would be better suited for the chief's company.

"Are in Scotland," he said, looking directly at her. Odd, but though he'd not given her leave to address him by his given name, Juliette already thought of him as Toren in her mind. It was a fine name. She tried to keep her expression neutral. Surely everyone could hear her wildly beating heart, or did the sound invade her ears only?

"I am—" he began.

"The chief of Clan Kerr," Lord Hedford finished. Juliette caught his quick reproachful glance across the table, but could not tell if it was directed at their new guest or the pompous lord beside him.

"'Twould be difficult for the man who has championed his country more than any other at this event to remain anonymous."

Juliette had lured him to another meeting with the promise of revealing herself. Would he reveal her misdeeds? Did he mean to call off their assignation?

"Lord Hedford and my wife, Lady Christina, at your service. And her dear friend—"

"We've met." Toren said and inclined his head in greeting. "My lady."

He had purposely cut off Hedford to keep her name a secret. Did that mean he intended to keep to their plan after all?

Though she looked away, she could feel the chief's gaze on her still. She looked up and found she was right.

"I trust you are well this evening?" His voice was low and

hinted at another meaning. Juliette knew she should stop staring but could not.

"I am. And trust you are as well." She took her hands from the goblet, folded them onto her lap, and looked at the musicians, who had just begun a new song. From her seat, Juliette could see everything. The lord's table, the army of servants emerging from the kitchens with trays of food, the massive arrangements of flowers just about everywhere. "Our view is quite spectacular."

She gave her attention back to the others.

"Indeed," Lord Blake muttered to himself, although she could hear him clearly. The man was not looking toward the front of the hall but rather at her. Though not at her face, exactly.

Juliette wanted to bring her hands up to cover the exposed skin on her chest, but she kept them on her lap instead, not wanting to bring undue attention to herself.

She chanced another glance at Toren, whose eyes were conspicuously hooded. Indeed, he looked as if he would like to give Blake the throttling he deserved. But his expression changed so quickly, Juliette wondered if she had imagined it.

The main course was served without further incident, despite Lord Blake's increasingly drunken state. Juliette spent most of the course attempting to divert her attention from the Scotsman she'd arranged to meet after dinner. She watched the harpist's fingers glide across the strings. She smiled as the earl and his wife laughed together, looking every bit the perfect hosts. She did manage to eat a few morsels until a piece of cheese nearly caught in her throat at Christina's proclamation.

"Look! They're setting up a stage."

Sure enough, the musicians were moving to the side as servants cleared the space in front of the high table.

The play.

Her head whipped around to find Toren Kerr already standing.

"Good eve, my lords. Ladies. I fear I must retire early this eve."

He didn't so much as glance at her. With that, the Scot turned and left as quickly as he came.

For a moment, Juliette was baffled—had he changed his mind? —but then she realized he'd likely left to meet her, which meant it was time for her to leave, too. Juliette placed her hand over her chest. There was no need to feign illness, as she really did feel quite lightheaded.

"I fear I must do the same. Pardon, my lords, I suddenly feel overwrought."

Christina had fought her all afternoon over her "foolish plan," but her friend came through, just as she always did.

"You do look quite pale. Perhaps you should take a rest before the dancing begins. Or even retire early if you must. Tomorrow will be another long day, is that not right, husband?"

Hedford looked back and forth between them, his eyebrows drawn up, likely trying to determine if they were up to any mischief. Juliette and Christina were known to get into some trouble when they were together, though perhaps Christina had not told him that.

"Aye," he said. "I will escort you, Lady Juliette."

He began to stand, but Juliette could not accept his offer. While she could go to her bedchamber and then return, she worried the Scot would not wait that long.

"No need, my lord. I know the way."

She expected him to argue. To tell her there were too many strangers lurking about. But after delivering a quick fare thee well to the young couple and her unwanted companion for the evening, who was now openly gaping at her bosom, Juliette fairly ran from the table.

She skirted men and women shouting and clapping as they prepared for the night's entertainment. Servants cleared the last course as she wove her way through them, turning into the corridor that would lead to the opening she'd used for her escape the evening before.

She stopped at its entrance and stared at the light from a nearby wall torch. The flickering light and distant sounds of celebration gave her pause.

What if Christina was right to be concerned? This was not a story, and the man waiting for her was not Sir Gawain. Maybe instead he was the Green Knight, thinking to test her but really preparing to chop off her head.

Nay. He was no monster but a mere man. Well, mayhap not a 'mere' man. Had there been more time, she never would have behaved so rashly. But there was not, and Juliette would listen to Sister Heloise's advice. She would not docilely accept the small life her father wished to give to her—she wanted her cup full, overflowing.

Of course, when the nun had told Juliette to choose her own path, the abbess very likely had not realized it would steer her to a private nook in a strange castle with a Scotsman she'd met but twice.

Juliette took a deep breath, placed her hand on the stone wall, and took a hesitant step forward.

6

She wasn't coming.

Toren had suspected as much at dinner. After learning Hallington was not yet at the tournament—if, indeed, he was coming at all—he should have left straightaway. Although it was not ideal, he would need to travel to Chauncy Manor to find him.

But he had not liked the thought of the Englishwoman waiting for him, not knowing what had become of him. He had stayed because he was courteous. For all his faults, and there were many, rudeness was not one of them. His decision had nothing to do with his desire to see her. Or his yearning to touch her, so strong he'd nearly reached for her when she'd approached him in the field.

And yet something told him there was more to it. He'd desired plenty of women, lain with many, and cared little for any of them. Never before had he put a mission on hold for any woman, and the thought that he'd do so for an Englishwoman was enough to give him pause.

Granted, this lass was not his mother, the Englishwoman who'd fled Scotland two days after his father's death.

His sister would be thrilled to hear he'd waited for a lass.

"Toren," Catrina had said on her last visit to Brockburg, "no less than three alliances have been proposed, none of which you'll even consider. What is wrong with you?"

The question was a common one, and he'd answered it the same way every time.

"I have no need for a wife. If something happens to me, Alex will become chief. And then Reid. The Kerr line will remain strong."

"We need more allies."

Toren had turned from her then, and looked below, across the open landscape at Brockburg. Lush, rolling hills in the distance. A hundreds-year-old tower walled and heavily guarded. Brockburg Castle was well fortified. It had not been attacked in years despite its proximity to the border. They needed no one.

"Allies to betray us? Nay—"

"You're more than a mite stubborn, brother."

"And you've a short memory."

They'd ended the conversation there, but Catrina's words hadn't failed to move him. He thought of them even now, standing against this stone wall for the second time, thinking of the blonde beauty who'd sat across from him earlier.

He should leave, but instead he stayed and looked up into the night sky. He thought of the sun and stars revolving around them. He ached to return home.

He ached to touch *her*.

Toren heard the footsteps before the sound of her voice met his ears. "The abbess would say God must truly be happy to give us a night such as this."

"The abbess?"

She turned the corner to meet him, and Toren sucked in his breath.

Holy hell, she was lovely.

She looked just as she had earlier, her pale blue gown

somehow outshining all of the other bright colors festooning the gathering of nobles. Though it was understated, unadorned but for simple embroidery with a shiny white thread, the woman who wore it was anything but.

Her expression, as usual, was welcoming. Her smile was contagious.

"Sister Heloise. She tutors me each day at the convent adjacent to—" her smile broadened, "—my home."

"If you think to withhold your identity forever," Toren pushed himself away from the wall, "I can simply go back down to the hall and ask—"

"Nay, do not." She grabbed his arm to stop him, and when she began to let it drop, he stopped her with his own.

He turned her hand over with her palm facing upward and lowered his own palm to touch it. Her fingers were so much smaller than his own. And softer. The feel of her skin against his rough palm instantly hardened him. This slip of a woman affected him so strangely.

"So small," he thought aloud.

She allowed his touch. An intimate touch for two strangers, but this was the same woman who'd asked him for a kiss on their second meeting.

"Yours are so large. And rough. They're very different than mine."

Toren swallowed. He shouldn't be here. Though undoubtedly alluring, his Englishwoman was an innocent. Her forward suggestion aside, how could he have ever doubted the fact?

"*We* are very different," he said.

He reluctantly pulled his hand away and looked at her. Thanks to the moonlight, he could see her face clearly. Her eyes betrayed her. She was nervous. Rightly so. It was foolish of her to be here, but he'd put her at ease nonetheless.

"Do you mean that I am English?"

He wasn't thinking that exactly. But it was a safer conversation than the one he'd been imagining. The one that involved the removal of their clothing to explore.

"Aye. And a woman, of course." He would stop there.

Her laugh, a deep and almost sensual sound, forced a smile from him.

"And you are much bigger than I am."

He would very much like to prove that she was right on that particular account.

"Let us see," she was clearly warming to the topic of their differences. "Do you have siblings?"

"Two brothers and a sister."

"Well then, we both have a brother. Kelvin is nine. Yours?"

Toren tried to remember his siblings at that age, although it was becoming more and more difficult. Although not young children when his father died and his mother left, they were still of an age to be cared for. It was his most important job, and the one he took most seriously.

"Both are full grown. My brothers Alex and Reid are back home. My sister Catrina is here in England. She was recently married. To an Englishman."

"And you don't like him."

Toren sighed. "It's a complicated matter."

"I see."

But it was clear that she did not, and he had no desire to speak of his brother-in-law or Bristol or any of it.

Toren leaned back against the wall and tried to think of a difference between them that would be a bit safer to discuss. "You're well educated."

"How did you. . . oh yes, the abbess. Aye. My father insisted upon it, and the convent borders our property, making it quite convenient. I've grown up with the nuns and Sister Heloise."

"So you can read and write?"

She shrugged, and Toren attempted to avert his eyes from the tempting swell just above the neckline of her gown.

"Aye."

He sensed she was being modest.

"Aye?"

Another shrug. God help him, he wanted to crush her against him and touch the creamy skin that seemed to glow in the moonlight.

"In three languages."

"Let me guess. English, French, and—"

"Latin." She rushed to finish his thought. "Sister has very strong beliefs about reading manuscripts in their original language. She says the translations sometimes change their meanings. Like *Le Livre de la Cité des Dames*. Pizan uses Latin-style conventions, but her very French writings would not. . . why are you looking at me so strangely?"

"Not strangely. With fascination. It's as if you've just come alive."

His Englishwoman bowed her head in what looked like shame.

"I'm sorry. 'Tis just that I do love Pizan. She's a champion of women an —"

He had not meant to offend her. The opposite actually. She fascinated him. He almost reached a hand out to comfort her, but physical contact would not be a good idea.

"Why are you sorry?" he asked instead.

"Everyone says I read too much. They keep telling me that I don't live in a story."

Though she tried to keep her tone light, Toren could tell the words had hurt her, that they still hurt her.

"Everyone? Who says such things? Not your friend?" He gestured toward the hall where drinking and dancing would last well into the night.

"Nay, not Christina. Well, not most of the time. But most everyone else. Except Sister, of course."

"Your parents?"

"My father mostly. He blames books for my unmarried state."

Now he was confused. Wouldn't her intelligence make her more desirable as a wife?

"Please don't think ill of my father. He loves me very much."

"But why—"

"So 'tis a difference between us?" she interrupted him. "Being able to read, I mean."

It was clear she didn't want to discuss the topic any further. Or perhaps it was her father she didn't wish to discuss. He could press her, but he didn't wish to do so. There was something about the lass that made him want to protect her.

"Aye, unfortunately. My brothers and I spent our childhoods training to protect our clan. My sister was tutored, though, and enjoyed reading to us."

Why was he telling her so much?

"Is she the eldest then?"

"Nay. Catrina is the youngest of our family. But no doubt the most intelligent."

His sister would very much like this Englishwoman.

"I can tell you're very fond of her."

The lass turned from him, lifted her skirts, and ventured toward the semicircle that enclosed the space they occupied.

"What do you suppose is up there?"

She pointed to the set of stone steps behind them, the ones that led to a parapet.

"The inner bailey lays beyond. But I'd not venture there if you wish to remain unseen. Two guards are stationed not far from that tower."

She nodded, as if he'd satisfied a piece of curiosity for her. This lass seemed curious about everything and forced him to question more things than he was accustomed.

He had so many questions for her, but one more important than all the others.

"Why did you ask me to kiss you? And to meet you here tonight?"

She opened her mouth to answer, but then closed it. He wanted so badly to reach out and touch those perfectly formed lips. To run his finger along the same path as her tongue, which had darted out briefly and retreated.

"Would it make you more comfortable if I answered a question for you first?"

"Aye," she said, her mouth tipping into the suggestion of a smile. She thought for a moment, then said, "Would your siblings say you're kind?"

That was not the question he'd expected.

"I suppose." *Although they may describe me in other ways first.*

"And you love them all very much?"

Love his siblings? What kind of question was that?

"Of course, but what—"

"Oh dear. It did not even occur to me that you might be married?"

He laughed at her stricken look. This was, without compare, the strangest conversation he'd ever had with any woman—it was even the strangest of the conversations he'd had with her.

"I would not be here with you right now if I were a married man."

Clearly, that answer pleased her—she smiled broadly and nodded. "I think mayhap you should kiss me just once more, if you please, just to be sure."

Granted, Toren hadn't much experience with English women. But he didn't think the ladies of his southern neighbors were much different than the ones he knew in Scotland. Unmarried gentlewomen simply did not make such requests. She was a lady, of that there could be no doubt, and one who did not appear to be free with her wares.

But damn if he didn't want to kiss her again.

"It would be my pleasure," he said. And meant it. "But first, you promised me a name?"

Why did she hesitate?

"If I tell you and we do not. . . that is to say, if I change my mind and decide you will not—"

Toren could not take this sweet torture any longer. Cutting off her nonsensical explanation, he took advantage of the fact that her mouth was open and plunged his tongue inside. He sought *her* tongue and, finding it, coaxed her to understand what to do.

When she responded in kind, he was lost.

He pulled her close, finally able to feel those ample breasts crushed against him. Every move she made was unsure, from the soft caress of her hands on his arms to the feather-light touch of her tongue.

Toren decreased the pressure of his mouth to give her time to adjust to the sensations he could tell were new to her. Cupping her face, he slowed the frantic pace and kissed her more slowly.

The effect her soft moan had on his body made him pull away. She was an innocent, and if he let himself savor much more of this, he was likely to forget the fact.

"You've not done that before."

He cupped her cheek and tipped up her face, an angel's face. So soft and smooth. So perfect.

"Nay, I've not."

She swallowed, and Toren wanted nothing more than to continue where they'd left off. But he was no deflowerer of maids.

"Why not? Surely you've had suitors who have stolen kisses?"

He dropped his hands and took a step back lest he become too tempted.

Before she answered that question, he asked another. "What is it you want to be sure of?" And then it occurred to him she hadn't revealed herself yet. "And what is your name?"

She took a deep breath and cocked her head to the side, watching him.

"I've had suitors, one my father is pressing more than others. But I've never wanted any of them to kiss me."

So she was all but betrothed.

"I can't tell you why I asked you to kiss me just yet."

A curious statement.

"You may want to reconsider. I leave on the morn."

"Leave?" The stricken look on her face left no doubt for interpretation. She wanted something from him, and Toren was beginning to understand what that might be.

It was something he could never give.

"I don't understand. Why would you leave? What about the remainder of the tournament?"

Since he couldn't very well tell her the truth, he said, "I'm looking for a man whom I expected to be here. . . someone I must speak with immediately. I fear our discussion is more important than remaining here."

He hadn't meant for his tone to sound so harsh, but he didn't want her to ask any more questions.

She was clearly not pleased with this news.

"I believe there's another question you've yet to answer," he pressed.

Lifting her head, the forlorn expression still in place, she said, "Lady Juliette Hallington, daughter of Stewart Hallington, at your service." She grabbed handfuls of her gown and curtsied formally, some of the light-hearted wit he'd witnessed returning despite her evident disappointment.

Dear God, no. Toren felt as if she'd taken a poleaxe to his stomach.

He was leaving.

Juliette should not feel so disappointed. She hardly knew the man. Her father would almost certainly not approve. Toren was more than a bit intimidating, and he was, after all, Scottish.

Most importantly, they were not in love. But she still didn't want him to leave. Especially not after *that.* Did Christina's husband kiss her that way? Is that what Lord Wytham would have done if she'd allowed him to steal a kiss when he'd hunted her down in the stables on his last visit?

Her thoughts were so muddled, Juliette did not quite know what to say. At least she was not alone in that. His face had lost all color. She couldn't understand his reaction.

"Is there something amiss about my name?" He didn't answer that question, so she followed it up with another. "Do you know of my father?"

He was slow to respond. Juliette listened to the far-off sounds of the banquet. From the sound of music that floated to her from the hall, the celebrations were just beginning. For now, they were safe.

"I do," he said. His voice was low and... commanding.

"Brockburg lies on the border, just north of Bristol," he said by way of explanation.

A border lord! Perhaps his interests would ally with theirs. "Are you a borderer who aims for peace or discord?"

"Lady Juliette—"

"Juliette." She'd blurted it without thinking. "There is a curious tradition in my family to not use titles."

He drew his eyebrows together. She likely could have come up with a better explanation, but that one would have to suffice. The truth was simple—she wished to hear her name from his lips unfettered by any title.

Best to change the subject.

"Of course, I would never presume to call you—"

"Toren."

"Aye, Toren. I would never—"

"You may call me Toren."

"I suppose you aren't able to have a shortened name?"

Toren leaned back against the stone wall. If he was truly leaving on the morrow, he certainly didn't appear to be in a hurry to begin his journey at the moment. Which was just as well. Somehow, she'd have to convince him to stay.

"What need would I have for a shortened name?"

Would he always be this exasperating?

"You don't *need* one. But my brother calls me Jules."

"Jules," he repeated. "I very much desire peace along the border, but I fail to understand—"

"Perfect!"

She clasped her hands together. Just one problem remained.

"On the matter of you leaving. . ."

What could she say that would not scare him directly back to the Cheviot Hills? Though she knew little of courtship, he was likely not prepared for talk of marriage just yet.

"I don't know who you're looking for. Or what could be so important that you'd leave the tournament after one day. But you should consider staying. Many are already saying that you—"

"I'll stay."

"Are favored to be champion. And I'd very much like. . . what did you say?"

Though part of his face was shadowed, the other half was touched by moonlight. It was the first time she'd seen him as the warrior from earlier in the day, the one who'd unhorsed a man as if he weighed no more than a bale of hay, rather than the man she'd been speaking to this evening.

"I'll stay."

No explanation. No easy smiles. Just a proclamation that should have made her happy. But why had he agreed so readily? And why did he appear unhappy about the decision?

"Juliette?" A frantic voice whispered from the stairwell beside them.

She groaned inwardly. "Christina?"

A moment later, her friend peeked her head out from around the entranceway. She glanced at her, and then Toren, and then back again.

"Come, quickly. Matthew insisted I check on you. I think he suspects something."

Juliette glanced from her friend to Toren. Would he truly stay?

There was nothing she could do about it should he indeed choose to leave. If Lord Hedford suspected she was up to something, he would watch her more closely, something she could not allow.

"I—"

"Go, Lady Juliette," he said. "We will speak again on the morrow."

"Hurry." Christina tugged on her hand, and Juliette allowed herself to be pulled away.

She knew her friend would ask questions, but she would have much preferred to retire to her chamber, close her eyes, and imagine Toren's lips on hers again.

She'd dreamed of what a lover's kiss may be like, but for once, her tales had all paled in comparison to the real thing.

Aye, he was the one.

The man she would marry.

7

"Chief, there's a woman out here asking to see you."

Toren had just returned from a joust and was preparing to make use of the lake that bordered the tented city. His armor lay in the corner of the tent, a space large enough to hold his sparse equipment and the bedroll.

A woman. Juliette?

After revealing her identity, she'd fled with her friend, leaving him in a stricken state of disbelief. Hallington's daughter? What were the chances? The fates were cruel indeed.

It appeared his bad luck had followed him to England. He blamed Douglas for getting him involved in the first place. If the king wanted the warden dead, he could have chosen any number of men to do the deed. He knew Toren wanted nothing more than to be left alone, to protect his own clan and leave the border troubles and politics far behind.

He should have left before meeting Juliette, but stubborn arse that he was, he'd stayed at Condren to rendezvous with an Englishwoman he knew to be an innocent. . . and he was still unclear as to why. Had he expected anything good to come from such a meeting?

Bloody hell. Why did she have to be Hallington's daughter?

Now he was stuck participating in this bloody tournament, and only the Lord knew where Hallington was hiding. She had not said when her father would be joining her, but the fact that she was here made the man's attendance at the tournament inevitable.

Which meant there was only one thing he could do.

Avoid her.

Toren's plan was simple. He would participate in each day's match and spend the rest of his time in the tent city, as the knights called it, or in Condren's village. He would avoid the castle, avoid Juliette, and wait for her father to arrive. The timing of his joust this morning had worked in his favor—it had been the first of the day, too early for most spectators.

Unfortunately, his body was not in full accordance with his plan. He'd awoken hard and ready, thinking of her innocent response to that damned kiss.

And now she was here. Did she not realize how dangerous it was to come to this place unaccompanied? The only women who spent any time near the tents were far less reputable and innocent than Juliette.

Dressed only in hose and a loose tunic, he lifted the flap of the tent and blinked at the sunlight that greeted him.

"Lady Christina?"

Juliette's friend, quite pretty in a demure sort of way, was clearly nervous. As she should be.

"Did you come here alone?"

"Aye, I did."

She lifted her skirts and sat quite properly on the stool in front of his tent. Where had that come from?

The squire, Alfred, rushed toward them with another small wooden stool and handed it to him. The boy was proving to be quite handy.

He nodded his thanks and sat.

"You're quite large, even for a Scotsman."

Toren raised his eyebrows. It seemed the lady shared her friend's penchant for addressing indelicate topics.

"So I'm told."

She strained her neck to look around him. The closest tent was too far for conversation to be overheard, but if she hoped to avoid attracting attention, he feared it might be too late.

"Does your husband know you're here?"

She shook her head vehemently. "Nay, he would be properly appalled. But I had no other choice. I was told you'd already won your joust, and I needed to speak with you before your meeting with Juliette."

Meeting? They'd not arranged a meeting.

"I'm afraid for her and saw no other way."

She held her hands together on her lap, and Toren could see they were trembling ever so slightly.

"You're quite brave to come here for your friend."

And he meant it.

"Juliette is like a sister to me. She's the best friend I've ever had. Which is what I came to speak with you about."

She took a deep breath and then let out a great rush of words. "I've never seen Juliette quite this way. She's behaving recklessly. Her stories have always given her some strange ideas, but I'm afraid this one will get her hurt. You see. . ."

She peered around once again, so Toren looked behind him. He saw nothing out of the ordinary, just a few squires tending fires off in the distance and grooms attending to their masters' mounts.

"I've never been in such a place," she offered by way of explanation. "As I was saying," Christina rushed to continue, "I'm worried about her. Worried her father won't approve, and she will be devastated."

She was making no sense.

"Can you start from the beginning?" he asked.

She sighed. "I should not be telling you this, but Juliette is quite determined, and I can see no other way. You see, she's terrified she will be trapped in a loveless marriage like her parents. Her father, her mother, and even sometimes her younger brother. . . they don't agree with her penchant for tales of chivalric love. Juliette spends much time studying with. . ."

"Sister Heloise," he finished.

Christina looked at him with surprise.

"Aye, and the nuns," she continued. "She's done so for years, and even her parents are unaware of the range of her interests. Books about history, religion, travel—Juliette reads them all. Because of it, she believes some. . . unusual things."

He imagined her friend was being kind.

"One of which is that she can avoid her parents' fate and marry for love. Which is absurd, of course, since her father will choose her husband. As mine did. As it is for every noblewoman. But Juliette. . ."

He already understood.

"Is here to find love," he finished.

Christina nodded. "Her father has all but betrothed her to Lord Wytham. Last eve, Juliette told me of your meeting. You saved her on that first day even though she was a stranger. You didn't take advantage of her, and for a man so large and intimidating, you seem very kind."

Kind was not the word most people would use to describe him, and in this instance, it was not completely unwelcome. He was ashamed of his behavior with the girl.

"Why did you risk yourself to tell me this?" he asked.

It changed nothing. It *could* change nothing.

"I don't want her to get hurt. Juliette is the kindest, most giving person you'll ever meet. She may have some odd notions about women—and marriage—but please treat her gently. I don't presume to know what her father may think. He's so concerned with keeping peace on the border, perhaps marriage to a Scottish border lord would not be unwelcome. But I do know Juliette is most vulnerable. I don't know your intentions, but I'd ask for them now."

He nearly smiled. "You're a mite protective."

She sat up straight on the small stool and stuck her chin out as regally as a queen. He'd seen that expression before. The women were good friends indeed.

"Obviously I know about your meeting last eve—"

"My lady," he said, cutting her off. "She asked to meet me, and you'll admit it was an odd request coming from an unmarried lady—"

Lady Christina had the decency to blush on her friend's behalf.

"So I did. As you said yourself, I did not take advantage of her. Nor do I intend to."

He stopped before mentioning he had no intention of marrying anyone, especially not the daughter of the warden he had been sent to kill.

Toren imagined his sister sitting across from a man, appealing to him on behalf of a friend, such as Lady Sara. He owed her the same kindness he would want someone else to show his sister. "I can assure you, your friend is safe. I have no intentions of hurting her. You have my word."

She eyed him with suspicion, but it appeared that she believed him, maybe because he'd spoken the truth. . . or as close to the truth as he could manage. Juliette would be hurt, there was no helping that, but not directly by him. And she would be extremely safe with him, as he had no intention on being alone with her or ever seeing her again if he could help it.

Her father, however, would not meet the same fate.

Christina was up to something.

She had excused herself from the midday meal, saying she felt ill. But her friend had looked perfectly fine, albeit a bit worried. They'd been going back and forth all morning, but Juliette refused to be dissuaded from her plan.

As soon as Condren's hosts took their leave and the meal ended, Juliette started to make her way from the hall to check on Christina. Lord Hedford had given her leave to do so.

Servants were already scurrying about, clearing tables and preparing for another meal.

She couldn't imagine the expense involved in hosting such an event. Sister Heloise had told her about a southern earl who'd once hosted a different tournament, the Tournament of the King, and lost everything but his title after lavish banquets and celebrations that lasted for nearly a month.

She wasn't sure the tale was true, but Juliette knew a tournament such as this one would put a serious strain on Chauncy Manor. Though it was very much a castle in all but name, and her father's land spread far enough to keep their family comfortable, their estate could never support such a lavish expense.

"My lady, a word if you please?" a gentleman asked her. She'd been so caught up in her thoughts, she hadn't even noticed his approach.

This Englishman reminded her of the lord they'd dined with the previous evening. Though not quite as dandified, he was nevertheless dressed in a bright red surcoat with gold trim, and his face, though attractive enough, was just too... pretty.

"Allow me to introduce myself." He bowed prettily. "Lord Blackburn of Anglewood."

Was she expected to know him?

"I'm pleased to meet you, Lord Blackburn."

He tucked his dark blond hair neatly behind his ears.

"You don't remember me."

At times like these she wished her maid had been able to accompany her on this journey. Or that Christina could remain by her side at all times.

"I fear I do not, my lord."

Juliette moved aside for a servant who was attempting to serve ale to a table of knights behind her. Apparently they did not care that the meal had ended.

"I visited your father and Henry Rode, who was once the bailiff at Blackburn, nigh more than two summers ago."

Though Juliette still could not place him, she did not want the man to feel insulted.

"Yes, Henry. I didn't realize he held that position anywhere else before coming to us."

Henry was Chauncy's bailiff, and her father relied on him to collect rents and supervise the peasants who lived and worked on their land. He rarely spent time at the manor, but she wasn't surprised to learn this man was connected to their bailiff in some way. Henry was. . . shifty. She never cared much for the man.

"Where is your escort?"

The question took her by surprise.

"I—"

"Here."

Lord Hedford's voice startled her. She'd left him behind, promising to return with news of Christina's welfare, and hadn't expected to see him so soon.

"Lady Juliette was just inquiring after my wife. Good day, Blackburn."

He took her elbow and guided her away before Juliette could bid the man farewell.

"I planned to—"

"I know. I saw Blackburn waylay you. Come, we'll check on Christina together."

They wove through the exodus as people left the hall to return to the lists—the afternoon jousts would begin shortly. As they climbed the winding stone stairs that led to the upper floor, Hedford warned her against her unwanted companion.

"You would do well to avoid him. The man is a lecher at best."

She shuddered, remembering the question he had posed to her.

"He says he visited Chauncy Manor, though I don't remember him. So you know the man?"

"I know of him. 'Tis said he colludes with those who attempt to destabilize the border for profit. His reputation makes him popular with those who feel the Scots belong in their own country and resent any attempt at peace."

"Why do you tell me all this?" Her father would never have been so forthcoming.

He pushed open the heavy oak door that led to their private chambers. "Because you asked."

Juliette was about to reply that she'd asked her father on plenty of occasions for more information, only to be told it was the business of men. Worse, her mother usually sided with her father on such matters. For a couple who did nothing more than cohabitate, they often shared the same opinion.

She was about to commend the man—not that she wasn't still suspicious of him—when the door fully opened. And the sight that greeted them made her heart leap in fear.

The empty chamber was devoid of Christina and her maid.

Hedford glanced at her, and Juliette shrugged, trying to appear casual. But she knew Christina, and this did not bode well. She was normally exactly where she was supposed to be.

Without another word, they both turned and walked back toward the hall. As they made their way down the stairs to find her friend, the very person they sought ran up the stairs toward them.

Christina halted as she turned the corner. "Oh!"

I knew it!

Her friend looked as hearty as she had at the meal. Her ailment was obviously temporary. Other than the flush that was creeping up her delicate cheeks, she looked perfectly fine.

She looked from Juliette to Hedford.

"I believe we need to talk." Hedford took his wife's hand and guided her back toward the private chambers.

It seemed she would have to learn about Christina's true whereabouts later.

In the meantime, Juliette would take advantage of her freedom to seek the man she'd dreamt of all last eve. She'd awoken from a fitful sleep to the imagined sensation of his lips on hers. He had invaded her thoughts both asleep and awake.

His joust had been too early to attend this morn, though Juliette had spied his shield on the wall of shields, so she knew he'd won his match.

As she walked back through the hall and down the flight of stairs that led to the castle's entranceway, she prayed Lord Blackburn had moved on. She had no desire to meet him again without a champion. Her distrust of that man was as strong as her trust of Toren—both were instinctive feelings she couldn't quite explain.

It was a warm day, and the sun hung high and bright in the sky, seeming to smile down on the event. Not a cloud in the sky to mar its perfect blue hue. She walked with purpose to the lists, enjoying the freedom, even if it was temporary. Toren had not appeared at the midday meal. Nor had she seen him watching the jousts. Juliette scanned the galleries, though she didn't expect to find him there. Most of the knights who were not participating stood off to the side as they shouted for their favorites.

Makeshift marketplaces had been built into both the inner and outer baileys for the tourney. On her way to the lists, Juliette had passed stands of fruits and vegetables, tables with merchant's wares, and even acrobats and stilt-walkers who were vying for the attention of potential customers.

Perhaps she would return to peruse the stalls, though somehow she didn't think Toren Kerr would be shopping for wood carvings or spices. On the other hand, she wasn't foolish enough to venture too far from the center of activity alone.

"We meet again. 'Tis indeed my lucky day."

It was certainly not hers. Had Lord Blackburn followed her?

"Well met, my lord." She tried to nod politely and walk past him, but he moved to block her path.

"Indeed. Has Hedford lost his charge?"

Though the question was innocent enough, his tone was edged with sarcasm. She tried again to pass.

"I was just returning to him—"

"Nay," he took her by the elbow, "come with me to watch the next match."

She would do no such thing.

"My lord, I must be—"

"I won't hear of anything but your assent, my lady. Come."

He tugged her more forcefully, and this time she was more firmly dismissive.

"Please let go of my arm."

She was proud that her voice sounded so strong and unwavering.

"Where do you—"

"She asked you to let go of her arm."

Toren.

She couldn't see him—the voice had come from behind her—but the expression on Blackburn's face left no doubt. He dropped her arm as if it were on fire. And though his eyes narrowed, Blackburn took a step away from her.

Juliette stood frozen to the spot.

"If you don't hurry, you'll miss the next match you dearly wished to watch," Toren said.

He must have overheard their conversation.

"Filthy Scot." Blackburn walked away, but not before giving Toren a look that said their conversation was not finished.

Juliette turned then and felt like she'd just fallen from a castle turret. He was dressed in a cream tunic, the sleeves of which were rolled to his elbows and a pair of tight—what did they call them in his country—breeks?

This look suited him.

Oddly, he didn't seem bothered by Blackburn's parting remark.

"Did you hear—"

"Are you unharmed?"

He wasn't smiling. In fact, it was the most serious she'd ever seen him. With the exception of during his joust, of course. But his helmet had hidden his face. Mayhap he had been grinning from ear to ear under it.

"Aye," she said, and tried again. "You don't look—"

"I'll bid you a good day," Toren said, departing.

"Wait!"

She grabbed his bare forearm on instinct, eager to keep him with her. She pulled away immediately, but not before she noticed how his arm felt below her hand. Hard, not unlike his personality in some ways. While the Scottish chief was normally quick to smile, something was clearly bothering him.

"I must to speak with you."

"My lady—"

"Juliette."

He was so different today. "Have I done something to offend you?"

"Nay, lass. You have not." But his actions proclaimed otherwise.

"Why did you agree to stay?"

She didn't mean to sound as demanding as a steward reprimanding his staff, but something was not right. The man who kissed her, who'd invaded her thoughts and rescued her—*twice*—was not the one who stood before her now.

This was the man she'd seen a glimpse of last night. The chief.

The hardened border lord. The kind of man, perhaps, who did not fall in love with his wife.

Could she have misjudged him so?

"I told you, I need to speak with someone."

Why was he being so frustrating? "Aye, and you said he was not here. Why did you decide to stay?"

A horn sounded, signaling the beginning of a match.

"I would suggest you not attend the joust unescorted with Blackburn on the loose. Good day, my lady."

Without giving her time to react, he walked away. The brute—perhaps her first assessment had been accurate after all—was gone. He was certainly no Erec, and she was feeling less and less like Enide each moment. She'd always fantasized about that knight, who'd won a tournament just to defend the assertion that his lady was the most beautiful.

Mayhap the story was just that. A fantasy.

But she intended to find out.

"Kerr! How does it go, you wee beast?"

The slap on the back that accompanied the greeting would have knocked down a smaller man. Toren wasn't looking for company, but in his rush to put distance between himself and Juliette, he had nearly run straight into the reiver.

Clan MacAdder had come upon hard times. Once a powerful border family, their already small numbers had been decimated, and the fierce chieftain had become a notorious border reiver.

He returned the favor, only he *did* manage to disengage MacAdder's feet from the ground.

"Better than you," Toren said.

The crowd had thinned as two popular contestants were facing each other in the nearby lists. Applause and shouts of encouragement could be heard even at this distance.

"I'll be thanking you not to remind me."

Toren pointed to the man's head, which was devoid of hair. "Reiving has not been easy on you, I see. Your hair's gone missing."

The chieftain laughed, a hearty sound Toren remembered from his youth. Clan Kerr had few allies thanks to his father's mistrust of anyone beyond his own kin, but he liked to think of MacAdder as an old family friend. His father had thought highly of the man and would be disappointed to see how his clan fared recently.

"Survivin' just fine, laddie, my hair be damned."

MacAdder's grandfather was a Highlander who'd settled along the border, bringing his kinsman with him. Toren remembered his father telling stories of the "savage brute" who'd terrorized the borderlands. Toren suspected the truth was not quite as entertaining.

"Though not as well as you, from what this old man can see."

"Old man," he frowned, dismissing the idea. "A few grey hairs in your beard doesn't make you old, MacAdder. Though your eyesight is failing if you think Clan Kerr is without its own troubles."

There was an expression along the border: 'living so close to the English has a way of making even the brightest day seem dark and grey.'

"Och, my failing eyes did not blind me to the fair lassie I saw you with earlier."

Juliette. Toren's stomach roiled at the thought of what he was going to do to her.

He hadn't planned on seeing her, certainly hadn't planned on talking to her. When he saw Blackburn near her, though, every muscle in his body had prepared for a fight. Everything he knew of the man put him on his guard. The coward had even cried foul after Toren had laid him out in the first pass of their match.

He was a coward, the kind of man who likely mishandled women because he could.

Blackburn was lucky Toren hadn't killed him.

"She's the English warden's daughter."

"Ahh, of course. Her reputation is warranted."

More so than MacAdder realized.

"Where is that traitor anyway?"

So Hallington's reputation had been spreading.

He shrugged. "Not here apparently. Why do you call him a traitor?"

He had to gather information on his target from as many people as he could.

"Surely you've heard. 'Tis said he's taking bribes, allowing innocent Scotsmen to be hung. Some are calling for a boycott of the Day of Truce. Others aren't so friendly in their judgments."

So the rumors that had reached Scotland's ear were true. More importantly, the borderers believed they were true.

"I may have heard something similar. But you know—"

"Clan Kerr," MacAdder said, interrupting him, "*sero sed serio*. And if you haven't heard of Hallington's duplicity, you're certainly late to this one."

"Aye, but you've forgotten the second part of our motto. Late *but* in earnest."

If only MacAdder knew.

"Come with me." He clapped Toren's back and pushed him toward the cheers. "I hear young MacDonald is matched against Thornhurst. Should be quite a joust."

Toren hadn't planned on being a spectator. But if he had to wait for Hallington anyway. . .

"If the man is as skilled as he's reputed to be, MacDonald may just end the Day of Truce today," he said, allowing himself to be pulled toward the lists.

The rash laird had nearly gotten himself killed the year before in the melee, famously taking off his helmet and throwing it at an opponent.

"With the Waryn men not participating this year, some are betting on Thornhurst as English champion."

Toren couldn't help but frown.

"Ah, laddie, I'll be apologizing for that. Forgot you are related to Waryn now."

MacAdder laughed as only a man whose sister hadn't fallen for an Englishman could do. "Bristol is too far south. The king was a fool for havin' you take it."

Though he agreed, Toren was loath to say so. He'd only taken the holding on his king's orders, but he'd never intended to lose it. It was the first time he had ever failed at anything, save being a good enough son to keep his mother from running back to England.

"So you know of the youngest Waryn's reputation then? 'Tis said the boy is becoming a man like his brothers."

Toren had heard. His own sister extolled the family's merits on every occasion she had to do so. Some said Neill Waryn was as skilled as Bryce but as ruthless as Geoffrey. A combination he'd like to see for himself. He was the Waryn sibling Toren had yet to meet.

"There he is." Toren pointed to the English knight who was seneschal of Camburg Castle, one of Lady Sara Caiser's holdings. The wife of the elder Waryn brother, Sir Geoffrey, was indirectly related to him now as well. It seemed his future was inextricably entwined with the Waryns whether he liked it or not.

And he definitely did not.

"He's not a small man," MacAdder said.

Toren followed his countryman to a wooden fence lined with spectators. But rather than watch the fight, he found himself turning his head up toward the galleries. The glint of jewels and the vibrant colors of the ladies' gowns was a sight to behold, but when he found himself seeking the blonde hair of a particular English rose, Toren turned back to the match.

He would not allow himself to think of the softness of a particular woman's lips, let alone the way his hands itched to explore every inch of her luscious body. He would not think of her lying next to him, naked, as he explored the quirks of her most interesting personality.

The horn's blast pulled him from his thoughts. Dangerous thoughts given her identity.

At least she was not here, and with any luck would stay out of trouble.

Not bloody likely.

8

"You *what?*"

Juliette must have misheard her friend. It had sounded very much like, 'I went to see the Scot in the tent city.'

"When you caught me returning to my chamber. Matthew was none too happy. He's threatened to have us both—"

"Christina, please start from the beginning."

They sat on Juliette's bed. Though her room wasn't overly large, it was near miraculous both she and her "chaperones" had been given private rooms. If not for her father's position, it never would have happened. The most important men and women in Northumbria, and others from across England, were in attendance. Wealthy, prominent families were housed here, while still others had found rooms in the nearby village. Nearly all of the tournament participants were relegated to the tent city.

"And do stop rolling your eyes."

Juliette had spent the day considering her problem. Realizing Toren wanted naught to do with her, she had attempted to give serious consideration to other gentlemen in attendance.

But after that futile and disheartening exercise, she'd spent most of the evening's meal attempting to coax Christina into sharing the reason for her strange behavior—all while trying to avoid eye contact with the very men she'd considered earlier that day.

When she wasn't looking for Toren, of course. And attempting to dissuade herself from admitting she had, in fact, been looking for him.

After saving her from the wretched Lord Blackburn, he'd disappeared for the remainder of the day, confirming his suspected disinterest in her.

Finally, she'd gotten Christina up to her room and convinced her to tell her the truth.

"So that's why Hedford insisted on escorting us up here when we begged to retire early? But you've yet to explain what you could possibly have been thinking to go there unescorted. Not to mention. . . *why?*"

"Shhhh," Christina admonished. "Helen likely has her ears to the door right now. Matthew told her not to let me out of her sight. She insisted on stationing herself outside your door when I told her I was coming over here."

Juliette smiled. She imagined the woman cross-legged against the door. Though not much older than she and Christina, the woman's ever-present stern expression made her appear twice their age. "Do you remember when Helen caught us sneaking out to the abbey? I was no more than ten and two."

Christina tucked her robe under her slippers and leaned forward. "Aye, she told her mother and none other. Thank the heavens."

Though they both adored Helen, whose family had served Christina's for generations, they could have done without the extra pair of eyes throughout the years.

Which would have made walking to the abbey after dark, alone, extremely dangerous.

"Speaking of sneaking off. . ."

"Right, that," Christina said.

She looked at the door once more and lowered her voice. "It was a bit foolish. But I'm so worried for you, Juliette. I just wanted to speak to the man. You know, to tell him not to hurt you."

Juliette grabbed a fistful of her hair, swept it to one side, and began to braid it. "I assumed as much." She knew her friend had meant well, and once Christina had admitted to the visit, it had been easy enough to guess her purpose. "What did he say?"

Christina raised her eyebrows.

So her casual tone had not been so casual after all.

"Christina!"

"He said he had no intention of hurting you. Aren't you afraid of him?"

Not since the first time they'd met, and even then, she'd been more intimidated than afraid. "Nay. He does look quite fierce though."

"Something about him. . ." Christina shifted on the bed, the cream-and-lilac coverlet barely visible in the sparse light from the candle sitting beside the bed.

"Did he say much else?"

Christina shook her head. "Nay, he was quite guarded with his words. You said you spoke with him earlier. Did he give you any indication of his intentions?"

"Aye, that he had none whatsoever. He fairly ran off the moment we met."

A knock at the door meant Matthew was back.

"What will you do?"

That was the very question that had plagued Juliette all afternoon. With less than a week to find a husband she could love—one who was capable of loving her in return—her choices were narrowing every day. None of the other men made her feel quite the way the Scottish chief did whenever she was in his presence. But he clearly had been avoiding her. If he had wished to see her again, he need only have made an appearance at supper.

Then why had he kissed her? Twice.

Because you asked him to. Simple as that.

"I have to go." Christina bounded off the bed and made her way to the door.

She heard Hedford's voice as Christina opened the door.

"Conspiring against my. . ."

Juliette couldn't hear the rest, for Christina closed the door behind her, but Hedford didn't sound angry. Perhaps her friend had gotten lucky after all. Husband and wife seemed to get along well enough, and Christina had confided in her that the marital act was actually quite enjoyable, although she refused to elaborate. Christina had always been the proper one, Juliette the hoyden.

She was the one who'd always gotten them into trouble more often than not.

Emboldened by tales of ladies doing far greater things than she had ever accomplished, she'd often get her friend into trouble. It was she who had suggested putting a dittany of crete in her father's oats once as a lark, though the herb had no discernable effect on his affections for her mother. It was she who'd given the first jeweled necklace she'd ever received to a serving girl without realizing the girl's parents would question such a prize. That incident had not at all pleased Juliette's mother, but she'd overheard the girl telling another she would never own such a bauble. What else was she to do?

And yet Christina was the one who had taken the real risk. She'd made her way to the tent city to speak with Toren.

The idea that was taking place in her mind was outrageous. So much could go wrong.

But who would stop her?

If Christina had made her way there, surely she could do it too. Granted, it was dark and likely much more dangerous at this time of night. But what choice did she have?

She had to know. Had she misread Toren's feelings toward her? Should she forget about him and concentrate on finding love elsewhere? If so, she would know this night and not spend another precious moment pining for a man who wanted nothing to do with her.

She moved quickly.

Juliette dressed simply in a kirtle and sleeveless surcoat, leaving her hair braided and uncovered. She slipped on a pair of soft leather shoes and took the small, jeweled dagger her mother had given her. It had seemed an unusual gift at the time, especially coming from her mild-mannered mother. Her mother had explained that even though the abbey lay on the south border of their property, and Juliette always traveled with a guard, it would make her feel better to know she had the dagger with her.

Her father had refused to offer her lessons on how to use such a weapon, so she had turned to the armorer, who was like a second father to her.

Slipping the dagger into a pocket sewn into her kirtle, she took the lantern each guest was given for occasions such as these. Well, maybe not quite exactly like this one.

Although no one gave her a second glance as she strode through the outer edge of the hall where the evening's celebrations had finally begun to break up, she had no illusions that it would be as easy to find Toren's tent safely.

To him that will, ways are not wanting.

A fine saying that she'd once read and oft repeated to herself, but staring out into the dark night from the enormous keep, Juliette wasn't so sure about the truth of those words.

Fires dotted the landscape. The men unwilling to attend the feast kept council here in the tent city. Toren was one of a handful of Scotsmen who had ventured to the earl's domain, but tonight he had eaten with the men here, a simple meal of roasted duck. All hunting regulations had been lifted for the duration of the tournament, a fact both guests and servants of Condren were taking full advantage of.

Though he'd managed to avoid Juliette for the remainder of the day, he had not stopped thinking of her. The sweetness of her kiss. Her innocence despite the fact that she seemed to entangle herself in very unladylike predicaments. On each occasion they'd met, she was either being harassed by an overzealous man or escaping the notice of her chaperone in situations bound to get her into trouble. It made him want to protect her, to tell the world that she was not to be trifled with.

Where the devil was her father? He had thought to ask her directly that afternoon, but the rush of emotion he felt when Blackburn had laid hands on her. . . He had to get away from her. No doubt the father would arrive on the morrow, and though he didn't like it, knowing the daughter would work in his favor. He wanted the deed done as quickly as possible.

Before leaving for the night, his hired squire, who had already fed his horse and polished his armor, had left him a tankard of ale. His doubts had been alleviated. Toren would offer the lad a position in his household. Alfred was competent and obviously wanting for such a position. He'd speak with him on the morrow.

He stood from the stool Alfred had fetched, a noise near MacDuff's tent capturing his attention. Something was afoot, but before he could decide whether or not to involve himself, it seemed the fray was coming to him.

As the outline of two people moved closer, he dropped the mug and grabbed his sword, which was never far from his hand. Though the shapes didn't appear to be moving quickly, an abundance of caution was nearly always warranted.

"You lost something, Kerr."

MacDuff. With. . . a woman?

Nay, it couldn't be.

"Ye best tell her 'tis not safe to be conspiring with the enemy alone at night."

Juliette. What in God's name was the woman doing here?

"Thank you for your assistance, sir," Juliette said, "but I believe you've mentioned that fact on more than one occasion."

"Ha! Sir. Do you hear that, Kerr? If I—"

"My thanks, MacDuff."

With a final glance at Toren and Juliette, the aging laird, who participated in the tournament's revelries but not the actual fighting, retreated to his own tent.

"Bloody hell, woman, what were you thinking?"

Not one, but two visits from English ladies today. The sparsely wooded field adjacent to the wall of the castle's outer bailey was no place for any woman day or night. Married men who brought their wives to the tournament found shelter in the village, unless of course they were honored guests residing within the castle.

His heart raced thinking about the dangers that could have befallen her. Juliette's simple dress did nothing to temper her beauty. In fact, without any jewels or elaborate hairstyles, she looked even more lovely.

His cock stirred, reminding him that he was alone with the very woman who'd haunted his dreams the last two mornings. He'd pictured her lips on his own more than once, and despite her last name, he looked at those lips now. Her tongue peeked out to wet them, and Toren imagined tracing that same path with his own.

She had to leave.

"I don't know why you're here, but you must—"

"I'm not leaving."

"Not. . ." He took a deep breath. "Juliette, this is no place for—"

"Until you answer a question."

She stood close enough for him to reach out and touch her. His hand ached to feel the softness of her bare skin under his rough, battle-hardened hands.

"Does your friend know you're here? Does anyone?"

She was either extremely foolish or very naive.

"Nay." She stuck out her dainty chin and crossed her arms over her chest.

"One question," he agreed.

He glanced back at MacDuff's tent, but no one moved within it. Beyond that he could see only the light of several fires and the outline of the Condren Castle's gatehouse. It was quiet, thankfully, for most of the men had retreated to their tents to prepare for the next day's activities.

"Why did you kiss me?"

Had he heard her correctly? She came to ask. . .

"Why did I kiss you? Because you asked me to."

He glanced down at her breasts, which climbed higher as she tightened her arms about her chest.

"Oh."

Her lips formed a perfect circle. She blinked, clearly not having expected that answer.

To be fair, it was not entirely true. It was mad of him to say anything else, particularly when she seemed inclined to accept his lie, but he found himself speaking nonetheless.

"I kissed you because I wanted to." And because he wanted *her*. Now. "Come, I'll take you back—"

"You planned to leave but decided to stay. You wanted to kiss me but didn't return to the castle this evening. Please help me understand."

She could never understand.

"You shouldn't be here."

"Nay, I should not. But I had to know."

A rider approached from the edge of camp, and though he turned before coming close enough to see them clearly, Toren lifted the flap of the tent and pulled his reckless Englishwoman inside.

"You're lucky it was MacDuff who found you. Do you have no care for your reputation? If you were found here. . ."

Juliette held up her small metal lantern, the candle inside flickering.

"'Tis small," she said of the inside of his tent.

Undeniably true. Although it offered enough room to stand, it didn't afford much else.

"I hadn't planned on having company here."

The small space felt even smaller now. He'd reacted rashly, which was unlike him. But it really would serve no purpose for her to be seen here alone. Particularly not at this time of night.

"Your—"

"I know, my reputation. The carefully cultivated, always protected reputation of a lady nobly born. Mayhap I no longer wish to abide by rules that were made solely for the advancement of men. This is my only chance at adventure, and if you think I—"

"Oh!"

He took the lantern from her hand and placed it on the ground beside them. Pulling her to him, Toren cut off the rest of her speech short with the kiss he'd wanted to give her all day.

He cupped Juliette's face with his hands and guided her lips to his own. Capturing them, he continued where they had left off the night before. This time, he pressed harder, plunged deeper. The rage he had felt at seeing her mishandled finally subsided as he drank from her lips, their softness his undoing.

Aye, he wanted her—in a way he hadn't experienced before. His body simply responded whenever she was near.

He broke away, needing to see her.

"Jules." He didn't even recognize his own voice, thick with desire.

She licked the lips he had just kissed so thoroughly. Her willing response emboldened his hands to explore, to touch the creamy bare skin above the kirtle that peeked out beneath her plain cream surcoat.

She watched him as he touched her, the whites of her eyes flickering through the darkness courtesy of the candlelight from the ground below. His hand dipped below the material, pushing it aside, sliding it lower.

He withdrew, or tried to, but her hand covered his own.

"Show me."

Ah God, the lass would be the death of him.

Her hand still on his, he dipped his fingers below her neckline and let his thumb extend as far down as the garment would allow.

It was just enough. Slipping his thumb over the hard nipple below, he moved it back and forth but then promptly pulled his hand away as if it had been burned.

"I cannot."

"Cannot, or will not?"

Both.

"Juli—"

"I rather like Jules instead."

He took a step back, just to be safe. Toren found it difficult to control himself when she was near.

"Jules, you don't understand."

"Make me understand. Is it because I'm English?"

He shook his head. "Nay. I'm not here to—"

"Aye, I know, you're here to speak to someone. Both the tournament and I are distractions."

What could he possibly say to that?

"And I thought my father stubborn."

It was the opening he needed.

"Your father," he repeated. "I imagine it will be more difficult for you to frolic about the countryside once he arrives."

"I don't frolic. And we've already established why I'm here."

Toren took a deep breath. A few more moments and he would forget the fact that she was Hallington's daughter. Forget his mission. Forget everything save the feeling of this woman in his arms. He couldn't afford to forget.

"I don't believe we have."

Her eyes narrowed. "Aye, I would imagine frolicking about the countryside would be more difficult with my father in attendance. Alas, that won't be a problem since—"

"I came here to speak with him."

Toren wasn't exactly sure why he'd told her. . . except that he felt he owed this woman, who offered everything and took nothing, as much truth as he could give her.

"This is why I was so surprised last eve to learn your identity."

Her father?

Toren made no sense. Nothing about this meeting made any sense. Granted, she was far from skilled in the art of courtship, but this was not exactly what she had planned back at Chauncy Manor.

She'd hoped for a chance to taunt the fates. To find love. To escape her parents' destiny. Aye. But a reticent Scotsman had kissed her, making her forget everything in the world save the feeling of his lips on hers. A man clearly bred for war but who had shown her as much kindness in two days as all of her potential suitors combined.

Nay.

And yet that very man had just admitted to his own mistruth.

"You lied to me."

"I didn't—"

"Aye, you did. Why are you looking for my father? Why didn't you tell me this last eve?"

She had so many more questions, but those would be sufficient to start.

His face hardened. The softness was gone, and the clan chief was back.

"You surprised me, and I'm rarely taken by surprise."

She disliked his harsh tone and would have turned and walked away if her curiosity had not been piqued.

"And?"

She crossed her arms as she was wont to do when miffed. And waited.

If the man hadn't been so handsome, she could have concentrated a bit more easily. She found herself staring at his frown, wondering how it was possible those pursed lips were the same ones that had moved so expertly over hers just moments earlier.

"I am a border lord. Your father is warden."

"What is that supposed to mean?" His lack of an answer was all she needed. She'd thought him different. But when it came to politics, he was the same as any man. "Matters too complicated for my woman's mind. Is that it?"

She was frustrating him, but she didn't care. "Which topic exactly did you plan to speak to him about? Let me take a guess, shall I? Is it the recent unrest? Rumors of a boycott on the Day of Truce? My father taking bribes?"

The look on his face...

She'd managed to surprise him. Good! And yet, she was so weary of the constant unease that threatened the tenuous peace their kings both seemed so determined to destroy.

"How do you—"

She'd had enough. He was not the man she'd thought he was after all.

Juliette turned to lift the tent flap, but Toren grabbed her hand. She unwittingly turned to face him.

"I am leaving."

She pulled her hand away, and this time he let her go. Ducking under the flap, she breathed in the warm summer air, belatedly realizing she'd left the lantern inside his tent.

At least she had the moonlight to guide her. Which was not as helpful as one might think. No more than two feet from the tent, she realized her error. It was quite a bit darker without the single candle to guide her way. As if he'd heard the silent plea, a light suddenly appeared from behind her. She turned, but he had already backed away, leaving the lantern on the ground beside her.

Like she'd done earlier, Juliette traversed the perimeter of the tent city, and this time no one stopped her. When she reached the gatehouse, a partial truth was all that was needed to get her through.

"I visited the tent city to speak with one of the contestants."

Though Juliette was forced to endure the same guffaws and jeering comments she'd been subjected to on her way there, she was nevertheless allowed entry. At least they could not see her face clearly, as she'd pulled a hood over her head prior to both encounters with the guards. Apparently a lone woman of loose morals was not seen as a threat. But as she made her way toward the main keep, traversing the eerie silence so at odds with the bustle of the bailey at daytime, her bravado began to wane. Juliette's cheeks tingled as she fought tears that she would allow to fall once she was inside the sanctuary of her bedchamber.

Toren Kerr wasn't the one for her after all.

9

He should not have told her.

Nor should he be sitting in the hall watching her now, but it seemed he'd left his good sense in Scotland.

After following Juliette back to the castle last eve to ensure her safety, Toren had returned to an empty tent, unsure exactly what had just occurred. Up until now, there'd been precisely three times in his life he'd felt out of control. When he watched his father die on the battlefield in front of him. The day his mother admitted to hating everything about his country and fled for England, leaving him and his young siblings behind. And when he lost Bristol and Bryce Waryn took his sister captive.

Toren's every decision was based on his desire to shield Catrina, Alex, and Reid from harm. To keep his clan safe. He forged no relationships with women other than to warm his bed. He allowed Clan Kerr few allies, not trusting many beyond his own clansmen. Yet here he was, in enemy territory, giving too much information to a virtual stranger simply because she could speak as easily of border politics as she could of ancient tales most did not know existed. Because he couldn't banish the memory of her body pressed against his.

Or the feel of her lips. The brush of his fingers on her soft flesh, her perfect mound cupped in his hand.

Stop!

He was a fool. But instead of waiting patiently for her father to arrive, using her anger to distance himself, here he was—sitting through another of the earl's feasts, this time hidden across the hall from her. Waiting, watching.

After winning his third match, Toren had escaped to the village for the afternoon. His squire, proving ever capable, had accompanied him and managed to negotiate better prices on badly needed supplies, including a new roundel. He'd overused his jousting dagger, but initially he had not planned on staying long enough to need one.

He had thought to return to the tent city for a light repast, but instead his feet had brought him here. The English knights at his table had tried to engage him in their discussion after realizing he was the champion favorite, a designation marked by the placement of his shield on the wall of shields. A representative from both sides met after each day's events to rank and announce contests for the next day. If Toren had needed additional equipment, or desired prominence, he could have entered additional events. But he had no use for either, only the excuse to remain until the melee, waiting for a chance to carry out his mission.

He ignored their bawdy comments about the serving wench who repeatedly tried to earn his favor and concentrated instead on the woman seated not far from the great table.

Jules's gown was more elaborate than usual this eve. The deep purple contrasted beautifully with the blonde waves cascading down her dress in every direction. A gold circlet around her head was the only adornment he could see from this distance.

The meal finally ended, and two loud claps from the host indicated the musicians should begin to play a different type of music, one that ensured some guests would rise from their seats. This was the moment Toren had awaited, and it seemed luck was finally on his side. A circle dance, but a slow one.

Toren made his way quickly across the hall, approaching Jules from behind.

"My lady, may I escort you in this dance?"

She and her two companions turned at once. He waited for her to refuse him.

"You may," she answered, happily surprising him. She stood from her seat and smoothed out the velvet dress he'd been staring at all evening. He resisted the urge to reach out and touch it. To touch her. Instead he held out his elbow, and she took it.

They walked arm in arm to the provisional dance floor, a large opening at the foot of the dais. Enough couples had paired off to form a large circle.

Thank you, Catrina, for forcing me to learn this abhorrent dance.

His sister had civilized him. Or tried to, at least.

"I'm surprised you accepted my offer," he said as they began to move.

He looked straight ahead and spoke loud enough for her alone to hear. Toren wished he could see her expression.

"I welcome any opportunity to name you a lout and liar."

The casual tone did not fool him. His lady was furious, and rightly so.

"I'm sorry, Jules." It was what he had come here to say—or so he thought. He wasn't quite certain about anything when it came to her. "I did not mean to offend you."

Of course, it was inevitable that he would. He had lain awake most of the night dwelling on the way she'd looked at him after leaving the tent. And she'd only known he needed to speak to her father. If she knew the full truth. . .

Though he should not have told her, it was too late for regrets. But he wanted her to understand.

"I need you to know I would never believe you were lesser because of your sex."

He took her left hand in his own, marveling, once again, on how small and delicate it felt. He spun her once around and was able to steal a quick look at her face.

Still furious.

"I respect my sister Catrina as much as any man. She's always asked to be treated the same as my brothers, and we've honored that request. Because of it, she is as capable, more so in many ways, as me and my two brothers."

He turned to the woman on his right, bowed, and took her arm in his. She smiled. And though she was beautiful, her dark hair contrasted too starkly to his other dance partner's gleaming blonde locks. This lady paled in comparison. All others paled in comparison.

He spun back around, as eager as a laddie, to face Jules. It was the moment he'd been waiting for. As the dance dictated, he clasped her around the waist with both hands and lifted her slightly into the air. Placing her back down, he released one hand and allowed the other to stay, grabbing her free hand with his own.

They spun to the slow, sensual sound of the music.

His heart raced as he looked into her eyes. Pleading. "Please believe me. I did not mean to hurt you, Jules."

How had he not noticed the small, faint mark under the left side of her chin. Some said such marks were from the devil. To him it made her appear more real. At times, when he looked at her, Toren could almost believe she had been carved from stone, so perfect were her features.

"I believe you."

He didn't want to let her go.

He never wanted to let her go.

"Let me come to you."

Damn, Toren! Is there no end to your foolishness?

She'd likely never agree anyway. . .

"Okay," she whispered. "I am--"

"I will find you." He had to get out of here. Now. Luckily, the song ended and Jules walked away before he could make an even greater fool of himself.

What had he been thinking?

"Kerr. . . dancing? I don't believe it."

The voice behind him was familiar.

Turning, Toren smiled for the first time since he'd disappointed Jules the evening before.

"Gregory! What the devil—"

"Dancing? Toren Kerr?"

The men moved aside for the dancers as a more lively tune than the last began to play. Toren forced himself not to glance back at the tables as guests continued to drink from the earl's deep stores of wine and ale. Instead, he focused on his fellow Scotsman, who looked quite comfortable in the Earl of Condren's hall.

Though they were very different, Gregory Campbell having been practically raised at court, Toren would be forever indebted to the man.

"Have you been here since the start of the tournament? What news from the Eastern Marches?" Toren asked.

True to his nature, Gregory winked at an obviously married Englishwoman who brushed past him on her way to join the dance with her husband.

"I've no wish to defend your non-existent honor to a cuckolded Englishman, Gregory."

A few years his junior, the chief's son smiled in a way that told Toren he wasn't far off the mark.

"Then perhaps you should reconsider your own suit." Gregory looked in the direction Toren had been avoiding. "Hallington's daughter? Isn't one English in your family enough?"

"One too many, if truth be told."

Whether in reference to his brother-in-law or his mother, Toren could not be sure. Either way, he'd not tolerate a reference to his English mother from most people. But the Battle of Largs had forged an unbreakable friendship between him and Gregory.

"They say she's refused so many suitors her father recently settled on Lord Wytham as a husband. I wonder if her intended knows of Hallington's duplicity?"

He was not particularly fond of the idea that Juliette was betrothed to be married.

"I care less about the girl than I do her father." If Toren had known Gregory was in attendance, he'd have asked him for an accounting of Hallington from the start. The man knew every move made by every important noble in both countries.

"So the rumors are true?" he asked instead.

Gregory smiled at yet another woman. This lady appeared quite distracted by his friend's good looks—she missed a step and earned a sharp glance from her dancing partner.

"'Tis more than rumor," his friend said. "Blackburn brags of killing two Scotsmen at The Wild Boar. 'Tis a borderer inn, and everyone knows to avoid bloodshed there. Apparently, the men he attacked did nothing more than glance his way. But he's not being held accountable for his crimes. Especially after the incident at the last truce day, and now this, his name should appear on the list of those being brought to trial. But it does not."

Though Toren hadn't heard of this particular incident, the story was a familiar one. Englishmen paying off the warden to avoid being brought to trial at the Day of Truce for crimes against Scotsmen. . . it was the very reason the king had sent him here.

"Have you heard why the warden is not in attendance?"

Jules had not told him when her father planned to arrive, and he did not want to raise her suspicions any further by asking outright. But if anyone knew, it would be Gregory.

"Nay, just that he's expected to be here, of course. Some are saying the rumors may have reached his ears and the man is too cowardly to make an appearance. But others vouch for his character and insist he'd never compromise his position."

"Exactly why the English king refuses to appoint another warden. He insists the man is innocent and refuses to investigate."

"Och, well, something must be done. 'Tis said one of the dead men is related to Douglas."

Why hadn't Douglas mentioned it if he'd lost family to the corruption?

"There'll be hell to pay when he finds out," Gregory continued. "'Tis rumored the man leaves behind a wife and five children."

The words sent a shiver down his spine. "When did this happen?"

Gregory didn't appear to have heard him. He was too busy flirting. He watched as his friend met the gaze of the married Englishwoman and nodded his head to indicate the very corridor where Toren had met Jules the evening before. Toren groaned inwardly.

"Dammit man, you need a wife to keep you out of trouble."

Gregory smiled. "I'll take one when you do, Kerr. Now if you'll excuse me. . ."

He placed his hand on Toren's arm and squeezed it. Remembering that his question had not yet been answered, he called out,"When did this incident happen?" to Gregory's retreating back.

The impatient lover turned just enough to call out, "More than ten days ago if memory serves."

Toren froze. So Douglas had known about his kin when he'd sent Toren to the tourney yet decided not to relay that particular bit of information.

Although he was not fond of learning information had been withheld, that bastard could not get away with such insolence any longer.

As much as Toren despised his mission, Douglas and his king were right. The warden could not be allowed to let murderers keep their freedom. Left unchecked, these incidents would destroy any chance of peace along the border.

Hallington had to be replaced.

And unfortunately, it was up to him to ensure it happened.

"You *what?*" Christina asked.

Juliette paced back and forth, pulling her robe tighter around her shoulders. She'd changed into a soft white chemise, though if Toren was truly coming to call, she would need to wear a proper dress. She opened the trunk where her gowns were stored, attempting to find one that would not require the assistance of a maid.

She'd made a mistake.

What is wrong with me? One moment I want to slit the man's throat for his duplicity, and as soon as he offers a few fancy words of apology, I find myself welcoming him to my private chambers.

She stopped looking in the trunk and glanced at Christina, who was dressed in a similar manner. She hadn't planned on telling her friend about this particular predicament, but the anxiety that had welled up in her as she waited for Toren had changed her mind.

Despite her reservations, she was beginning to quite like Hedford. Another man might have railed at her for knocking on his door late at night, but after answering her insistent knock—the sword in his hand had seemed unnecessary; all the same, she was grateful he was protective of his wife—he'd sent Christina over to her bedchamber. Now Christina sat on a cushioned chair before the small hearth, staring at her in open disbelief.

"When you said you wanted an adventure, I suppose you quite meant it. Seeking out a man in the tent city, alone, at night. Inviting him to your bedchamber. Have you truly gone mad?"

Juliette forgot the gowns and began to pace again.

"I believe so. But I may remind you, I'm not the only guilty one. Someone gave me the idea to seek him out there."

"Oh, *no*! That was during the day, and he hasn't shown a predilection to kiss me every time I'm near him."

Juliette shuddered at the thought of her friend in Toren's arms. Or any other woman for that matter. And if he thought she hadn't seen him flirt with nearly every maiden in the hall that eve, the man was sorely mistaken. Her efforts to keep from looking at him had failed miserably.

"The man is like my very own Vivienne of the Lake."

She stopped pacing long enough to see Christina's confused expression.

"Vivienne of the Lake. She raised Lancelot. Merlin *knew* she would entrap him once she had all of his secrets of magic, but he was still powerless to stop her. The entrancement she'd cast on him was too strong. And so, after learning all she could from the wizard, the Lady of the Lake trapped him in a tree!"

Christina's laugh forced Juliette to smile despite herself.

"Tell your Scotsman he is akin to your own Lady of the Lake, and you'll no longer need to worry about what to do with him. He'll likely run for the hills of Scotland, leaving you—"

"With no prospects for love." And that was the crux of it, wasn't it? That was why she had so readily accepted his apology even after swearing to do no such thing.

Christina leaned forward to place her hands closer to the fire. Though it was a warm summer night outside, the thick stone walls of the castle lent a chill to the rooms once the sun set. This particular bedchamber was adorned with tapestries on every wall and was not lacking for any luxuries. But the fire still offered a welcome warmth.

"Since you refuse to tell me what he did to warrant an apology, I can't comment. But I *can* advise you not to entertain a man you've known for a few days in your private chambers. If anyone were to find out—"

"Who would know unless Toren announces it on his way here? This is one of the most remote corridors in the castle. Aside from us and Hedford, none are housed here. And all the servants are downstairs in the hall." Then it occurred to her. "You won't tell—"

"Nay, of course not. But what if he overhears voices in here? The walls are thick, but—"

"I haven't heard one sound from your chamber yet. Which reminds me. . . I've been meaning to ask a bit more about the marriage bed. What exactly—"

A knock at the door nearly startled her off her feet.

What have I done?

"Christina." She implored her friend, but didn't know why. . . or what she wanted from her.

They stared at one another. The longer Toren stood outside, if it were truly him, the greater the possibly he would be caught. That could not be allowed.

Her friend's nod was so slight she nearly missed it.

Juliette rushed to the door and pulled the iron handle toward her.

She stood staring at Toren for what seemed like an eternity. She hadn't truly believed he would come. But he stood before her nonetheless, dressed in the same black and silver-trimmed surcoat he'd worn at dinner. His frame was nearly as large as the opening of the door itself.

A cough behind her reminded her they weren't alone.

"Sir, I ask the same of you now as I did yesterday. Good eve." With that, Christina brushed past Toren, who continued in the doorway. "And I suggest you not remain standing there for much longer unless you're looking to be the subject of quite a scandal."

Juliette opened the door wider in invitation and Toren walked through it. As he brushed past her, a flood of warmth seemed to creep from her toes upward. She closed the door and turned, not knowing what to say.

"Good evening, Jules."

10

How did one force a casual tone with a man standing in one's bedchamber? Should she ask him to take a seat? What exactly was the protocol?

There is no protocol, fool. You've broken every rule.

"Your friend does not object to me being here?" Toren asked.

"I wouldn't say that exactly."

He smiled. A devastating, sensual smile that reached his eyes. It really was quite warm in here.

"Do you mind?"

He indicated the chair Christina had vacated a moment earlier. Juliette nodded and made her way to the one adjacent to it. She sat and folded her hands on her lap.

"You're nervous."

"I've never entertained a man in my bedchamber before."

"Hmmm." He leaned forward, close enough that his distinct but pleasant smell overpowered the fumes emitted by the fire. "I would expect not."

"Why are you here?"

She had her suspicions, of course—and they both frightened and excited her—but Juliette cautioned herself to remain calm.

"I wanted to see you. To speak to you. Our brief conversation below stairs left some things unsaid."

She decided to be blunt. "You're here to talk?"

She was *not* disappointed.

Toren stood and took a step toward the fire. He picked up the iron and moved a log that had begun to suffocate the flames below it.

When he was done, he turned and looked at her.

"I would seduce you if I could, Jules. I'd show you what it's like between a man and a woman."

She could not breathe.

"But I will not dishonor you in that way. I'm here because I wished to see you. Speak to you. Hold you in my arms for a brief moment before my good sense returns."

She couldn't see his eyes, but Juliette sensed he was being truthful. And she didn't know what to make of it. Of course that's what she wanted as well. She couldn't give herself to a man who was not her husband. And Toren Kerr was certainly not her husband.

But could he be?

"I do not understand you," she admitted.

Not knowing what to do with her hands, she reached behind her to gather her unruly locks and pulled them to one side.

He stared at her in such a way that a strange feeling between her legs demanded her attention. It was like a family of butterflies had invaded her body.

"From the moment I caught you running from that wayward knight, I've been drawn to you in a way I've never been drawn to a woman."

"And that is bad?"

She had planned to question him again for lying about his purpose here, but instead found herself wanting to avoid the topic altogether.

"Aye, it is."

"Why?"

"Shall I be honest with you?"

Juliette held her breath. Something about his tone had changed. It was more serious, more ominous, and she nearly said no.

"Aye."

He sat back once more and simply looked at her.

"I have not once lied to you, Toren, and don't intend to. Please give me the same courtesy."

Still, he was silent.

Finally, he leaned forward and took her hand. "I want you. I want to be with you. But we could never marry. Which is why this unnatural desire for you is dangerous. In truth, I should not be here right now."

If she were to place her hand on her chest, Juliette knew she would be able to feel her heart beneath the thick fabric of her ermine-lined robe. It thudded a hard and fast rhythm. The words she wished to say were dangerous. Her father would disown her. Her mother would be appalled. Sister Heloise and the nuns would pray for her soul.

"Show me anyway."

"Jules, you don't understand—"

"I understand perfectly well, so please do not treat me like a wayward child. You are prepared for the time when you do marry. I—"

"It has nothing to do with—"

She took her hand from his and raised it into the air, palm outward. Juliette may not be wise to many things, but she did know this. If Toren did not want to marry her, then she would not shame herself by trying to convince him otherwise.

But by all that was holy, she would not marry Lord Wytham or enter a nunnery without ever having known what it was like to be with a man who desired her—one whom she desired in return.

"If I'm to be doomed to a loveless marriage, I would like to first know what it feels like to be with a man of my choosing."

Toren began pacing back and forth along the foot of her bed, following in her footsteps, as it were, though he didn't seem to realize what he was doing. He stopped and looked at her as if wondering how she could bear to sit so still.

All of her doubts seemed to float into the air and disappear like the ash that periodically floated up from the fire.

"What you're asking is impossible. What of Lord Wytham?"

"How do you know his name?"

Toren Kerr surprised her even now.

She was thankful when he returned to his chair. The man was making her dizzy, and her room felt twice as small with him in it.

"An old friend may have mentioned it earlier. So you are, in truth, all but betrothed? I thought you came here to find—"

"Love. I came with Christina and her husband, knowing it would be my final chance to follow a destiny of my own choosing. We're not yet betrothed, but my father plans to make it official as soon as I return. I suppose there are worse candidates."

That was honesty. Of sorts. She couldn't bear to voice her convent plan aloud just yet.

"When you return? Isn't your father coming here? Don't you mean when you both return?"

She opened her mouth to answer and then closed it. There was something about his choice of words that stilled her tongue.

"I want to know why you are here to speak to my father before answering that."

The turn of their conversation was a welcome one. Speaking so openly of being intimate with him was exciting. . . but also uncomfortable.

He cocked his head to the side, as if measuring her response. At times, even though she fully trusted him not to harm her, Juliette was reminded that Toren was very much a border lord, chief of his clan and a true warrior.

This was one of those times.

"I will have your word—"

"I would not speak of it to anyone," she interrupted.

He didn't look convinced, but he continued nonetheless. "Those rumors you mentioned—"

"That he is taking bribes to protect Englishmen from being brought to justice on truce days."

"Aye. I'm here to treat with him. Ensure—"

"He's not."

Juliette crossed her arms and prepared to defend her father. He was harsh at times, but in his peculiar way, Juliette knew he did love her. Moreover, he was a good man who intended to use everything in his power to establish peace along the border. She refused to hear anything untoward said against him.

"He's not taking bribes. My father has spent his entire life cultivating peace for the people who live in fear that lawless reivers, English and Scottish alike, will steal their goods, rape their women, or raze their lands. I know my father, have lived with him my whole life, and can tell you the rumors are not true. He—"

"What?" Toren stood and walked toward her. "What, Juliette?"

Juliette stood too, for she would not let him intimidate her.

They were so close she could hear him breathing. She wanted to reach out to touch him. His face. His hair. The broad shoulders that she could see rising and falling with each breath he took.

"I don't know." She was no longer thinking of her father.

"You don't. . ."

He stopped talking. Instead he pulled her to him.

He wrapped his hands around her back and brought his mouth down to hers. Covering it, he kissed her so passionately she forgot to breathe. His hands moved to the front of her robe, untied the string that held it together, and shoved the material from her shoulders. She heard a soft "whoosh" as it hit the floor.

Suddenly, his hands were everywhere. They moved up the

front of her chemise to grasp both breasts, and that tingling feeling she'd felt earlier, deep within her core, returned. The gentle squeezing made her want to get closer to him. She tightened her hands around his neck, pulling him toward her, deepening their kiss. His mouth moved so expertly over her own she vaguely wondered where he'd learned such a skill.

His groan emboldened her. She tugged at the hem of his surcoat, and he pulled away just long enough to rid himself of the offending garment. Kissing her once again, Toren pressed against her until she could clearly feel the evidence of his need.

Everywhere her hands explored there was muscle. She boldly moved her hands under his shirt to explore his bare chest and was rewarded with an expanse of warm, tight flesh very much unlike her own. She moved her hands up his back, delighting in the play of his muscles under her fingers.

But then he pulled away, taking all the wonderful sensations with him.

"Ah God, lass. I want you so badly."

"Then why did you stop?"

He ran his hand through his hair and closed his eyes, breathing deeply.

"I want you to be sure."

"I am—"

"Nay, I want you to have time to think about the ramifications of what you're offering. You'll not go to your husband a virgin, and that's no small matter."

"There are ways—"

"It takes but just one time for a man and woman to be together for a babe to result."

"Have you lain with women before?"

He scowled. "Aye, but—"

"And do you have any children?"

"Nay, but the women I've—"

"Then we're settled." She would not be swayed on this.

"Nay, lass, we're not settled. Think on it. Let your friend dissuade you from such foolishness."

"I will, and she may try, but—"

"If you still feel this way on the morrow, give me your favor during the joust. I will come to you then."

She felt at peace with her decision and did not need to wait until the morrow to tell him that her favor was his. But she sensed the stubborn man would not take her word for it.

"Then I shall see you tomorrow on the lists."

Toren looked at her for a moment longer. Would he kiss her again?

Nay, he tore his gaze away and walked to his discarded surcoat. Picking it up and donning it once again, he turned toward her but did not come close. He nodded instead, and turned and left her chamber.

Her favor. Tomorrow she would give him that and quite a bit more.

Christ, what was wrong with him?

He hated feeling so out of control. This was precisely why he should not have gone to her chamber last eve. And why he was a fool to even consider riding toward her now and announcing their connection so publicly.

Already, she could connect him to her father's death when it happened—he'd admitted to being here to speak with the man. If he took her favor today, others might make that same connection. And yet. . . in a perverse way, he was eager to declare his intentions. A thought that was utterly irrational—his mission precluded any real connection between them, and Juliette was all but betrothed.

Toren hadn't visited her chamber last night intending to schedule an assignation. He'd simply wanted, *needed,* to talk with her for longer than the brief dance had allowed.

Who was he really fooling?

But to take her virginity? He couldn't do it. Nay, shouldn't do it. It mattered not that Juliette seemed resolved in her decision. Who could blame her? But while it wasn't unheard of for a woman to lose her virginity before marriage, and there were indeed ways around both of the problems he had mentioned, there was a barrier between them most did not have.

He was supposed to kill her father.

Toren reached for his steel-tipped lance. Alfred, now sworn to the service of Clan Kerr, struggled to keep it upright. He was a nimble lad, and quite resourceful, though not the strongest of young men. Alex would train him. The most patient of Toren's brothers, Alex excelled at building both character and skill in others.

They'd reached the fifth day of the tourney, which meant the remaining participants in the joust would be the most skilled. Without the Waryn brothers in attendance, only Lord Thornhurst would give Toren any real competition. But that didn't mean he couldn't be beat. One slip of the hand or lapse in concentration could mean defeat.

"Lord Covington to match against Toren Kerr," the herald shouted. He didn't recognize the standard, but he did recognize the name.

Now that the crowd of knights had been reduced to a mere fifty men, twenty-five on each side, the formalities had become even more pronounced. It was the first day favors were to be given, and nearly everyone attending the tournament had come out to watch the day's matches. The earl and his countess sat above all others under a canopy, which was hardly necessary on this grey, sunless day. Rain threatened at any moment.

When he entered the lists, Toren spotted Jules immediately. She sat in the middle of the galleries, her white gown in stark contrast to the bright colors around her. He knew accepting her favor was wrong. For so many reasons, he should look away. Avoid her completely.

But he was powerless to do so. Instead, he found himself nudging his horse forward, the animal's hooves kicking up dirt and grass with every step. The crowd cheered as his opponent accepted a favor from a noblewoman in the crowd.

The prospect of facing the highly skilled, armored knight on his massive destrier did not trouble him, while the sight of Jules lifting a small, pure white ribbon into the air made his heart beat faster.

He should not take it.

Toren stopped in front of her. Without his helmet, he could see her features quite clearly. She smiled, a secret, perfect smile, and reached out as he tipped his lance toward her. Toren did not see her companions' expressions, for he could not look away from her as she tied the ribbon to the tip of his lance.

The crowd cheered once again as he pulled the lance toward him, straightening it into the air, and returned to the start line. Assisted by Alfred, Toren donned his tourney helmet, and once prepared for the joust, moved back into position and awaited the sound of the trumpet.

The joust was not much of a contest. Although he failed to unseat Covington on the first pass, it only took one more for the man to fall—and he did so in a frighteningly awkward manner. Toren returned to the field after two blasts of the trumpet declared him the winner. He jumped from his mount and tossed his lance aside, making his way to the injured knight who still had not moved.

It would not be the first death at a tournament, though Toren had never before had the bad luck to kill a man in sport.

A physician ran to his opponent's side and lifted the helmet off his head. There were no apparent signs of injury, but that meant nothing.

"Step aside. Move along."

Toren took a step back, relieved to see movement in the man's legs. A moment later, the knight opened his eyes.

"Very good," the physician said. "Now sit up. Slowly. That's right, sit up."

Confident that the man would live, Toren walked away, looking up into the galleries once more. He nodded to Jules, who appeared just as relieved as he felt. Anxious for any cause for celebration, the crowd cheered again when his opponent stood and made his away off the field to allow for the next match.

"A shame," a voice murmured from behind him.

Blackburn.

"A shame he lived?" Toren's hand instinctively moved to his side.

"A shame you both lived."

He knew better than to challenge the English knight on English soil in front of a few hundred witnesses.

"Turning on your own countrymen too? It doesn't seem wise to instigate both sides of the border, Blackburn."

He started to walk away.

"Tell that to the Hallington wench."

He was going to kill the man.

Toren spun, hand on his sword, and stood so close to Blackburn their faces were nearly touching.

"Spew your hate elsewhere, Blackburn. Or this tournament will be your last."

He would not let the man goad him into violence.

Toren walked away, his fists clenched so hard his forearms ached. It was as much restraint as he could muster. Letting Alfred attend to his equipment, he left the field as cheers began for the next match.

And then he froze.

In the heat of the moment, his only thought had been to defend Juliette against the cad, but something had just occurred to him. If Hallington had accepted a bribe from Blackburn to ensure he wouldn't be brought to trial during the next Truce, wouldn't he be grateful to the man? Why would he speak ill of the daughter? Something wasn't right.

Though she was very much biased, it was hard to deny Juliette's intelligence. He must balance her relationship to Hallington against her assessment of the situation.

He would get answers.

Tonight.

11

"Lady Juliette, may we speak in private?"

She looked at Christina, whose shrug indicated she knew not what her husband intended. They had just finished the midday meal and were making their way through the castle's entrance into the crowded courtyard.

Hedford smiled at his wife and offered his arm to Juliette, who took it without hesitation. Her best friend's husband was rising in her esteem, but she still had more questions about him than she did answers. Why did he refuse to speak about his travels? How had he been injured? And why had he agreed to escort her to the tournament? To placate Christina? Her father? Perhaps this would be her chance to have a frank talk with him.

"We've not yet been given the opportunity to speak in private," Lord Hedford said with a smile. "Although you and my wife seem to do so quite frequently."

He appeared amused rather than upset.

"We are more akin to sisters than friends. 'Tis my hope —"

"Nay, you've no need to explain. As your chaperone, I merely wish to ensure you're being well-treated."

"Aye, my lord." She wasn't sure what was he asking, but it seemed best to be agreeable.

"Your affinity for a certain Scottish chief—"

"Affinity? I would hardly call it thus. The man in question is—"

"My lady, I mean no offense."

He knew. She wasn't sure how much, but his steady gaze indicated he had not been as oblivious as she'd thought—nay, hoped.

"It's my duty to ensure your safety. I would be remiss if I failed to speak to you about the dangers of being alone with a man who is not your husband."

Oh God! Did he know about last eve?

"Especially in the Scots' tented city. At night."

Oh. That. So he didn't know of Toren's visit to her chamber.

"How do you. . . did Christina—"

He chuckled, a pleasant sound coming from this very proper man who was serious more oft than not.

"Nay, never. She would sooner toss herself from a turret than break your confidence, as I'm sure you know. Which makes it even more imperative that you understand your position."

"My position?"

He lifted his hand to Christina, who was watching a juggler with a growing crowd of spectators. The festivities stretched from the inner bailey of the main keep well into the field beyond it. Juliette had really never seen anything like it.

"As an unmarried maiden." Hedford was most definitely measuring his words. "And as the daughter of a man whose actions impact the tenuous peace along the border."

"How is my father's position related to my safety here at Condren? There's something you're keeping from me, Hedford."

Though she was certainly sheltered, Juliette was not stupid. If only everyone would stop treating her as if she were. She looked toward the crowd surrounding the juggler. The group of English —and some Scottish—knights, ladies, and servants smiled and clapped, uncaring of matters of allegiances and peace. All knew of the dangers that lurked just beyond the borders of this demesne, yet they had set their worries aside for a brief moment.

Could she not do the same?

She thought of how Sister Heloise might respond.

"I thank you for your concern, Lord Hedford, but I can assure you I am taking care to ensure my safety. You will no doubt deliver me to the confines of Chauncy Manor at the conclusion of the tournament, or mayhap direct to Wytham if my father has a say in the matter. And I will live quite peacefully inside yet another prison hidden away from the Scottish brutes and lawless reivers who would cause me harm. Now, if you will excuse me."

He called out her name, but she ignored him as she made her way to the juggler. This talk of family and clan, English and Scottish. . . she'd heard it her entire life. Today, she wanted to forget all of it.

Today, she wanted to enjoy all this tournament had to offer. Its abundance and jollity. Its deliberate attempt to deny that dangers lurked so close they were mimicked within these very walls, on the lists and later this week on the mock battlefield.

She was not a fool, but for one day she would be happy to act like one. There would be plenty of time for responsibility. An entire lifetime, to be precise. She could wait to bear the yoke.

"Juliette, have you ever seen anything like him?"

Christina pointed to the juggler, easily the most talented one she'd ever seen.

"Nay, he's quite good!"

Although the sun had failed to peek through the clouds, the rain had not yet come. It was a fine day indeed, and the evening that followed would be even more interesting. Her heart skipped a beat thinking of it.

"I need to speak to you," she implored her friend.

Christina must have recognized the urgency in her voice.

Lord Hedford stood at a small distance, already engaged in

another discussion. Christina took her hand and pulled her toward him.

"My lord, we will return shortly."

Christina didn't wait for a response before guiding Juliette toward the castle gardens behind the main keep.

"I've been wishing to see their gardens," Juliette exclaimed. She smiled at the sight before them. Though not quite as grand as this vibrant display, the abbey's gardens were every bit as beautiful. Lush and green, flowers peeking out from every corner, it was one of her favorite sanctuaries, and the nuns allowed her to read alone there once a week. It made her feel more at home to have found a similar haven here.

"Come, sit." She gestured to an ornate marble bench next to a patch of bright lavender-blue asters in full bloom.

Christina smoothed her dress as she sat. "Is this about Matthew? What did he say to you?"

Juliette glanced around the garden, lowering her voice even though they appeared to be alone. "Nay. He knew of my visit to the tent city, but not that Toren came to see me last night."

"But you said nothing happened?"

"Nothing did. But that doesn't mean your husband would approve of me entertaining him in my bedchamber!"

"Why, of course he wouldn't. Then what—"

"Tell me more about lovemaking."

Christina clearly hadn't been prepared for that particular request. "Juliette, what... that is to say... please tell me you're not serious."

"I have never been more serious in my life."

Christina grabbed both of her hands, pulling her closer. "You can't do it. I won't allow it. You'll be ruined. Your future husband—"

"Will marry me, and all will be well. Christina, what would you have me do?"

"I would have you marry the Scots chief if you're intent on being with him. Or at least--"

"He won't marry me."

Christina released her hands and stood. Now it was *she* who paced, their roles from the previous evening reversed.

"What do you mean, *won't* marry you?"

"He does not wish to marry, and I can hardly force him to do so. And if I'm never to know a man, then I would like--"

"Oh Juliette, this is not a story. We speak of your life, your real life, and I fear you're making a grave mistake."

"Please stop and sit."

Although she listened, Juliette could tell her friend was having a difficult time understanding.

"Christina, please. Hedford will be looking for us. Please. Tell me more than you have in the past."

Her mother had never spoken to her of what happened between a man and a woman, and while Juliette had overheard the servants speaking freely about such matters, she wanted to understand.

"I don't know what will happen when Toren returns, but—"

"*When* he. . ."

Christina trailed off, and she appeared quite incapable of speaking.

"When he's near, I find it difficult to think straight," Juliette said. "My hands shook as I tied the ribbon around the tip of his lance earlier. I've never felt this way before, and I may never do so again. Christina, please. . ."

As she stared into the eyes of the one person she trusted above all others, Juliette felt a rush of gratitude.

"Thank you for being my friend."

Christina's eyes filled with unshed tears. "Oh, Juliette. I do adore you so. I just want you to be happy. And safe."

"And I want the same for you. Now tell me, are you happy? Does Hedford make you feel the way Toren does for me?"

Christina's smile was her answer.

"I am very grateful to have been given such a man. I know not all ladies are so lucky. But yes, he does. And I am very much beginning to care for him as well. And lovemaking. . ."

Her cheeks turned pink. They'd never discussed such a thing in detail before.

"It is. . . very pleasant. The first time," she winced, "hurt a bit. But after that. . . it's quite nice. Matthew is quite skilled with his—"

Juliette's eyes widened.

"Hands." Christina smiled, likely knowing the direction of her thoughts. His hands? How precisely? She was prepared to ask when a rustling sound interrupted them, followed by a man's voice saying, "Come my dear, we won't be noticed here."

The lady's only reply was a giggle—so, a pair of lovers planned to rendezvous in the garden.

There was more murmuring, and Juliette and Christina exchanged a glance. "Let's go," Christina whispered, tugging on her hand.

They ran from the garden and spilled out into the courtyard where they continued their conversation. By the time Hedford discovered them, Juliette could not look the man in the eyes.

"Ladies. . ." He looked from his wife to Juliette and back to Christina. Neither of them could stop smiling. "What in the devil?"

Juliette was about to make an excuse for their behavior when a commotion near the blacksmith's forge drew their attention. A crowd gathered, and though Hedford tried to stop her from joining it, Juliette was too curious to heed him. As she made her way to the outer ring of people, a man shouted at the edge of the crowd. Everyone turned toward the sound, and Juliette shivered when she saw him, sword raised, pushing his way toward the forge.

Toren.

Spectators parted, and Juliette took advantage of the dispersion by running forward rather than edging backward. What was he doing?

Then she saw what the crowd had concealed—two men on the ground, rolling from side to side as they pummeled each other. She'd never seen a fight this close before and was struck by the violence of it. The second thing that caught her attention was that other knights, all with weapons drawn, had formed two lines on either side of the fighting men. Her eyes sought Toren's. He stood shoulder to shoulder with three other men, one of whom she recognized.

All of the warriors on Toren's side were Scottish, and the men who stood opposite them were English knights. So much for peace. It was clear the fight between two men was about to turn into much more if someone didn't stop them.

And then one man stepped forward.

At first Toren had thought to stay out of the fight. Staying out of others' arguments was how he ensured his clan's survival. With the exception of Bristol and this current mission, but those had both been edicts from his king.

But that was before he saw Juliette standing calmly at the edge of the crowd. He was hurrying forward to pull her away when he heard someone yell, "Saw his wife with Campbell. . ."

Gregory!

Pushing through the crowd, Toren groaned when he saw the men gathering on either side of the fray. Fights between English and Scottish were not uncommon at this annual tournament, but this year, with the Day of Truce rumored to be in jeopardy, tensions were even higher.

By the time they fought in the melee, it would be an outright tournament of war.

Aware that Juliette was still in the crowd, Toren rushed toward the fight. Barely glancing at his friend tumbling on the ground with an unknown Englishman, he drew from his experience on the battlefield and the countless times he'd stopped his own clansmen from re-arranging their opponents' features, he shouted out a few orders. Men from both sides rushed to break the men apart and he finished the job, reaching between them and receiving a blow to the shoulder for his efforts. Moments later, he'd stopped the fight and convinced the other men to stand down.

Before he could pull Gregory away to give him a talking-to, someone called to him from behind.

"Kerr," the male voice shouted.

Toren, still practically holding his friend in an upright position, turned to find Juliette's guardian following him.

"Can you stand?" Toren asked Gregory.

"Aye, I can walk, but the bastard nearly broke my damn knee when he kicked me from behind. Coward."

Though his friend stumbled at first—the fight had left him battered and bloody—he caught himself and stood tall.

Gregory reached over and clasped his arm. "Many thanks for the rescue, Kerr. Though it was unnecessary."

Lord Hedford looked from him to Gregory and frowned.

"May I have a word?" he asked, clearly not wanting an audience.

Toren nodded and turned to Gregory, making a downward gesture. "Can you keep that from other men's wives? I've no wish to do battle off the lists again, Campbell."

True to his nature, Gregory grinned. "I'll do my best, but no promises, laddie."

He limped away, garnering curious glances from the remaining spectators.

"You know that man?"

Toren watched Gregory make his way toward the back of the

keep and prayed he would heed his advice, at least for the remainder of the day.

"I had the good fortune of fighting alongside him at Largs."

It was best Hedford knew straightaway that, despite Gregory's lack of judgment, he would defend the man to the death.

"Ahh, I see."

Hedford nodded to indicate they should move away from the center of activity, and Toren followed him, looking toward the crowd, looking for Juliette.

"She's returned to her chamber to prepare for the evening meal."

He didn't attempt to deny that he had been looking for her.

"How did the warden's daughter come to be your responsibility this week?"

Toren wasn't a man for idle chatter. And though he was not certain of the Englishman's purpose for this discussion, he had an inkling of what it might be.

"How did she so quickly become the object of your curiosity?" Hedford shot back.

Toren eyed the man more carefully. Well dressed and with a slight limp, more permanent than the one Gregory had recently attained, Lord Hedford appeared to be of an age with him, or close. The inquiries he'd made about Juliette's chaperone had shed precious few details. The man was a minor baron whose father had died suddenly last year. His land bordered Lady Christina's to the north, making theirs a marriage of convenience, though they seemed to get along well enough.

But Lord Hedford had apparently spent much of the last few years overseas, and no one seemed to know why. It was particularly unusual in that he'd stayed away from Hedford Manor for some time after his father's death.

"Circumstances of the tournament celebrations," he responded, purposefully vague.

"Circumstances of proximity," Hedford said, answering his

original question. Giving Toren a pointed look, he added, "Warning Lady Juliette of dallying with a strange man is akin to preaching the dangers of excess to our host."

Though he had only known her for a matter of days, Toren had already surmised as much.

"So you thought to warn the man against said dalliance."

Hedford's actions were honorable but misguided. Neither he nor his wife would dissuade him from Lady Juliette. He took orders from no one with the exception, in this instance, of Jules. The matter of their relationship was between the two of them and no one else.

Well, perhaps his sister warranted another exception, but damned if he'd let the chit know it.

"Your warning is duly noted, if not heeded."

Hedford's eyebrows rose.

"You misunderstand me. I'd learn your intentions concerning Juliette, not dissuade you from pursuing her suit."

Toren was rarely surprised, yet it took a moment for those words to penetrate.

"Why?"

Hedford adjusted the sword at his side, reminding Toren he was not participating in the tournament. Because of his injury?

"You stopped a fight that could have seen men from both of our countries killed." He paused, staring intently at him as if taking his measure. "You are reticent. Cut off from your neighbors, mistrusting even your own countrymen as allies."

"What do you—"

"And you lost Bristol to the Waryns."

Toren gritted his teeth but somehow kept his anger in check.

"Otherwise, both you and your clan have a reputation for peace. Bristol was a rash act taken by your king when the border lines were less stable. And before you defend him. . ."

Hedford was wrong if he thought taking Bristol was an action he would defend. King or nay.

"Ours has made the same foolish mistakes in this never-ending quest to secure dominance between our countries. But despite missteps by leaders on both sides, a more than thirty-year agreement has stood, so far, because of men such as you and I. Ones who care more about the lives of our families or clans than we do about what we call ourselves."

"What do you want from me?"

More importantly, how much did Hedford know about the rumors surrounding Juliette's father. Did he suspect Toren's interest in Juliette was more than just personal?

"I want you to conduct yourself with the honor you're reputed to have. And to understand Juliette has been sheltered. And though she may be naïve, the woman is far from ignorant."

Toren wouldn't reveal any more than he already had. Hedford wanted something, that much was clear, but it was impossible to offer anything in the way of assurances, especially since Toren himself didn't yet understand his motivations when it came to Juliette Hallington.

"So your wife has already mentioned. Good day, Lord Hedford."

12

The world had opened for Juliette, truly opened, when she was ten and seven. She'd finished her lessons with Sister Heloise, and the nun told her that henceforth she would be given free rein in the library. But, she admonished, Juliette could remove only one book at a time to take home with her. And she had to promise to read in every language and every genre.

Until then, Juliette hadn't known the abbey's extensive library included non-religious manuscripts. So it was she found herself exploring French poems, English history, and fairytales penned in Latin. Even one that she was sure was donated to the abbey but never read by its nuns. One that detailed the act between a married man and woman. One that she'd wondered about many times since she'd read it. But more than all others, there was one type of manuscript that held her attention.

Tales of courtly love.

Now, at one and twenty, she sat on the edge of her seat in her chamber, waiting for her life to change again. After this night, she would no longer be a maiden.

Without windows in her chamber, Juliette couldn't tell how much time had passed, but she'd stayed at the meal for as long as she could bear before excusing herself for the evening. Anxiety and excitement made her heart race, so she forced herself to think about a story, her usual way of calming herself.

The first tale that had made her eager for love was that of Melior and Guilaume. Melior, the daughter of the emperor, was promised to Alphonso, a Greek prince, but Melior's stepmother turned Alphonso into a werewolf so the girl could marry the man she loved. If Guilaume, a commoner, could marry the daughter of the emperor, surely she could have some say in her choice of husband?

She wasn't asking her parents to turn anyone into a wolf, but she certainly wished they would take her desire for love more seriously.

Did she love Toren? She wasn't sure. Nor did it matter since he obviously did not love her. Why else would he refuse to consider marriage? But he did desire her. And for now, that was enough.

The knock was so low Juliette hardly heard it. She rushed to the door and opened it, remembering belatedly that she had not wished to appear too anxious.

"You gave me your ribbon," he said as he walked into the room.

Her heart beat wildly, his unique smell assaulting her as he came toward her. She stepped to the side and closed the door behind her. When she turned back around, the first thing she noticed was that his tunic sleeves were rolled back, revealing the thick muscle underneath.

She had an intense urge to touch him there.

"Aye," she murmured, mesmerized. "I told you I would."

She lifted her head and shivered. His expression left no question as to his mood.

"You're not a wolf," she blurted, immediately wishing she could take the ridiculous comment back.

He laughed. Such a deep, sensual sound.

"I wouldn't be so sure."

Toren took a step toward her.

"I. . . I was just thinking of Alphonso. And—"

"Melior?"

She tilted her head back to look him in the eyes. "You know the story?"

"Aye," he said, moving even closer. "But I would think my role is more akin to Guilaume, is it not?'

What was he saying? Was it a proclamation that he felt something for her after all?

"Who do you want me to be, Jules?"

Oh God, if he took one more step she'd be unable to stand.

"Just yourself," she managed as Toren reached for her. He pulled her to him and wrapped one arm around her waist.

"'Tis all that I know," he said as his head bowed toward hers.

He covered her lips with his own, coaxing her to open for him. When she did, his tongue plunged into her mouth. It teased and tormented, and she reached up to wrap her arms around his neck.

Toren groaned, pulling her even closer.

"Please." She didn't know what she asked for, but he seemed to understand.

He reached between them and began to untie the belt at her waist. Too curious to do otherwise, she placed her hands on his forearms, stroking them as the hard muscles tensed beneath her fingers. The belt dropped to the floor, and then he lifted the heavy gown in one swift movement, pulling the heavy fabric over her head. She hadn't been expecting that, but when he tossed the offending garment to the side and pulled her to him once again, Juliette could immediately understand the benefits. With only her shift and his tunic to separate them, she could feel him pressed against her.

And God help her, she wanted to get closer.

His mouth moved from her lips to her neck, and Juliette bent her head to the side to allow the access.

"Are you—"

"Please, not again. I'm sure, Toren."

The fluttery feeling returned, and she pressed against him, wanting something. Wanting everything.

"Keep at that, and you'll not be a maiden for long."

She'd resigned her maidenhood to him the moment she tied the favor on his lance. Hadn't that been their agreement?

Toren reached behind her and scooped her up into his arms. She found herself floating, or at least felt that way, to the bed.

He lowered her onto it, the feather mattress sinking under his weight as he lay next to her.

And then, nothing.

Propped on an elbow, he simply stared at her until she became aware of the state of her dress. Or lack of it.

She shifted, not knowing what to do.

He reached out and grabbed a strand of her long hair, twisting it around his fingers.

"When we first met, I had such an intense urge to touch you." He slid his fingers down until they rested just above her breast. "Everywhere."

His hand cupped her and squeezed gently. He never took his eyes off hers.

And then that talented hand moved lower, over the thin cotton shift and across her stomach. It moved lower still, and Juliette was reminded of their first kiss. He had that same look now, as if he would devour her.

But this time, she'd let him.

Without looking away, he placed his hand between her legs, and Juliette instinctively closed them. But he pressed anyway, his palm circling. He lowered his head, and though she did not understand why, the tantalizing sensation of his lips against her neck made her press into his hand. Pleasurable sensations radiated from every place he touched her, pooling in her core.

A desperate moan spilled out of her, and his lips burned a path across her neck and to her mouth. He kissed her, deeply and fully, and she writhed against him. Suddenly, the pressure of his hand was gone, but before she could ask why, he lifted her shift, removing the only remaining obstacle between them. He touched her in that private place again and then shocked her by putting a finger inside her.

Slowly at first, he mimicked the movement of his tongue in her mouth. Juliette was sure she'd never survive the sensations tumbling through her. His mouth, so firm and unyielding yet somehow still gentle. His wicked finger, sending pulses of pleasure through her.

"Please," she asked against his mouth.

He didn't seem to hear her. Or mayhap he did, for he moved even closer to her, his manhood pressing against the side of her leg. She could hardly even think of *that.* How could she when the sensations he wrought demanded her full attention?

Without warning, the building intensity shattered around her. The butterflies exploded and forced her eyes to fly open. She stared at him in wonder.

He smiled but kept his hand there. Between her legs, at the most intimate part of her.

As suddenly as the feeling began, it ebbed away from her. She wanted to catch it, but a delicious calm took its place. Nothing seemed more appropriate than to smile back at him.

"I've read about this."

He took his hand away, pulled down her shift, and propped his head up on his elbow again.

"Have you now?"

She must sound absurd.

"Well, not exactly about *that.* The whole act, really."

Toren's hand rested on her leg in such a natural way that she couldn't imagine it being anywhere else.

Well, maybe one other place.

"I read a lot."

He raised his eyebrows.

"But I'll admit to being completely unprepared for. . . well. . . what was that exactly?"

"That, my dear Jules, was your body's way of saying it enjoys my company."

She rolled her eyes.

"I'm not a child, Toren."

Neither of them smiled.

"That is quite clear."

He didn't move toward her. Didn't kiss her or even touch her anywhere other than the hand that lay so innocuously on her upper thigh.

And then she knew. Somehow, though he hadn't yet said a word, she knew.

He would not be swayed.

"You're not going to make love to me. Are you?"

Her voice was flat. She had tried to sound uncaring but hadn't quite succeeded.

"No, I am not."

And yet he did not move.

"You've never deflowered a maid before?"

Every action he'd taken in their acquaintance had told her this man was too honorable to take her virginity. It was why she'd felt so safe with him.

"Nay. Though I sorely wish I could this eve."

It should not feel so, but lying here with this man felt perfectly natural. She should feel embarrassed by what they'd just done. But she didn't.

"This is perfect," she blurted.

"*You* are perfect."

Though it was a compliment, his tone was not light.

"Something is troubling you."

Then again, something always seemed to be troubling him.

"You came here to find love and instead are willing to give yourself to a man who could never be your husband. Why?"

Could never be.

She looked away, staring at the fire across the room, the only source of light in the otherwise darkened chamber. Juliette couldn't expect him to understand.

"You are your people's chief," she said, looking toward him once again.

"I am."

He moved his fingers ever so slightly.

"Everyone must listen to you."

Toren sighed. "Must? Should perhaps. But my brothers argue with me as much now as when we were children. And Catrina listens even less."

A smile had stolen across his face again. He was clearly fond of his siblings despite his words.

"But your clan?"

She could tell he finally understood what she was saying.

"Aye, lass. My clan listens to me."

"They take their orders from you. And have likely done so for some time, you being the eldest son of a clan chief. But try to imagine what it would be like to have to take orders rather than give them. From everyone. Your mother and father. Your tutors. Your chaperones. Telling you how you should dress. Whom you should speak to. And whom you should marry."

She shuddered.

"Is your intended that bad then?"

She preferred not to answer.

"Lord Hedford mentioned--"

"Hedford? She sat up in the bed. "When did you speak to him? Why did you speak to him?"

Toren didn't move but lay there oh so casually. He seemed to take up the entirety of her bed, filling it just as he had filled the small room upon entering it.

He was exceedingly handsome.

"He attempted to warn me away from you. Of sorts."

"What do you mean?"

"I'm not sure exactly. I assumed he was trying to warn me off. But instead he pleaded for me to act with honor."

She crossed her feet, tucking her legs under her.

"Did you find anything. . . unusual. . . about that? About him?" she asked.

Toren lay back and folded his hands behind his head.

"I thought it odd he didn't forbid me to speak with you. I've made some inquiries of him as well."

"Inquires? Of whom? What did you find?"

He turned toward her, his lips turning up ever so slightly. She was sure this was the most relaxed she'd seen him.

"So many questions. I'd imagine you know the man quite a bit better than I do?"

She shook her head. "Nay, not well at all. Christina's father only told her of the betrothal six months before Lord Hedford returned from France. They met on their wedding day, which was just four months past. Christina knew him when they were young, before he left. But I had only met him twice before the tourney—once at their wedding and then on a visit a few weeks ago. I was glad my father allowed him and Christina to accompany me here."

"Your father obviously trusts the man."

She shrugged. "Enough to allow me here with him."

Toren frowned.

"Do you trust him?"

"Every time I ask Christina why Hedford was away for so long and what he was doing in France, she speaks of something else. I've attempted to question her about his background, but she's shared precious few facts about the man. I'm not sure she knows herself. But I'll admit, despite the air of mystery surrounding him, the man is quite beginning to win my affections for his treatment of Christina."

"I'm sure he's glad of it. And if I find anything about him, I'll share it with you," he said.

She stared at him. He said it so casually, it seemed as if Toren had no idea the implications of such a gesture. She tried to imagine her father sharing anything other than a flagon of wine at dinner with her. The idea was unfathomable.

"Jules?"

She continued to stare. "You will?"

His eyes narrowed. "Is something amiss?"

"Nay." She didn't want him to know how little she was ever consulted on matters of importance. "'Tis just not something my father would ever say."

Toren smiled again, but this time it looked different, slow and sensual and almost predatory. "I am not your father."

That was quite clear.

For a moment, it seemed he was going to reach for her. Mayhap kiss her again. But then he pulled back and asked, "Will he arrive soon?"

She wanted him to kiss her again, but Juliette refused to be disappointed. He was not coming, and she planned to say as much. But she did not want to talk of her father and instead attempted to dismiss the matter. "He is Lord Warden of the Middle Marches. A powerful man, and much too busy to inform his daughter of his plans." She tried, and failed, to keep the resentment from her voice.

"You dislike your father's treatment of you?"

Did he sound. . . hopeful?

"Aye, at times. I also love my father very much. But he is not a man to share his plans with a 'mere' female. My mother sometimes doesn't even know which holding he visits or what month he will return. But he is my father."

Something had changed between them. The easy banter was gone. Toren no longer seemed quite so relaxed.

"Is something amiss?"

For a moment, she feared he would get up to leave. But just as quickly as his mood had shifted before, so it shifted again. His features softened, and he reached for her. Juliette gave him her hand.

He rolled onto his elbow once again and pulled her hand, along with the rest of her, toward him.

"I cannot take your virginity, my fair maiden. But there are some other things I can show you."

Reluctantly, Toren replaced the fine linen sheets over the woman who slept soundly next to him and stood from the canopied bed. He walked toward the dying fire, placed two logs on top, and began to stir it back to life.

Much the same as Jules had done for him.

He turned to watch her sleeping. From his position, he could see only a form lying on the bed. Nay, not just a form, but a goddess sent to torment him. Though he wasn't as well read as his English rose, Toren knew some stories. His sister had once commissioned a traveling Irish bard to perform for May Day at Bristol, and Toren remembered vividly the man's tale of Clíodhna. The goddess of love, more beautiful than all others, remained chaste until she met the mortal Ciabahn. She left Tir Tairngire, the land of the gods, to be with him, and the Gods took her away in a tidal wave.

This dalliance with Jules was destined to end just as poorly.

But he could not keep pretending it was simply a dalliance.

It was something more.

He had tried to stay away but could not. He had come here intending to make love to her, but he hadn't been able to do that either. She was an extraordinary lass. Beautiful, aye. But also kind, fiercely intelligent, innocent. . . brave and caring. The kind of woman he could marry. He'd told her he could not marry her, and though it was true, it was the first time in his life he mourned such a fact.

But Jules was a different sort of woman. She was nothing like the mother who'd fled his family in their time of need. It was obvious she would do anything to protect the people she cared for—Christina, her mother and brother, and even her father. . .

The father he had been sent here to kill.

But after asking questions all day, he was further from the answers he sought. None seemed to know when, or indeed if, Hallington was coming. And when he inquired into the rumors, it appeared Jules' father was indeed dedicated to peace along the border.

"So deep in thought."

He'd turned back to the fire and hadn't heard her leave the bed. The hand that settled so gently on his shoulder reminded him of why he should leave.

Toren turned and instantly hardened. God, how he wanted to be inside her. Claim her as his own. She looked as if she'd been properly bedded, but she'd not been. He had not even trusted himself enough to remove her shift, knowing it would be his undoing.

But he'd pleased her nonetheless.

"Something is wrong," she said.

Aye, everything.

"Nay, lass. Not any longer."

He pulled her into his arms at the same moment he told himself, again, to leave.

She came willingly and wrapped her delicate hands around his back. He held her like that for too long.

Toren inhaled and, oddly, found himself thinking of his brother-in-law. How he had railed against the man for dishonoring his sister. Upon learning the Englishman had taken Catrina's virginity, he'd been so consumed with rage, it had taken all three of his siblings to convince him not to rampage back to England to slay the man.

Catrina had insisted she loved him. That despite the differences between them—ones that must have seemed as impossible to resolve as his budding relationship with Jules did—she had given herself to him freely.

He was beginning to understand.

"I must leave," he forced himself to say.

"Aye," she murmured, making no move to release him.

In response, he pulled her closer.

"It wouldn't do for the household to stir and your handmaiden to catch us here."

"It would be quite difficult as she remains at Chauncy Manor."

He pulled back just enough to look at her.

"That is an unusual arrangement, is it not?"

Toren watched as her eyelashes fluttered open and shut as she blinked. God, everything about her fascinated him. "She took ill on the eve of our departure here. Helen, Christina's maid, has been assisting me. She likely already knows you are here."

"And that doesn't bother you?" She was unusual in so many ways.

"Nay, she does not gossip. She'd likely tell Christina, who already knows."

He couldn't resist smoothing her hair, touching the long, silky locks that fell in waves all around her.

"Your friend disapproves, of course."

Jules shrugged. "She doesn't understand."

He moved his hand under her chin and lifted it so he could see her face more clearly.

"What does she not understand?"

He knew he should not ask. Just as he knew he should have already left hours ago. Somehow all the 'shoulds' in the world had ceased to matter.

"I've told you. This is my only chance to make a decision about my life. And I choose you."

He felt as if she'd punched him in the stomach.

"I can't offer you much, but I promise you this." He leaned down and kissed the tip of her nose. "I'll not take what is your husband's by right, but I will give you everything else I can. All I have, while I'm here at Condren, is yours."

She looked confused, and rightly so. He was confused, and yet he wanted to love her in all the ways that he could.

Love.

Could it be?

"If you'll have me, I will come to you every night. Give you pleasure and leave us both with memories to last a lifetime."

He sounded like a damn poet rather than a hardened warrior. Soon he'd be swooning like his brother-in-law.

You already are.

"I wish for more but will take what you offer, Toren. I'd be a fool to do otherwise."

Nay, he was a fool to think a few days of pleasure would erase the pain he'd cause her. But what other choice did he have?

His doubts would wait until tomorrow.

13

"I will change his mind."

Juliette and Christina walked toward the lists two mornings after Toren had made his pledge to visit her bedchamber nightly. She'd spent the better part of the previous day in turmoil.

Christina knew everything, of course, and while her friend had tried to talk her out of seeing him again, she'd at least agreed Toren was honorable for not taking her virginity. At first, Juliette had resigned herself to their unusual relationship, accepting that theirs would be nothing more than a fleeting dalliance.

And yet. . . that resignation quickly faded, replaced by the desire to keep this wonderful thing she'd found for herself. The day before, she'd overheard a conversation at the midday meal about a wedding that was to take place between the daughter of a Scottish chieftain and an English noblewoman, which had reminded her such things did indeed happen.

"Despite the ban, marriages do take place between English and Scots," she had told Christina.

"Of course they do," her friend had answered. "But you already knew that, Juliette."

This morn, Christina, dressed in the same bright blue color as Juliette, looked vibrant. Marriage seemed to agree with her.

Why should Juliette give up on it so easily?

"Aye, but to have the evidence there in front of me. My father speaks of peace with Scotland. Well, what better way to show he means it than to give his daughter to a border chief in marriage? Toren says we cannot marry. But that's only because his mother left them. He fears it, Christina. Even with the evidence of his sister's happiness in front of him, he doesn't truly believe a peaceable union is possible. He despises asking for anything. Wants to be independent of the border politics, even his own country's troubles. All he cares about is keeping his clan safe. But even the great Toren Kerr needs allies."

Christina lifted her hand to shield her face from the sun, which had finally deemed it time to make an appearance.

"You seem to know much about your Scots chief."

Juliette thought about that. Did she really? He'd shared much during their last two nights together. He'd said it was more than he'd ever told any woman before her. He'd told her of his upbringing and his siblings—and how he'd finished raising them after their mother's abandonment.

While Juliette's own mother had never truly understood her, she'd always listened to her. And her mother loved both her and her brother very much. She couldn't imagine a mother simply leaving her children, grown or nay. It was unthinkable.

She stopped, and Christina did the same. They watched as Lord Hedford, who didn't seem to notice they were no longer behind him, continued to make his way toward the galleries. Flags of various colors waved in the wind, the wooden spectator bench seats filling with spectators.

"I don't know if he loves me, or I him for that matter. But I do know he cares for me. I can tell by the way he looks at me. And mayhap that is enough. Besides, it's not as if he lives in the Highlands. I'm accustomed to life at the border. I just have to convince him I'll not leave him."

"And you're sure that is the only barrier? The only reason for his resistance?"

Nay, she wasn't sure of that at all. There was something else that held him back. If only she could discover the source of his resistance.

"Come," Christina took her hand. "You don't want to miss him."

Toren would be participating in two jousts that day. By tomorrow, only two Scots and two Englishman would remain. The winner would be announced that evening, and the most important event of the tournament would begin the following day.

"Oh. . . I failed to mention," Christina said. "Matthew received word from your father this morning. I don't know the contents of the missive, but I thought you should know."

Juliette stopped but neglected to let go of her friend's hand.

"Oh," Christina exclaimed when she was pulled backward toward her.

"Sorry," she murmured. "It's just. . . why did he not send word to me?"

Although her father wasn't known for being forthright with her, that he would communicate with a man he hardly knew but not his daughter. . . it rankled.

"And then there is the matter of getting his permission to marry Toren."

Christina laughed and tugged her forward.

"Mayhap you should get your intended's permission first?"

They resumed walking, moving more quickly as the crowd was already cheering the first participants of the day.

"Mayhap."

Not for the first time she wondered what her father was doing. For the warden to miss a tournament that embodied peace at a time when border relations were tenuous... something important must be keeping him. Did it have anything to do with those rumors? Toren had told her he needed to speak with her father... mayhap he knew something?

She would ask him this night.

By the time they arrived, the two opponents had already taken their positions. Juliette and Christina made their way to the opposite side of the lists where Hedford was sitting. He waved to them, and Juliette tried to navigate through the narrow wooden planks without stepping on a gown. This was the first time the crowd had swelled to capacity. These last two days before the melee, all the other contests had finished, and only the jousts remained.

The abhorrent Lord Blackburn had been declared winner of the archery contest, and Toren's friend, the man who'd been involved in the fight, had bested all others in sword fighting. She'd attempted to ask Toren why he had not participated in those other events, but they'd been alone in her chamber at the time. Instead of answering, he'd slipped his hand under her chemise and made her forget to ask again.

Later, she'd asked him if it was normal to retain one's clothes during such an encounter. Toren had only laughed and tossed her onto the bed. He'd kissed her so thoroughly she'd begged him to take her in truth.

Again, he had refused.

Whether they were merely lucky or Hedford and the maid looked the other way, she couldn't be sure. Either way, they'd been able to keep their liaisons a secret. Toren left as soon as the sun rose, heading down to the hall to join the morning meal, where none would question the presence of an outsider. All tourney participants were welcome at any meal, even though they were primarily attended by the inhabitants of the castle.

"There he is."

Although it was not the first time she'd seen him fully

armored, the sight of Toren atop his mighty tournament horse made her squirm in her seat. At first she had thought it was fear for his safety that made her anxious. Men died in tournaments like these regularly. But having watched his matches, she'd begun to think it wasn't possible for him to lose. He was methodical. Striking.

His sheer size and power were what made her heart race with excitement. . . and something else.

"I can see why you're drawn to him," Christina whispered.

She swallowed. He was coming this way, just as he'd done yesterday and the day before.

He tipped the lance toward her, and Juliette tied the ribbon she'd brought around the tip. She could feel all eyes on her and knew, with each passing day, the whispers only grew louder. What did she care? Though her father would likely learn of it, she hoped by then it would not matter.

And if she could not convince Toren his notion of marriage was incongruous?

Well, she'd have larger problems than her parents learning of her supposed indiscretions: the choice between a vow to the church or to a man who would control rather than love her.

Toren smiled and thrust the heavy lance into the air as if it were a small dagger. The crowd cheered, and Juliette refused to meet anyone's gaze but his.

"He's declaring himself for you in front of everyone," Christina whispered.

"Nay," she whispered back, watching Toren as he maneuvered his horse into position. "He cares little for convention. To anyone else, it would be a declaration. To him, it's nothing more than his way of flaunting their expectations."

"Say what you will. He clearly has a tendre for you."

She very much hoped so.

As they watched the joust begin, Juliette held her breath. Then, suddenly, the unthinkable happened.

She was so confident Toren would knock his opponent to the ground that, when the exact opposite happened, she bounded up from her seat without realizing it.

Toren lay on the ground. Unmoving.

Dear God, was he dead? She nearly leapt over the couple in front of her in her eagerness to get to him, but her friend pulled her back into her seat.

"Juliette!" Christina's frantic tone finally penetrated her mind. She was urging her not to rush down the galleries. But Juliette didn't care who was watching. Toren was hurt!

"Juliette, sit down!" Christina muttered again, speaking for her ears only.

Her hands began to shake. Tears formed in her eyes, and when she tried to blink them away, it was Hedford's voice that finally penetrated. "Lady Juliette, he's fine. Look."

Sure enough, though she'd been staring at him the whole time, it was just then that she saw his arms move. The rules dictated an opponent could not strike a felled man, so even though his opponent had already dismounted, he did not make a move toward him.

Until Toren suddenly sprang to his feet and unsheathed his sword.

And then panic welled in her once again. Their swords rang out so loudly she could probably have heard them back at the castle. While those around her cheered, Juliette had to force herself to sit as the English knight attempted to run his sword through Toren's body. That their broadswords were blunted offered little comfort. The men aimed to inflict serious damage on each other, and Juliette couldn't watch any longer.

She closed her eyes.

"What's happening?"

Clang! Clang! Clang!

"What do you mean— Dear lord, open your eyes and look."

She did. It appeared Toren was in control. He had backed the other man up against the tilt. While his small round shield—where had that come from?—seemed maddeningly inferior to his opponent's, Toren didn't seem to have much need of it. The power and control he displayed atop his horse had fluidly transferred to his sword-fighting abilities. The other man was clearly weakening. On the defensive now, his last attempt to knock Toren's sword from his hand was met with a swing so forceful it not only knocked the sword from his hand but dropped him to the ground as well.

And now it was he who did not move.

Though the crowd cheered, the audience's appreciation had been much louder when Toren's competitor had toppled him from his mount. Although this was to be a neutral event, its location promised that the English were always slightly favored. Her father had explained that since they treated across the border in Scotland each month for the Day of Truce, the yearly tournament was always held in England.

Nevertheless, they did cheer when the earl himself stood and clapped. Toren's power was a sight to behold, and all present, including Juliette, had no doubt who the champion of the joust would be. None were as skilled as her Scotsman.

As Toren moved toward his squire, Juliette squinted to get a closer look. He'd mentioned the boy to her, and something about the lad roused her curiosity. He was so small and moved differently. More gracefully perhaps.

She wanted so badly to go to Toren, but even she knew there were limitations to their affair. Instead, she pretended to scan the field while shooting glances at Toren, the squire, and the attending grooms. As the ground crew cleared the field, picking up pieces of wood from the broken lances, she waited for Toren to look up.

When he did, she let out the breath she'd been holding. He was fine. She'd already guessed as much, but her nerves hadn't settled until *he* gave her the signal. The Knight Marshal announced the next combatants, and a new match began.

"Extraordinary," the woman seated in front of them said loudly.

Indeed.

"Juliette, are you all right?" Christina had not taken her eyes off her.

"Aye, splendid. 'Tis a fine day for a joust."

A fine day to finally learn what it meant to fall in love.

For there was no way to deny that, for the briefest of moments, she had thought her life was over, every chance of happiness gone. When she'd believed Toren dead. . .

If *this* was love, did she want any part of it?

Toren sat across the hall from Juliette, much the same as he had that first night. Gregory was beside him, at a table that was a mix of English and Scottish. A wealthy baron and his wife sat in their midst, sharing a flagon of wine with them and several knights who likely had nothing more than the armor they'd worn to this event.

While the wealthiest or most prestigious guests typically sat closest to the host, this event was intended to bring borderers together regardless of rank or nationality—a notion that seemed more heartily embraced by the baron than his wife. For the whole meal, she'd stared in obvious horror at the man across from her, as if he were a barbarian and not a knight.

"Imagine bedding that old witch," Gregory whispered.

Toren shuddered. Though the woman was handsome for her age, it was clear from the lines around her mouth that she rarely smiled.

"I'd rather not."

He popped a piece of meat into his mouth and looked at Jules. Again. She had not glanced his way all night. Or perhaps she had but he'd not noticed.

"Toren Kerr. In love with an Englishwoman."

He placed a well-positioned elbow into his friend's side, caring not that Gregory choked on his dinner.

"I am not—"

"Ha!" Everyone seated with them looked at Gregory, who simply shrugged. In a lower voice, he continued his verbal torment. "I've had the great fortune to be in love with many women. It's pure foolishness to get stuck on one."

Of all the men who could have done him honor on the battlefield, why must this cad have been the one?

"Why don't you marry her? Pride for having condemned your sister for choosing an Englishman? Will she not have you?"

Though Gregory was clearly attempting to goad him, Toren refused to allow it. He didn't react in any way.

"No matter. It appears she's found another to take your place."

Toren shifted his gaze to her in alarm, watching as the earl's nephew held out a hand to her. She stood, tucked her elbow in his, and joined the other dancers. Music played throughout the meal. The dancers needed only wait for the main course to finish, and now that the hosts' table had been cleared, the night's revelries had begun in truth.

As the song ended and the next one began, Toren began to stand.

"Toren." Gregory pulled him back down. "You will dance La Rursus? You will turn every head in this hall if you do anything other than sit and watch. Unless, of course, you're prepared to declare for her."

Declare for her? That was not possible.

"Well? Are you?" his friend pressed.

"Nay."

He sat.

"I thought as much."

Though he would sooner slit the earl's nephew's throat, Toren watched instead as he circled Juliette in the most erotic dance allowed in polite society. Outlawed by the church for that very reason, the La Rursus was only acceptable since Queen Eleanor, much to King Henry's dismay, had declared it as her favorite. He watched as the young man circled Juliette with his hand at his sides. When the pace of the song increased, he placed his hand on her back. They turned, along with the other couples.

His torment must have been evident, because Gregory clapped him on the back. "You've no claim on her," he said, his tone no longer taunting.

Toren shifted on the bench, grateful for his friend. Without someone to intervene, he would have stormed onto the dance floor. But Gregory was right, and he'd do best not to forget it.

Juliette laughed as her partner lifted her into the air. Her hair swung around her, its golden hue in stark contrast to her blue velvet gown. They spun in a circle, laughing and clearly enjoying themselves.

He could not watch this any longer.

He clasped Gregory's shoulder and climbed to his feet.

"Fear not, my friend," he said, in answer to the questioning look in the other man's eyes. "I'm leaving."

Toren would not go to her again. The feelings she evoked in him were ones he'd do best to ignore. He forced himself not to look behind him as he strode through the hall toward the exit.

He did not unclench his fists until he emerged into the night air, a floor away from the perfumed excesses of the hall. Some impulse bid him to walk and keep walking, and he made his way through the tent city, passing his tent. Guided by moonlight alone, he took the well-worn path to the lake below. He heard the rush of water before he could see it.

The heat of the day had not entirely abated, and the prospect of a swim was too compelling to ignore. He took off his surcoat, glancing briefly at the crest his father had worn with such pride. At least his father had not lived to see him fail so miserably. Losing Bristol. Failing to retrieve Catrina until after she'd fallen in love with the enemy. Failing to complete the king's mission. Falling in love with his target's daughter...

The rage he'd felt while watching Juliette dance had startled him. That, and his desire to protect her from harm, his nearly uncontrollable urge to be with her whenever possible...

Bloody hell. He *did* love her, and he hadn't the faintest idea what to do about it.

"You didn't care to dance?"

He reached for the sword he'd discarded and swung it into position before realizing it was *her*. She had followed him without alerting him to her presence even with a lantern by her side.

That had never happened.

Ever.

He dropped the sword to his side.

"Jules... how?" It was all he could manage.

She lowered the voluminous folds of her dress she held to her sides. "I've read extensively on the subject of tracking."

"You've..." He took a deep breath. "*Read* about tracking?"

"Aye." She walked past him to the edge of the lake. He was about to admonish her to be careful when she stopped.

"As I've said, Sister was adamant I read in every language, on every topic imaginable. Once I became of an age to do so. Odd, don't you think? That she'd not have me concentrate on religious books? I read those too, of course. More often than the other. It is a convent, after all."

Her back was still to him. Only her hair and the lantern at her side was clearly visible.

"Of course, I'd not read about tracking people. But I imagined it would be quite the same as tracking animals. . . and it is, is it not? Without being able to see clearly, I simply did what any skilled tracker would do."

Anticipate the prey's movements.

"How could you possibly have known I would come here?"

She still did not turn toward him.

"You were angry, and likely restless. You mentioned having used this path to bathe each day in the lake. So I simply assumed."

Sheltered, not stupid, she'd said. And she was right.

"You're angry," he said.

She did turn then, and with the glimmer of the lake behind her, she looked to him like a wood nymph, ethereal and beautiful. She made no move toward him.

"I don't understand you, Toren. Help me understand."

Oh God. . . if only he could. He wanted to reach out, pull her toward him, but she deserved more from him. If he could not answer such a simple question, he did not deserve to touch her.

"Why do you hold back, even now?"

Another question he could not answer. And so he stayed silent.

"Tell me, Toren. Why? What is wrong with me? Why do you not want me?"

He could not let her believe that, not even for a moment, so he did step forward then. Taking the lantern from her, he replaced it with his hand.

"Nothing is wrong with you, Jules. Just the opposite. You are the kindest, most beautiful woman I've ever met. You're as smart as our priest at Brockburg, as resourceful as my sister, and more caring than I deserve."

He'd give her every truth he could. It wasn't enough, but it was the best he could do.

"Then why? Tell me, please."

"I can't—"

"I believe I may be falling in love with you."

His heart stopped, albeit for the briefest of moments. At least, it felt as though it had. He was the luckiest and most doomed man in all of England. And Scotland.

"Jules, you deserve so much more than I can give you."

She was so damn innocent. If loving her was the stupidest thing he'd ever done, what he was about to say was even stupider.

"Your father." God forgive him. "There are rumors. . ."

"What do they have to do with us?" She pulled her hand from his and gestured back and forth between them. "I meant what I said. He's innocent. I promise you. He would never, ever, do the things some are claiming he's done."

The conviction in her voice was a reason to love her.

"Sister Heloise knows everything, and she believes him to be innocent as well. When I overheard my father speaking to his steward, I immediately made inquiries."

He hadn't asked her to elaborate before, and as much as he wanted to know what she had to say, Toren refused to do so now. He would not exploit their relationship this way.

"Forget I said—"

"Nay, you'll hear me out on this. I spoke to my mother, who knew not a blessed thing, but Sister Heloise told me that what I'd overheard was true. Or at least the rumormongers believe it to be true. They say he has taken bribes from well-placed English nobles. They say he has guaranteed those who pay him exemption from being brought to trial on the Day of Truce. But hear me on this." Her voice rose in volume as she spoke. Jules was truly upset. He reached for her, but she took a step back.

"He did not do it, Toren Kerr. My father has spent his life ignoring everyone around him. My mother. Me. My brother. Everyone. All at the expense of securing peace along the border. He claims his greatest desire is to keep us safe. And maybe he believes that. But it's a game to him now. One he's determined to win. This is the quality King Henry saw in him. It is why he appointed a minor baron as Lord Warden of the Middle Marches —and why he has refused to consider these rumors."

He didn't dare question her. Instead, he waited for her to calm. When she did, he broke the silence between them.

"I believe you."

Either Douglas and his king were right, which meant Jules had not taken her father's measure correctly, an idea he was increasingly beginning to doubt, or they were both wrong, and an innocent man was being unfairly persecuted.

"But others may not. I'm here to learn the truth. When your father arrives—"

"He's not coming."

He could not have heard her correctly.

"Not coming?" he repeatedly numbly.

"Please do not point out the oddity of the warden not attending this tournament, or the obvious fact that his daughter should have some indication of his whereabouts."

He wasn't coming. Toren kept his expression neutral while he thought of what needed to be done. He needed to relay a message to Douglas before any further decisions could be made. He'd send a trusted messenger from Bristol. Which meant. . .

"I must leave on the morrow."

"Leave? You said you'd changed your mind. Is this because my father isn't coming? That's the *only* reason you're here? I'd thought—"

If anyone was within shouting distance, they would be upon them shortly.

Suddenly, she stopped talking—or, more precisely, shouting—and attempted to march past him. He caught her by the arm.

"It is not the only reason I am here. Jules, please. I want the same thing as your father. Peace for the borderers who see a lifetime of murder and bloodshed every year. I was sent here to save the process that has kept violence from spreading beyond the borders. To protect both countries from the death grip of an increasingly inevitable war."

She pulled her arm away.

"I thought you were different."

"Listen to me." Surprisingly, she stayed. The cries of crickets filled the air around them, and it suddenly struck him that they were arguing in the most peculiar of places.

"How did you get away? Are you always in the habit of placing yourself in such danger?"

She crossed her arms, reminding him he still had some convincing to do before she would answer his questions.

"I came here to speak with your father and to represent my country in this overly extravagant but necessary display of peace between England and Scotland. I never expected to meet someone as extraordinary as you."

"So that is why you fled the keep this eve rather than coming to me as planned."

"Did you enjoy your dance?" he countered. That he'd found it impossible to watch her in another man's arms was a thought he had planned to keep to himself.

"Will I ever see you again after you leave?"

If not for the mission that promised to keep them apart, the answer would be appallingly easy.

Unless he could prove that Hallington was not the man he'd been painted to be, her father would die—if not by his hand, then by someone else's—and it was possible Douglas would not be inclined to give the man the benefit of the doubt after the death of his nephew. So for now, he gave her the only answer he could possibly give her. "No."

It was the hardest thing he'd ever said, but he'd vowed not to lie to her, aside from his decision not to tell her the details of his mission.

The candle in her lantern flickered. It was the only movement between them. There was nothing more he could say.

She stared at him, her expression indiscernible. There was pain there, and something more.

"I would know you then, before you leave. And before you say no, tell me true: do you want to make love to me?"

"Yes, I do."

"Then allow me this one chance to control what happens to me."

He wanted to argue. To force her to see reason. Explain why they could not, should not be together. But she was making it difficult to deny her. To deny them both.

14

Juliette shivered despite the warm, dense summer air. Though she could hardly see his face, she knew he was going to do it.

She was scared.

And excited.

He reached for her and pulled her into his arms. His mouth covered hers in a demanding kiss that left no question as to his intentions.

His mouth slid across her own as it had the past two nights, but this time there was an urgency that had not been there before. Toren reached under the right side of her gown and began to unlace it before turning his attention to the opposite side of the cumbersome dress. Without taking his mouth from hers, he worked quickly enough to make a skilled handmaiden jealous.

Once loosened, he tore the laces apart and, in one quick motion, pulled the heavy velvet gown over her head.

"Clearly you've done that before."

She didn't mean to sound accusatory, but the memory from two nights prior of him flirting with ladies in the hall, or at least them flirting with him, sharpened her tone.

"I'd no sooner answer that question than I'd ask you, once again, if you're sure about this, Jules."

He discarded his surcoat and, for the first time since they'd been together, his shirt. In the past, he'd insisted they remain clothed for their encounters. Now, she understood why. Seeing him like this, it would be impossible to walk away without being fully satisfied.

Even though he was dimly lit, she could see the lines of each muscle in his chest and stomach. She stepped closer and ran her hands along his arms, reveling in the bumps and curves of his muscles.

"Ah God, lass..."

So this felt good for him?

"I will explore every bit of you before the night is through," she said.

He pulled her to him in response, and instinct drove her to wrap her arms around his back. Kissing her neck, he trailed a path toward the sensitive flesh behind her ear. She could feel the warmth of his breath as he teased her there. She gripped him, not embarrassed to beg.

"Please." She wanted... more.

He gave it to her.

Grasping her buttocks, he pressed into her until she could feel the full length of his manhood against her.

"It's time to cool off," he whispered.

"What—"

She felt the rush of air against her body before she realized what he had done. She was sure she'd never disrobed herself so quickly in her life. He stood back and simply stared. How odd it was to stand there before him, utterly naked as a needle.

He reached out, cupped her breast, and rubbed the tip with his thumb. It hardened instantly.

He'd reached beneath her shift before, but it felt different now that she was completely naked. More sensual. She closed her eyes and wondered if it would also feel more intense when his fingers played with her *down there*.

The pressure of his hand lifted suddenly, and when she opened her eyes, ready to protest, she realized he had only pulled away to remove the remainder of his own clothing. He stood in front of her, tall and proud.

She looked down.

Oh dear.

"You said it was time—"

"For a swim," he finished.

Was he serious?

Apparently, he was. Taking her by the hand, he pulled her toward the edge of the water, and before she could decide if this was a good idea, her toes were wet. The water was not frigid, but it was not very warm either.

"Don't think, just keep moving."

Hadn't she done that all night? Or all week, to be precise?

So she did. Before long, she was submerged up to her waist.

Toren released her hand and disappeared underwater with a splash, only to emerge right beside her.

Holding her breath, she ducked her head under the surface and swam away, but not too far. When she emerged, she turned to find Toren behind her. He grabbed her around the waist and pressed his body against hers. She could feel the evidence of his need against her again.

Juliette shuddered.

"Cold?" Moving her wet hair to one side, Toren kissed the sensitive spot below her neck. She wanted him to do what he'd done the past two nights in her chamber—to stroke her and fill her with his fingers—but could not bring herself to say such a thing aloud.

"Nay, I'm not cold." Just the opposite. She felt warm all over when he was this close to her.

He reached around to cup her breast once again. But his hand stayed there only briefly before lowering to the spot that had given her so much pleasure.

It was as if he'd heard her thoughts and thought only of pleasing her.

He slipped inside and moved. . . back and forth. His fingers circled and pressed.

"I. . ."

She wanted to say *something* but wasn't sure what exactly.

"What is it?" He continued to press into her with increasing speed. She grabbed his hand, needing to hold on to something.

"Show me," he said.

At first she didn't understand, but when he stopped moving his hand, only starting again when she reached down to guide him, she realized he wished for *her* to set the pace.

Everything ceased to exist besides the two of them. And then everything inside her tensed and an explosion pulsed through her, radiating wave after wave of sweet sensation. The sounds she made surely weren't her own.

"I'm going to make you mine, Jules."

What did that mean? He'd made it clear she was anything but his. Had he changed his mind?

Spinning her around, Toren moved his lips over hers, his tongue plunging inside to capture her own as water splashed around them. Jules belatedly understood what he had meant about making her "his" when he reached down below the water's surface and she could feel him pressing against her.

That was not his finger.

She wanted this. She wanted him. She didn't want a stranger to show her. Or to never know a man before committing herself to a life of servitude.

"Show me, Toren," she said, sensing his hesitancy and echoing his earlier words. He'd slowed his movements, and Juliette wanted to be sure he understood.

"Make me yours."

He grabbed her then, pulling her up so her legs wrapped around his waist. The man was holding her body weight up with one arm, acting as if it were effortless. With the other, he inched his hardness closer to her core, where his fingers had been.

"This is irreversible, Jules."

She didn't answer him. Couldn't if she'd wanted to. She felt a pressure then, a fullness as he pressed.

"This will hurt a bit."

"So I've been told."

"Ouch!" He'd thrust into her and stilled, his hands now both holding her buttocks. It would have been difficult to change her mind even if she'd wanted to.

Which she did not.

The initial sting gave way to an. . . interesting. . . sensation.

And then he began to move.

The warm water—had she ever thought it cold?—was like a blanket surrounding them on every side. He held her, moved her, thrust into her and with each movement, she wanted more.

Catching on to the pace quickly, Juliette helped as best she could.

"Kiss me," he asked, and she did so gladly.

This time it was she who captured the tip of his tongue with her own. As he moved faster, water splashed onto her from every side. The completely foreign but highly enjoyable sensations were every bit as powerful as before, but this time the knowledge that they were truly joined made it somehow. . . sweeter.

She pushed down onto him, and Toren tore his mouth from hers.

"Bloody hell, Jules."

That feeling was stealing up on her again, the building one that made her feel like she was nearing a cliff, only it would be safe to jump off the edge. To soar through the air and revel in her very aliveness.

"Please."

He guided her as she pulled on his hair, holding him close so she wouldn't fall into the dark recesses of the water beneath them.

"Toren! It's happening again."

And it was. She screamed—a most unladylike sound—though she wasn't alone. He did the same, making one final thrust as she pulsed around him.

She didn't want to move. Or want him to move. Juliette simply wanted to stay in this position forever.

Still breathing heavily, Toren looked at her, his expression solemn.

"You're a maiden no longer."

He regretted it.

"Good." She did not.

Somehow she had to make him understand she really had wanted this. That she didn't have the slightest care about how wrong it had supposedly been. Nothing in her life had ever felt more right.

He lifted her up and away from him, but then wrapped his arms around her. With her cheek pressed up against his chest, Juliette inhaled deeply, trying to remember the smell. Tomorrow, he would be gone.

"You know," she said, pulling back to look at him, "I thought earlier to convince you to keep me." The words had not come out as flippantly as she'd intended, so she rushed to finish. "I'd decided to keep you."

He raised his eyebrows.

"But since I can't, thank you for giving me this instead. It had to be with you."

His smile vanished.

"Nay, lass. Thank you for giving me the most precious gift anyone has ever bestowed on me. I don't deserve it. And should not have taken it. But it's done, and by God it was magnificent."

She did smile then. Whether he realized it or not, he complimented her constantly.

They stood in the waist-deep water, wrapped in each other's arms, for so long, Juliette began to shiver. But she would not be the one to end this night. Once they left this otherworldly haven, it would be the start of a long journey.

A lifetime of knowing desire. And love.

And having lost it forever.

Toren couldn't recall the exact moment he'd made the decision to become the very man he'd railed against. His brother-in-law would be vastly amused.

He walked to the bank of the lake hand in hand with Jules. If they could have stayed in that water forever, left their troubles on shore and began life anew together, Toren would have jumped at the chance.

She was shivering from cold, and he wrapped his tunic around her as soon as they reached their clothing.

"Use it to dry yourself," he instructed. Though she looked at him oddly, Jules did as he asked. They hastily picked up and shook out their discarded garments.

The water stood in stark contrast to the castle in the distance. The feast and dancing would continue late into the night, especially now that they were nearing the end of the tourney. But there was no glamour or glory here. Just nature and peace.

And love.

He'd fallen in love with the one woman he could never claim as his own. . . and he'd taken her despite knowing he shouldn't.

"How will I get this back on?"

Jules held the wrinkled velvet dress in her arms, carrying it to him as gently as if it were a wee bairn.

"Just so," he answered and proceeded to help her don the shift and gown, which required lacing up each side. With her soft leather shoes in place, she was completely clothed, though none who spied her in such a state would have any doubt as to her actions that night.

"Come to my tent. It's much too early for you to go back now. We'll wait until most of the guests are asleep. Besides," he wrapped the belt around his waist and secured his dagger and sword into place. "I can't very well escort you back like this."

His tunic was too wet for him to don, so he stood shirtless.

"I think it's a fine look for you."

He turned back to catch her appreciative glance at his muscles. Mayhap the tent would be a good idea for another reason as well.

"In that case, for my lady, I will fight in the last match as such tomorrow. For your viewing pleasure."

"You had not planned on participating, even so close to being named champion?"

He took her free hand and they walked away from the stream.

"Nay. But if it would bring you pleasure, I will do so. As I am."

"You wouldn't," she said.

"That, my fair maiden, is a challenge. Toren Kerr, third of his name and chief of Clan Kerr of Brockburg, accepts it as such."

15

After she made it back to the castle, escorted by Toren, Juliette slept deeply for just a few short hours before Christina burst into her chamber with Helen.

"Still sleeping? Juliette, hurry. We don't want to be late for the final match!" She tugged on her hand. "I've never known you lay abed beyond sunrise."

She allowed the maid to help her into a pale yellow gown lined with gold thread about the neckline, which plunged lower than most of her gowns. She normally allowed her hair to flow freely, but today the maid braided it, weaving small crystals into the plait to catch the sun's rays. It was a trick she'd read about in an ancient text that told the story of how one Egyptian servant had won the heart of a pharaoh. She carried them with her for just the right moment, and today was certainly that.

Toren was leaving. And after last eve, she was more certain than ever.

He was the one she'd come here to find.

Truly, in her heart, she hadn't expected to find love at the tournament. She had wished for it, aye, but to have actually met a man who made her feel as he did. . .

When they were finally alone, Christina grabbed her by the shoulders.

"What did you do?"

She simply smiled.

"Juliette, nay. Tell me you're jesting."

"I love him," she said simply.

"Love him—"

"It was my choice," she added quickly.

Her stomach turned as Christina's eyes took pity on her. She might as well tell her everything.

"He's leaving today."

"He's. . ."

Her poor friend's eyes widened bigger than Toren's tournament shield.

"So that's your plan? Give your virginity to a man you'll not be marrying. Wave goodbye as he heads back to Scotland. And then what?"

Christina feebly attempted to warm her hands by the dying embers of the fire.

"I don't know."

She didn't have a plan. Her heart urged her to make him stay, but Toren Kerr was not a man who could be *made* to do anything. But she was just so confused. He appeared to care for her as much as she cared for him, so why did he not wish to marry her? What was keeping them apart?

A hard knock on her door came at just the right moment.

It was Christina's husband waiting to escort them to the meal. Even the simple breaking of their fast was grand this morning. And while the crowning event, the melee, was still to come, this morning's event was just as revered.

Toren would be matched against the English champion, and none were pleased the scoundrel Blackburn would represent their country. If only the legendary Waryn men had been here to defend their titles. Lord Thornhurst, alas, had been injured in his last match.

If she thought the meal was grand, Christina fairly fainted when they reached the lists.

"Have you ever seen anything like it?" Christina asked.

"'Tis most impressive," her husband agreed. The crowd had swelled beyond capacity. It seemed every seat in the galleries and all the bench seats below were filled, but Christina spotted an opening in the berfrois. Many waved ribbons and colorful cloths in the air, and the crest of every important family in Northumbria was represented.

Musicians played as everyone awaited the two champions. Grooms, handlers, physicians, and tournament officials all gathered at the entrance to the lists. Juliette sat with her companions, scanning the crowd for him.

Cheers greeted both men as they entered the field simultaneously. Toren sat taller and more regal, even though it was supposedly *he* who was the barbarian.

It was impossible to carry on a conversation over the noise, but she smiled at Christina, who gave her a curious look in return. Did Christina judge her as others would? She was the one person whose good opinion truly mattered to Juliette. Her heart crumpled a little in her chest at the prospect, but her friend finally smiled back. Even though Christina was surprised, mayhap disappointed at what she'd done, she would support her, and Juliette loved her for it.

"He's coming this way! Juliette, your ribbon."

Sure enough, Toren maneuvered his mighty warhorse toward her once again. When he tipped his lance to her this time, she not only tied her favor to the end of it but waved to him as well. He raised his hand in greeting, and Juliette wondered if the galleries would open up and swallow her.

For that was how she felt. Consumed in every direction by light and happiness. In that moment, she decided she would not do it. Whatever happened, she would not let this man simply walk away.

After Blackburn took his favor from another, the men retreated to their respective recesses and prepared for the match. She tried to ignore the speculative eyes that were trained on her. Let them whisper about how she'd given her favor to Toren again and again. Juliette did not care.

"He will no doubt win," Christina shouted, and Juliette silently agreed.

"Blackburn is highly skilled," Hedford replied, also shouting. "He's won tournaments across the continent, though some question his methods."

Did he cheat to win? The possibility didn't surprise her given his behavior during the tourney, but there wasn't a chance for her to press Lord Hedford. The herald's horn blasted, signaling the start of the match.

Juliette couldn't watch.

She squeezed her eyes closed as the men met each other, but they flew open upon the first sound of wood and metal clashing.

Both men were still seated, though they had each lost their lances.

Back in the recesses, they were handed fresh lances—a pattern that occurred two more times, the last pass a clear point by Toren.

This joust was perfectly horrendous. She squirmed in her seat, alternating between opening and closing her eyes.

Finally, on the fourth pass, Toren knocked Blackburn to the ground, but the man immediately rose to take his sword from his squire. Though by rights Toren could have stayed seated, using the advantage of height in the ensuing swordfight, he did not.

Her chief had a peculiar sense of honor.

He raised his fist, indicating both opponents should return to their recesses, a move within his rights to properly secure his weapon. Spectators' necks strained to see what was happening, but since Toren was clear across the lists from where she sat, she only caught sight of him when he began walking back toward the center.

Whispers of surprise around her were matched with Christina's much more blunt comment, "By God's blood, what is he doing?"

What, indeed. She would kill him.

The daft man had removed his armor. And though his legs were still covered with the thick leather favored by the Scots, his chest was completely and utterly bare. Nothing. No shirt, no mail. . . nothing to shield him from his opponent.

She suddenly remembered his promise. She would have laughed aloud if she weren't so scared.

"What is he doing?" Christina asked.

In response, she reluctantly smiled. The man truly was like a Greek god who'd chosen to honor humankind with his presence. As he swung his sword upright in preparation for the fight, his muscles tensed. Juliette was sure she'd never see such an awe-inspiring sight again for the rest of her life. Some of the guests stared at her, but she pretended not to notice.

"He's attempting to intimidate his opponent," someone said.

"I told you, they're heathens," said another.

As comments swirled around them, Juliette had eyes only for the man who had put himself in jeopardy simply to please her. She didn't know if she wanted to kiss him or throttle him.

Mayhap both.

Fortunately, there was no reason for the rapid beating of her heart and the sweatiness of her palms. Toren used his considerable skills to ensure the match ended quickly, and it did. With nary more than a few clangs of metal, and one thrust from his opponent that convinced her Blackburn was there to kill, not for sport, the match was over.

Toren had won.

Blackburn lost his sword to Toren, and when he attempted to reach for the dagger at his side, a trick that could see him hung as a cheater, Toren moved surprisingly quickly for a man his size and kicked the cad's legs out from under him.

Lying on the ground, completely disarmed, Blackburn finally laid his head down in defeat. A horn sounded, and attendants rushed onto the field as the crowd cheered their champion. True to tradition, even though he hailed from north of the border, Toren was celebrated. He bowed before the earl and his wife, who led the rest of the guests in a deafening round of applause.

Finally, it was over.

Toren spun toward her, and as Juliette and her companions stood, she realized he was coming her way. Spectators watched with bated breath as he halted beneath her. She looked toward Lord Hedford, who nodded, although she would have gone to Toren even if he had not given permission. At least he'd allowed her the appearance of acquiescing to her chaperone's judgment.

Toren was looking at Hedford as well, and the men seemed to communicate silently. When she arrived at the bottom of the wooden stands, she reached for Toren's hand, for all to see, and allowed him to lead her away from the lists.

"What are you doing?" he asked.

She had played a dangerous game meeting with him each night. But this was different. Physical contact, in public. Her father would no doubt hear of it. But what did it matter? She had given the man her virginity last eve, and the nuns would surely take her anyway. That was, of course, unless she could convince Toren otherwise.

"You are mine," she proclaimed.

"Aye," he said. She glanced at him, her heart racing.

People cheered and slapped him on the back as they walked past him.

"Where are we going?" she asked.

He'd released her hand, and she deliberately walked slightly behind him. Not in deference, but in awe. She rather liked looking at the muscles on his back.

He did not speak but rather led beyond the lists toward the outer edge of the tents where the Scots made camp, though it was still quite a ways from his own. "Here," he said, indicating a tent near the edge of the field. It was more decorative than his own, and they slipped inside without notice.

"It's a friend's," he said simply, as if there wasn't time to say more. The moment the flap closed, he pulled her toward him.

"Oh!"

She wrapped her arms around his bare back, disregarding the sweat and dirt that covered his flesh, and Toren lowered his head and kissed her. She opened for him, her tongue gladly dueling with his as they melded into each other.

Her champion.

When he finally released her, she murmured, "Congratulations. But if you ever attempt such a stupid, idiotic. . . what's so funny?"

"You."

"I didn't say anything funny! I was chastising you, if you had not noticed."

He ran his thumb across her lips, parting them and staring in a way that made her insides tingle.

"I noticed."

His hand roamed downward until it reached her breast.

"This is much too low," he said, looking at the neckline of her gown.

"Too low?" she repeated.

He dipped his thumb beneath the cloth, teasing her.

"Aye, lass. Others may get ideas."

"What ideas?'

His hand stilled. And pulled away.

"The same ideas I've had all morning since I spied your hair glittering from across the lists." He reached up and touched one of the crystals in her hair. "Interesting."

"Mayhap they are the same thoughts I had when you so brazenly decided to engage in a swordfight without armor."

The corner of his mouth tipped up. "I keep my promises whenever possible."

She could lecture him, tell him his actions had been foolish and dangerous, but he likely already knew that.

"I didn't bring you here to seduce you. Again."

"Then why *did* you bring me here?"

"I must leave, Jules."

Knowing what he'd planned to say and hearing the words were not the same. She suddenly felt a bone-deep chill despite the day's heat. Her chest constricted, and Juliette knew not what to say. She'd prepared a pretty speech, but none of the words came to her now.

"I am the worst sort of man for having done what I—"

"Stop." She wanted to reach out, to touch him. Make him hold her the way he'd done last night. As if he cherished her. But this was a different man who stood before her.

This was the chief of Clan Kerr. The champion of one of England's greatest tournaments.

"You insult me by claiming it as your decision alone."

He looked surprised, but truly he had no reason to be. Juliette had never claimed to be ruled by conventional wisdom. Sometimes, she wished her thoughts were more akin to other ladies, but courtesy of the nuns and their learning, she would always be different.

He looked as if there were more he would like to say, but he did not. She vowed that morn not to let him just simply leave. Should she tell him how she felt? That she wished him to fight for her? That she'd decided to fight for him?

Her earlier conviction fled as quickly as it had taken hold. To what end? He had decided he was leaving, and the burden of her love would not change that.

"Where will you go?" It wasn't the question she wanted to ask, but she was curious nonetheless.

"To Bristol Manor," he said. And she knew he spoke the truth.

She forged ahead. "I just wish I understood why you need to leave so suddenly. What you need from my father."

Why we can't be together . . .

He stared at her so intently, for so long, Juliette thought perhaps he was finally going to explain everything.

"Toren," a male voice called from outside the tent.

Neither of them moved.

"I must go," he said. Taking her in his arms, he kissed her so gently on the lips she could hardly feel it.

And then he was gone.

Juliette stood there for a long time. She could feel the air grow warmer. She didn't know whose tent she stood in, but she was afraid to look outside for she knew he would be gone.

Why had they left so much unsaid?

Juliette lifted the flap and startled when a man she didn't recognize bowed to her.

"My lady."

She looked around, confirming what she already knew. There was nary a sign of him.

"This is yours, I presume?" She stepped into the sunlight.

"Aye, my lady." He offered his arm. "Gregory Campbell at your service. I am a friend of Toren's and am to escort you back to the keep."

Though she already knew he was gone, she found herself asking, "And he is?"

"Gone, my lady. Regretfully."

Gone. To his sister and brother-in-law. Juliette stood there, immobile, until she finally noticed the man's elbow extended to her.

She took it and allowed him to lead her away. Had this morning really happened? Had last eve? It all felt like a dream, and yet it was more real than the sunny day around her. How was she to act as if everything were normal? It was unthinkable to return to the revelry. Unthinkable to go home and fall in with her father's commands or join the nuns.

And yet what choice did she really have? She was the daughter of a border baron, a woman with few skills save the ones she read about in books. A dreamer, as her parents said.

You're as smart as our priest at Brockburg, as resourceful as my sister, and more caring than I deserve.

She *was* smart. And resourceful.

And she was not ready to accept her fate just yet.

Toren had ridden hard for nearly two days and was finally rewarded with a view of Bristol Manor. Alfred had kept pace quite nicely. He could have arrived a half day earlier if not for the pack horse that carried his equipment.

Built on a river basin two days' ride from the border, Bristol Manor was a solid structure. Though its main keep could have fit into one of Condren Castle's outer buildings, it was quite well appointed. Surrounded by not one but two curtain walls, the second added just recently, it was also well-defended.

Which was just as well since his sister now lived there with her new husband.

To think, just a few months before, Bristol had been his.

Riding through the gates, Toren should have felt awkward as the ousted master who was now nothing more than the manor's former lord. And brother to the lady of the manor.

Instead, he was quite relieved. Brockburg was his home, and though he had come to appreciate the people of Bristol, it had never felt quite right.

"What in God's bones are you. . . Toren Kerr, get down from that horse immediately." Dressed in a fashionable dark green kirtle with a cream tunic peeking out from underneath, Catrina was a little slip of a thing, and yet she had a way of talking that made her seem much larger.

He'd expected such a greeting, as the guards who'd allowed them entry would have sent word to Catrina.

He complied. Taking orders from this red-headed harridan was not unusual for him. Nor for any other man in her acquaintance, including her husband. As he dismounted, Toren found himself thinking again of Jules. How different it would have been if he could have brought her with him and introduced her to his sister as his intended.

Pushing the thought away, he embraced Catrina. "You rode directly past us on the way to the tournament, and you didn't think to stop and visit with your sister?" she scolded.

Toren tousled her hair as he'd done his entire life. She swatted his hand and smoothed the long, wild tresses.

"And then you fail to introduce me to your guest?"

She pointed at Alfred, who seemed wary of her, already leading the horses away. "Wait," she called to him.

The boy, ever shy, peeked up at her from beneath the strange cap he wore night and day.

"Why is he so dirty?" she whispered, her voice full of concern.

Toren shrugged. "He always seems to be so." He waved the lad over.

"Greetings, lad. What's your name?"

Without looking up, he answered quietly, "Alfred, my lady."

He could tell Catrina was a mite confused. "Alfred proved indispensable at the tournament. I've asked him home with me to train with Alex. I was lucky that he agreed."

"Alfred—" his sister moved closer to the squire, "—welcome to Bristol Manor. If it pleases you to lead the horses to the stable, Arthur will assist you. And please make yourself comfortable here."

Toren thought he saw the boy smile before he turned back toward the stables.

"He's quite unusual, is he not?" Catrina asked as they watched him walk away.

"He is certainly small for a squire. And aye, so painfully shy that he refuses to look me in the eye. But the lad is quick and competent."

"And in need," Catrina finished, quickly assessing the real reason he was here.

"Indeed," he turned to face his sister. "Catrina, I need a messenger. One who is trustworthy. And swift."

She took his hand and they walked together toward the manor.

"Something is wrong." It was not a question. Catrina already knew.

"Aye."

She stopped him steps away from the entrance to the main tower. The great hall was housed on the first floor here, something that was unusual in manors of this size.

It was getting dark, and Toren suddenly realized he was ravenous. For two days they'd eaten only bread and cheese, save the hare he'd cooked over the modest fire last eve. He looked forward to a proper meal. But this was more important than food.

"I've much to tell you. But I must get a message to Douglas. Quickly. Tonight."

He looked into the bright hazel eyes the exact shade as his own. Pulling her aside, he told her what he had not been able to share with Juliette. Or even Gregory.

"Douglas, on orders from the king, sent me to Condren to kill the English warden."

Her eyes widened.

"You're being punished. For me."

To ease her mind, he chucked her under the chin and said, "I believe it has more to do with my legendary sword-fighting skills."

At least she smiled.

"But he is still vexed about Bristol. Douglas mentioned it specifically." And the broken betrothal, but he'd keep that information to himself. Catrina should not be made to feel guilty for her happiness.

"However, Hallington never arrived at the tourney. When I learned he definitely would not be coming, I left immediately."

"To await further instructions," she finished.

"Nay, not exactly."

She cocked her head to the side. "Nay?"

He planned to tell her everything but couldn't find the words.

"What is it? Toren, what are you not telling me?"

A man approached them from the side of the manor. He was not smiling, but that was no great surprise. Bryce Waryn hardly ever smiled.

"My lord." He inclined his head, not unlike when they'd met for the first time, prepared to end each other's life in a judicial combat to settle the matter of Bristol Manor and its lordship. If it weren't for his sister, one of them would not be standing here right now.

Waryn slipped his hand behind Catrina's back, and the smile she bestowed on him was full of such pure happiness, he felt a begrudging appreciation for the English lord.

After a long awkward silence, Catrina finally pulled him toward the manor, linking one arm through his own and another through her husband's. "You need to eat. We'll speak more later."

This could not wait.

"The messenger?"

Catrina tugged him along. "Aye, we'll arrange it. Come." She then turned to her husband on her other side. "And quit glaring at my brother."

He would have laughed, but he was certain his brother-in-law wouldn't appreciate it. A small smile must have escaped, though, for as they walked through the entranceway, he was similarly chastised. "And you, stop taunting my husband."

He did laugh then and thought he spied a very slight upturn in the corners of his brother-in-law's mouth.

Leave it to Catrina to lighten his mood. If only for a short time.

16

Three days after arriving at Bristol, Toren had finished practicing in the lists and was watching a match between Bryce and his steward, Thomas, when he spied his sister running toward him. Lifting her kirtle as she ran, Catrina looked exactly as she had when they were children. She'd never quite embraced the idea of decorum, and he loved her for it.

When she got closer, he could see she kept glancing back to the manor. The confused look in her eyes alerted him that something was wrong.

"Clean yourself, Toren. And follow me."

"Clean myself?"

"Catrina?" Bryce said, having stopped his match. "What is this about?"

"Hurry, brother." She tugged on his hand. "'Tis fine, Bryce. We have visitors."

"Visitors?" both men said in unison.

"Toren!" Catrina continued to tug his hand, offering nothing more by way of an explanation.

He handed his sword to a squire—Alfred was nowhere to be found—and acquiesced. Fighting Catrina was a useless endeavor.

But he could not imagine why he needed to 'clean himself' for her guests, let alone what visitors could possibly require his attention.

He stopped and let go of his sister's hand.

It wasn't possible.

Waryn caught up with them. "Catrina, I will know immediately what—"

"Juliette," she said simply. It was all she needed to say. Waryn looked at him with an expression akin to pity in his eyes.

So Catrina had told him everything. Of course she had. There should be no secrets between a husband and wife, and though he didn't like Bryce, Toren knew he could be trusted. He had given her leave to tell Waryn everything after explaining the hopeless situation to her.

His sister had burst into tears upon learning about his ill-fated love.

Toren had not known Catrina to cry often, so her reaction had surprised him.

And now Jules was here? How had this happened?

He allowed his sister to lead him into the manor house where a young maid attended him in the bedchamber that had been his sister's when Bristol was in the hands of Clan Kerr.

"My lady says you'll be needing to wash?"

He'd already changed, although he could hear his sister chastising him for rolling up the sleeves on his loose cream tunic. Yet she was the one who'd occasionally been mistaken for a servant. It was only their mother who'd cared for pageantry and appearances, and after she left, he and his siblings had rebelled against the stringent English rules she favored.

"I don't believe we've met," Toren said to the maid.

She bobbed a curtsy. "Elise, if it pleases you."

So timid. It was a wonder Catrina didn't scare the poor girl away.

"Many thanks, Elise." He washed, drying himself on the cloth she offered, and then followed her down the circular staircase and into the great hall below.

Her back was to him, but he would have recognized her anywhere. She was dressed in a simple dark green riding gown, her hair pulled back into a single, long blonde braid.

She had not seen him yet. She stood with her companions, Lord and Lady Hedford, as well as his sister and her husband. And then, as if sensing his presence behind her, she turned to look at him.

Though clearly travel-weary, Jules had never looked more beautiful. Her cheeks had been kissed by the sun these past days, and she looked like an angel.

But then a memory of her wrapped around him in the lake was overlaid upon the image of the serene lady before him. Quick to respond to his touch and passionate enough to make him more than slightly uncomfortable as they stood silently staring at each other.

"Jules." He quickly corrected himself. "Lady Juliette," he said as he walked toward her.

He lifted her hand, so soft beneath his own, and touched his lips to it. He never wanted to let go of her again.

As if he had a choice.

"Toren," she finally responded.

No one else existed. Except Bryce, who apparently thought it an appropriate time for a rare display of mirth.

"I'll have your apology any time, Kerr."

The bastard was grinning from ear to ear. Catrina must have sensed his reaction to the ill-made jest because she stepped between them and took Juliette by one arm and Lady Hedford by the other.

"We've already finished the midday meal, but Cook will prepare you a light repast. In the meantime, Elise will look after your needs. My lord." She nodded to Lord Hedford as she walked away with Toren's English maiden.

His chest constricted.

No longer a maiden. Thanks to him.

Jules glanced over her shoulder at him, and Toren realized he still did not know why they were there. What would he say to her? It would be days before Douglas responded to the message he'd sent asking for leave to further investigate the matter of Hallington's guilt.

It wasn't just Juliette's words that had swayed him—though they had weighed the most—he had been asking questions since his arrival at Condren, and nothing added up.

By all accounts, Hallington had spent his life fighting for peace along the border. Just as Jules had said, his reputation was that of a hardened warrior whose relentless pursuit of peace had become almost an obsession. He suspected the man cared more for his legacy than he did for the safety of the English borderers he protected, but nothing he had heard pointed to a man who would jeopardize everything to line his pockets.

Then why the rumors? Was he being framed? And would it matter to the king either way?

He thought of Douglas's words to him. 'As long as he's alive, Stewart Hallington will remain English Lord Warden of the Middle Marches. A man increasingly distrusted, and one who will be the downfall of any modicum of peace along the border.'

The man's guilt or innocence may be as insignificant as the reason why Toren had been chosen for this mission, especially knowing Douglas's kin had been slain. When it came to taking orders from the king, only one thing truly mattered.

Compliance.

Tell that to the woman who had just disappeared from view. To the woman he loved.

Their hostess was beyond extraordinary.

Lady Catrina's greeting had been warm and kind, particularly since they were unannounced guests. Juliette was about to whisper as much to Christina when Lady Catrina muttered, "Leaving his guests waiting," followed by a word that made Juliette blush.

She'd never heard a lady speak so! If Sister Heloise were here, the poor woman would likely faint. Lady Catrina must have realized she'd shocked them, for she clasped her hand over her mouth and looked at her husband, who simply raised his brows.

Sir Bryce Waryn, who was reputed to be the most skilled tournament fighter in all of England, was a severe man. And yet he had a surprisingly tender look on his face whenever he glanced at his wife. An odd couple to be sure, and yet they were clearly in love.

Still reeling from the fact that they were here, being escorted by a virtual stranger, Toren's sister no less, Juliette took a steadying breath. She tried to listen to Lady Catrina and Christina's chatter, but she could not stop thinking of Toren. Of his touch. Of her feelings for him. And of the fact that she would see him soon.

After he left, whispers circulated of Lord Blackburn's attempt to injure Toren after the match had ended. Some called for an inquiry, but without his opponent present, most agreed it would amount to nothing.

Then he appeared behind her, and everything else ceased to exist—their hosts, her friend, Lord Hedford, and the very hall in which they stood. He was dressed casually, the sleeves of his tunic rolled to his elbows, as was his custom, yet Toren looked as in control as she'd ever seen him. Though no longer lord of Bristol Manor, his bearing proclaimed him an important man to be sure. Chief of an ancient clan. Ruler of her heart.

He kissed her hand, and the warmth of his lips sent a shiver down her spine. She wanted so many things—to rail at him for leaving, to throw herself into his arms, and to kick him for making her fall in love with him in the first place.

Instead, she did nothing.

Before she knew it, Juliette was being shuttled to the manor gardens. Catrina had offered to show them to her and Christina, and though Jules had been reluctant to leave Toren, there was no polite way to refuse.

"Yes, Juliette enjoys the gardens back home," Christina said as they followed their hostess. "She often reads to the servants, which vexes her parents. Most especially her father."

Then they were there, and despite the tug she felt to return to Toren, there was no denying the gardens were magnificent. Shrubs that rivaled her in height surrounded them on every side, and flowers she'd never seen before bloomed despite the summer's heat. It rivaled even Condren's gardens.

"This is beautiful," she said in awe.

Lady Catrina smiled.

"Our gardener at Brockburg taught me how to make flowers thrive, even in less than ideal conditions."

She stared at the woman, her eyes wide. "You did this?" She tried to imagine her very proper parents' reaction to Juliette assisting their gardener back home.

"Whenever I have time, aye. Being raised by three men, Toren in particular, left little time for the niceties one would expect a lady to engage in."

They sat on two stone benches, the delicate carvings evidence of a master mason's work. Their hostess looked at her. "Tell me, Juliette, why are you here?"

Her voice held only curiosity, and she had expected the question, of course. But she'd imagined explaining herself to Toren.

"Well, I. . . Toren and I. . ." Oh dear, this was not easy, however kind Catrina seemed.

Christina answered for her, likely spying the blush on her cheeks.

"Juliette's father is the Lord Warden of the Middle Marches. She learned Toren attended the Tournament of the North with the hopes of speaking with her father, who never arrived. He was delayed."

Juliette finished, "Just after Toren left, Christina's husband relayed information to me that I thought it important for Toren to hear."

She attempted to ease the look of confusion on her hostess's face. "Lord Hedford is well-acquainted with border politics." She hoped this next bit would not get her into trouble. "Toren advised me not to mention that he was looking for my father. But somehow Hedford already knew."

Oh, to hell with it.

"Your brother and I grew. . . close. Hedford knew that, and when he learned the reason for my father's delay, we both thought it prudent for Toren to receive the news as well."

She wasn't sure how much Lady Catrina knew of her father and the vicious rumors about him. So she stopped there.

"I see. You left the tournament early?"

She looked at Christina, who shrugged. It wasn't the question she'd expected.

"If truth be told, Juliette made a convincing argument to myself and my husband why we should travel here," Christina added.

Christina put it more delicately, but the simple fact was that she had begged until they relented. "Aye," Juliette said. "We left as soon as Hedford received the message from my father."

Juliette had begun to form her own opinion about the nature of Hedford's secretive past, but it was not her secret to tell. Although Christina finally welcomed this adventure, her husband was quite against traveling to Bristol Manor. He'd wanted to send a messenger, but she and Christina had worn him down with their relentless arguments.

"Did you not wish to be there for the melee?"

Juliette had the feeling she was being tested in some way. Though still gracious, Lady Catrina's expression was... intent.

"Nay. Watching your brother win the championship match, though it was quite a harrowing experience, was enough excitement for me. My lady, your brother is quite reckless. He took off his armor for the hand to hand combat and fought shirtless. In a swordfight! Christina, tell her."

Toren's sister didn't even appear the slightest bit alarmed. In fact, she smiled.

"Juliette does not exaggerate," Christina added.

"That does sound... interesting," Lady Catrina said.

"Interesting? Lady Catrina, you should really speak to your brother before he gets himself killed."

The lady's laugh was one of pure mirth, and Juliette couldn't help but smile back.

"Please, it's simply Catrina. And it appears you've spent some time with my brother, so you'll understand the futility of telling him to do anything."

"Catrina," she repeated. "I've found you are quite right. But I'd like to try, if it pleases you."

Evidently she'd passed the other woman's test, for Catrina wrapped her in an embrace and squeezed her so hard she nearly lost her balance.

"It pleases me very much," Catrina whispered.

And that was when Juliette realized...

Toren's sister knew everything.

After their discussion in the gardens, their hostess whisked them to their rooms, where a servant had been waiting with a stunning display of bread, cheese, and fruit on a table as large as one in the hall. As they ate, Catrina, a flurry of activity, handed Juliette the strangest garment she'd ever seen and insisted that she wear it.

"For the ride," she said, as if that explained all.

When Juliette asked where and with whom she would be riding, Catrina simply smiled and admonished her to eat.

The prospect of a ride did not appeal after the long voyage to Bristol, but the sparkle in her hostess's eyes told her this was a ride she would not wish to miss. Catrina had something planned.

"Tell me," she said instead, gesturing to the garment, "what exactly is that?"

Catrina looked down at the outfit. "Breeches, of sorts. They were made specifically for a woman's legs. Here."

Juliette took the garment and prepared herself for yet another ride. It was only when they were leaving the keep that she realized Catrina would not be coming. She instead pointed her to the stables, which was when she first saw him and realized what was happening.

Her pulse raced when she finally understood the ride would be with Toren, and he alone.

And so she found herself mounting a beautiful chestnut mare not long before the sun would set. She assumed Hedford had already relayed their information to Toren, but since this was the first opportunity for them to talk, she tried not to groan when she mounted.

"Where are we going?" she asked as they began to move.

"You'll see," Toren shouted back to her. They rode past the curtain walls and around the manor, in the opposite direction of the small village she and Christina and Hedford had passed this morning.

With the Cheviot Hills to her right and lush green grassland all around, Juliette tried to enjoy the last remaining vestiges of sunlight, but it was impossible to pay attention to anything other than Toren Kerr. They were finally alone together.

She heard the sound of the waterfall before she saw it. And then it was before her. Water tumbled down a series of rocky outcrops, a white blanket against the hillside. It almost appeared as if there were multiple falls with plumes of water spraying in every direction.

Toren stopped without speaking, dismounted, and held up a hand to help her do the same. She took his hand, reveling in his touch, and allowed him to help her off the horse. Together, hand in hand, they walked toward the pool of crystalline water at the foot of the falls, surrounded by mossy rocks that climbed up the side of the modest hill.

His arms encircled her from behind.

Juliette lay her head back on his chest and grasped his forearms, never wanting to let go.

This time, she would refuse to let go.

She sighed when he swept her hair to the side and leaned in close, his warm breath on her flesh. He moved the odd tunic Catrina had lent her aside and kissed her so gently on the back of her neck she wondered if it had actually happened.

His arms tightened, and this time the touch of his lips was unmistakable.

The sound of the waterfall, so powerful yet peaceful at the same time, had a calming effect. She'd been so worried about how Toren would welcome her—about *whether* he would welcome her—the relief she felt now was mixed with the raw emotion.

"I missed you," he said over the sound of the falls.

How she had longed to hear those words. She'd missed him as well. The days they spent apart were some of the longest of her life, as if each moment stretched into eternity.

"Mayhap you should not have left?"

Toren spun her around, his arms still wrapped around her.

"I had no choice."

She reached up to touch his cheek. "You could have told me the reason for it."

He covered her hand with his own. "I thought I had told you."

"I know everything."

His hand froze. His eyes widened, and Juliette could sense he was struggling to remain calm. A storm in his eyes raged.

Why does it matter that I know?

"Somehow Hedford learned of your intent at Condren. He's more aware of my father's dealings than I would have guessed."

His hand dropped, so she let her own fall. What was wrong with him?

"Toren, are you quite all right?"

Though his arms stayed loosely around her, she sensed a marked change in his mood.

"What exactly do you know?" he asked.

She looked quizzically at him. "That your king sent you to determine whether my father is taking bribes in exchange for failing to bring men to justice across the border on the Day of Truce. Your people are threatening not to honor the decades-long tradition because of it, which is threatening peace along the border. And that you were sent to right the wrong."

And yet there was something in his expression that told her there was more. She pulled away to look at him.

"I imagine Hedford told you about the message he received," she asked, though she already knew the answer.

"Aye, lass, he did."

"Well?"

He reached for her, but she avoided him, wanting to first know what he thought of this turn of events.

"'Tis. . . interesting."

"Interesting? You and your blasted countrymen have accused my father of deceit, only to find out it was his bailiff taking bribes without his knowledge. And that's all you have to say? 'Tis interesting?"

"Are you surprised, Jules?"

"That Henry Rode nearly succeeded in undermining my father and putting our entire family in danger because of it? Nay. I never liked the man. I'm glad he's been arrested and this matter of my father's guilt has finally been settled."

And there it was again. That look.

"What are you not telling me, Toren?" Mistakenly, she had believed that there would be no more secrets between them once he knew the truth. Disappointment weighed down on her.

Toren countered with a question of his own.

"What do you make of Hedford? Do you find it odd that he knows so much?"

She allowed him to distract her momentarily. "Aye. As I said, I hardly know the man, but there's something a bit odd about him."

He stared into the falls, and for a moment, she didn't think he intended to say anything else. Then he suddenly blurted out, "I believe Hedford is a spy."

She had guessed as much and was therefore not overly surprised.

"An English spy," she said. "His travel to France—"

"His reluctance to discuss personal matters," Toren finished. "Campbell confirmed it."

"The man whose tent you 'borrowed.'"

"Aye. I believe the injury forced him to retire. It would explain his numerous connections and access to information. Likely he was chosen very carefully as your chaperone."

"He was not chosen. He happens to be Christina's—"

"It may be possible this matter of Henry Rode was already being sorted before I left for Condren."

"Most likely. Do you remember the day of Gregory's fight? When Hedford spoke to me?"

"Aye."

"He knew of our 'relationship,' if you will. But he did not warn me off. I suspect he knew my purpose for being there. To speak with your father, that is. And he did not seem to disapprove, which raised my suspicions."

"Disapprove of what, exactly?"

She'd had a lifetime of border politics and was bone-achingly weary of it all. And though she was content to have her suspicions confirmed —did Christina know?—she was proud of herself. Her instincts about him had been right.

Toren reached her so quickly Juliette did not have time to react.

"This," he said as he lowered his mouth to hers.

All talk of spies and traitors ceased.

17

He was going to kill Catrina.

She had suggested that he bring Juliette here. Alone. With so little privacy at the manor, he'd agreed they needed to come to an understanding about their time here at Bristol. Toren planned to hear Hedford's revelations from *her* lips. He'd known the risks, but he'd assured himself his will was strong.

Unfortunately, that didn't apparently extend to this particular Englishwoman. He needed to touch her. He needed to make love to her. It was wrong—even with Hedford's revelations, there was much left to settle—but he didn't care.

He had to be inside her.

As she opened for him, he slipped his tongue into her mouth, claiming it in the same way he wanted to claim her body. Not holding back, Toren kissed her with all the pent-up passion that had tormented him since the moment he'd left Condren. Juliette began to writhe against him, and he encouraged it with his own movements.

Though he was not surprised that Catrina had lent Jules the breeches—his sister always wore them for riding now, a habit she'd picked up from Lady Sara, Geoffrey Waryn's wife—he'd wanted to throttle each and every man who'd looked at her. A possessive impulse demanded those were his curves to touch, and his alone. But now, with just a thin layer of fabric between them, he was glad she hadn't worn a shift and thick gown. He pressed against her, pulling her closer still.

"Jules," he whispered along her neck, having released her lips to prime her for what was to come. He kissed the sensitive flesh at the base of her neck and moved lower still, untying the woman's tunic Catrina had lent her. The garment gave him the access he hungered for. Dipping his hand beneath it, he lifted her perfect breast to his mouth. She gasped as he began to tease the hardened nipple. He flicked it with his tongue—lightly at first and then with increasing pressure—and then took it into his mouth completely.

As he suckled her, Toren grasped her other breast in his hand. He knew he'd succeeded in pleasuring her when she arched into him, moaning with pleasure from a slight nip with his teeth.

When he began to lift the loosened tunic, she raised her arms to allow him. He looked down and nearly lost control at the sight. They'd been together in the dark, and though the sun had already begun to wane, he could see her clearly. Two beautiful orbs tipped with beautiful rosy nipples that he couldn't resist touching once more. The waterfall rushed down around them, urging him to give in. Urging him to take her.

"I want you inside me," she said, staring into his eyes.

As always, he offered as much honesty as he could. "I don't know what will happen between us, Jules. I would be with you, always, but the king may not allow us to be together." Toren could tell she was confused, but it was the only explanation he could give her.

He'd sent another message to Douglas asking, nay, begging, for the king's order to be revoked. With the bailiff now in prison, Hallington's innocence had been proven. He'd been undermined by his own staff, and while it certainly didn't recommend him, the fact that he was not a traitor meant there was no longer a need to remove him as warden.

Certainly no longer a need to kill him.

And Lord help him, Toren didn't think he was capable of killing the man after what had transpired between him and Jules. He loved this woman, English or nay. His sister had guessed as much, and she'd begged him to tell Jules the truth about his mission.

Earlier, when she'd claimed to know all, his insides had frozen. Could it be true? But her knowledge was limited in a most important way. She did not know his mission had been to end her father's life. She couldn't ever know. If she did, she would never look at him this way again.

And he needed her to look at him this way. To see him as a good man.

When Jules reached for his shirt and pulled it up over his head, Toren was completely undone. He gladly assisted her, discarded the garment, and pulled her against him.

"I like how that feels," she said.

Though they were only partially unclothed, he couldn't agree more.

Her hands explored his bare shoulders and arms, and he stood still, letting her do as she wished. The look of pure joy on her face convinced him that she had not yet had her fill. He was hard and ready, had been since he'd first seen her golden braid in his sister's hall. Yet Toren was perfectly content to relish in the feeling of her fingers tracing his bare skin.

He was content to wait.

Or so he thought.

When her hand moved to his lower back and then trailed a path toward his front, he stiffened. She wouldn't. . .

She did.

Jules lowered her hand and rested it there, on top of his trews. His cock hardened even more, if such a thing were possible. It pounded beneath her hand, demanding more from him. She looked up at him, her gaze questioning whether it was advisable. He had just begun to unlace himself when a shout in the distance wrested him out of the haze of pleasure.

"Toren!"

He jumped away, pushed Jules behind him, and grabbed his sword from the ground even before he could determine where the shouts had originated.

A short time later, three riders approached, the sound of the horses' hooves drowned out by the waterfall.

His sister was riding toward them with two guards. Catrina dismounted and ran toward him. Toren positioned himself so Jules's state of undress was shielded from view.

"Bloody hell, woman. What are you—"

"Toren, you need to come quickly." She didn't so much as attempt to look beyond him, and his possessive anger shifted to fear. What had worried her so?

"There's been an incident," she continued.

"You're as maddening a lass as ever, sister. What kind of incident warrants—"

"Hallington."

He could feel Jules move behind him. "What happened?" she asked, her voice small but unwavering. She was likely mortified to have been caught in such a position, but she hadn't allowed it to hold her back.

Catrina didn't flinch. "Reivers," she said. "The injured party made their way to Bristol. One is badly off. He will not likely live, but Evelyn is with him."

If anyone could save a dying man, it was Bristol's old but competent healer.

"What does my father have to do with the attack?"

"One of the victims foolishly threatened the reivers would be brought to justice. The man apparently responded with, 'I've enough coin for the warden's deep pockets.'"

"Who are these men?" Toren asked. "Clearly they cannot be trusted? Hallington has been vindicated. They're likely—"

"Clergymen. They made their way west to Whithorn."

He froze.

"Whithorn? What are they doing this far south?"

Catrina shrugged. "Lost, I'd imagine. They don't appear properly prepared for such a journey. But you both should—"

"We're coming." He gave Catrina a pointed look. "We will meet you at the manor."

"Oh. Of course," she said, finally understanding. She turned and walked back to the other riders.

They quickly began to dress.

"These reivers could be lying. Or mayhap they've heard the rumors. Or—"

He kissed her, wanting more than anything to finish what they had started. There would be plenty of time to explore the implications of this attack. For now, he was sorry for the interruption.

"We'll speak to them," he assured her, reluctantly letting her go. "You can ask as many questions as you'd like."

She gave him a wide-eyed look, and he could tell she was surprised to have been included. It was not the first time Jules had been taken aback by such a thing.

"Of course. You are just as involved as I am. More so."

Her bright smile told him it had been the correct thing to say. Fully dressed, they made their way toward Catrina and the others. If only he was as optimistic about the outcome.

An attack on clergymen. Blatant disregard for border law. Something dangerous was afoot.

It was worse than he'd imagined.

Evelyn was not hopeful the injured man would live, and by rights, his attacker should be brought to justice. This was no mere cattle raising—the clerics had been robbed and beaten for no good reason. Reivers' blatant disregard for the law was the reason the Day of Truce had first been conceived thirty years earlier.

When Toren listened to the survivors' tale, he was inclined to believe it, including that an accusation had been made against Hallington. Only a man without fear of retribution would be brazen enough to say such a thing. The reiver, at least, believed he could bribe his way to continued freedom.

After a subdued meal, the household retired early, but Toren could not rest. He made his way to the top floor of the keep. Once a solitary building, the old tower house had originally been built for defense—a purpose it still served.

After capturing Bristol, Toren had often retreated here to look out toward his home. Odd to be back as a visitor. . . the guard stationed not far from him was the same one who'd nodded to him countless times as he stood on these very parapets. Against the advisement of his kinsman, he had retained as many men who wished to stay.

The sound of footsteps advised him that he was no longer alone. Toren turned, not overly excited about the intrusion—even less so when he saw it was Bryce Waryn. If it was company he sought, his brother-in-law would not have been his choice of companions.

"What will you do?" Bryce asked, stepping onto the parapets and coming to a stop beside him.

"If I knew, you'd not be the person with whom I'd share my plans."

The large black steel torch holders scattered around the parapets held flaming torches, giving the space a foreboding appearance. In the distance, lanterns were spaced on both stone walls, only one of which could be seen at this distance. Waryn had been busy since Toren had last been here.

"Keep in mind, Kerr, if your sister had not sent me up here, I would be in a warm bed with a willing— "

He glanced over his shoulder, daring the man to continue.

And so they stood at an impasse.

He understood why the Waryns held him in contempt. He'd overseen the raid in which their parents were killed. Though they had not died at his hand, and the raid had only been undertaken on the king's orders, he had apologized to the Waryns. He understood the pain of losing a parent, and they had lost their parents and their home on that same ill-fated day.

He was still sorry for it. Even so, his voice was bitter when he said, "So you're here to gloat?"

There was just enough light to make Waryn's face perceptible. He looked serious, as ever.

"We can continue to despise each other," the man said. "Or recognize that you and I are now related, thanks to the woman currently sprawled—"

"Waryn—"

Bryce's lips turned up ever so slightly. "Tell me your plan."

"You speak as if I have one."

Waryn waited. "You are very much like your sister, except in this."

He looked at the man Catrina had chosen to spend her life with. It had been obvious from the moment she had returned home to Brockburg that she'd left her heart behind. With Waryn. The Catrina he had helped to raise was full of life. A mite brazen, but intelligent and strong. The one who had returned to him had been sullen and silent. She'd spoken incessantly of Bryce Waryn even while claiming to despise him for his eagerness to kill her brother.

If only he were confident his own situation with Jules would end as happily.

"Except in what?"

Bryce paused and looked at him square in the face. "She believes in other people. Aye, perhaps she is trusting to a fault, but at least she gives them a chance."

"I don't need your lectures, *brother.*"

He trusted plenty of people. His siblings. His steward. Brockburg's priest. Gregory Campbell, to an extent.

And Jules.

"You can trust me, Kerr. Allow me to help you."

Toren cocked his head to the side. Trust the man he'd tried to kill? Who'd reciprocated with vigor?

It was becoming difficult not to do so despite himself.

The corners of Waryn's mouth tipped up and he shrugged. "Catrina said if we didn't make peace, she'd lock us both in the buttery until we were incoherent. And even then she may choose not to let us out."

Toren imagined the two of them in that small space surrounded by wine and had to admit it was not the worst plan he'd ever heard. "Very well," he relented. "I sent word to Douglas apprising him of Henry Rode's arrest. With information I managed to gather while at Condren, I'd begun to suspect Hallington's innocence, but having such proof should make my argument easier."

"And what is your argument?"

This was where his plan was questionable, at best. "That Hallington should remain warden. As unfortunate as it is, I don't believe the clergymen's account of the reivers counts as much more than rumor, albeit one the reivers, and others, obviously believe. Hedford claims Hallington was absent from the tournament because he was deep in a plan to reveal Rode as the traitor. The pieces had already been in place before the tournament started. Before I was sent on this fool's mission."

"So you'll not tell Douglas of what happened here today?"

"'Twould be a form of treason for me not to do so."

"You didn't answer the question."

Though he knew he could trust Waryn, it was uncomfortable for him to do so.

"Dammit," he muttered. Then, "Nay, I will not be relaying this particular incident."

The other man's response was automatic. "I agree you should not. Douglas may not care that the traitor has been uncovered for the same reason that these reivers think they're safe. Rumor can be as damaging as truth, and what happened today will only make it worse. If peace does not collapse, then Rode's actions will be forgotten. The rumors may not be."

It was exactly what he had been thinking.

"Of course, your role is still very much in question," Waryn continued. "If he orders you to carry out the mission nonetheless, you've a larger problem still."

And that was where this conversation would end. Damned if he'd take advice on love from this particular man.

"Tell Catrina I said your counsel was most welcome," he said sarcastically.

Waryn did not take offense. "If you'd like my advice, dear brother, on how to handle the matter of your future bride, you know where to find me."

Before he could reply, the Englishman began to walk away, but not before he called back, "Occupied in my chamber with the beautiful woman I call my wife."

Bastard.

18

After Juliette took mass with Catrina and Christina, she wandered the grounds. It was no surprise to her when she found herself in the gardens. At home, this was where she always went to think.

The reivers would be long gone by now, but the men had gone to track them. She suspected they were using it as an excuse to hone their precious battle skills.

Now that they had brought their message, Juliette assumed Christina, or at least her husband, would want to discuss their departure. Neither of them had mentioned it, and Juliette was eager to take all of the time they'd allow her.

Christina was fully supportive of her love for Toren now, and Juliette had passed Catrina's test. The waterfall ride had been her idea. Which meant she'd passed her test.

So there was only one person left to convince: Toren himself.

"There you are."

Juliette bowed her head in deference to her hostess.

"My lady."

"Nay. Catrina, remember?" The other woman pulled her toward a room opposite the entrance to the hall. One that had clearly been added onto the original tower and now served as the lord and lady's solar.

It was a handsomely appointed room. The furniture ornately carved and— "Oh my!"

Books... so many of them.

"Where are these from?" She raced to a shelf stacked with at least thirty manuscripts and ran her hand along the leather that bound one of them together.

"Some are from Brockburg," Catrina said with a smile. "I can read as well, but not in so many languages as you. Perhaps you can read for us this afternoon?"

Either Toren or Christina must have told her about that particular habit. Juliette was about to pull one from the shelf, but she turned first to seek permission.

Catrina waved her hand in acknowledgment, so Juliette took one down and opened it to an elaborately illuminated page. The gold-leafed scene was one immediately familiar to her, though she'd never seen such a rendition before. She touched it, feeling the edges carefully and admiring the bright reds and blues of the illumination.

"Le Chevalier de la Charrette," Juliette said breathlessly.

Catrina looked over her shoulder at the beautiful pages in her hands. "The Countess of Kenshire gave me that as a wedding gift." She was clearly amused. "Her idea of a jest. So you know this is the first tale to feature the love affair between Queen Guinevere and Lancelot?"

Juliette turned the page, marveling at the beauty and detail. This page was just as elaborate as the last. The scene featured the tower where Guinevere had been held prisoner.

"Aye," Juliette answered. "And Lancelot makes no apologies for being with a married woman."

She closed the book and carefully replaced it.

"So it is true?" Juliette asked. She had not thought she'd be so bold to ask, but Lady Catrina was easy to speak with, and the question slipped from her lips before she could stop it.

"Aye, '**tis true**. Bryce held me captive, originally planning to ransom me to Toren. 'Tis a complicated tale that I am happy to share with you one day."

But not now. Juliette could tell her hostess wished to speak with her on another matter, and she could guess the topic.

"Your brother," she said bluntly.

Catrina lifted her arm, pointing to the books. "You are welcome to them," she said. Then a voice—her husband's—called out her name from the hall, and she turned to leave the room. "And Toren," Catrina said with a smile, leaving as quickly as she'd come.

So. It was as she suspected. But gaining the permission of Toren's sister, although it was a quite nice and unexpected boon, was not her primary concern.

"Why am I not surprised?"

Her hand froze as it reached for another book.

He was her primary concern. She was weary of his vague explanations and half-promises. Weary of not understanding why this man who seemed to love her did not wish to be with her in truth. But some of that resolve melted when he reached down to touch her neck.

She began to turn around, but he whispered, "Nay. Don't let me disturb you."

Her fingers reached for the volume that most caught her eye. Rather than leather, the pages were bound together by some type of metal with an engraving that looked vaguely familiar.

Toren no longer touched her, but he stood so close she could feel his breath on her neck. She shivered visibly, eliciting a chuckle from behind her.

"Open it."

She did. And gasped.

"'Tis beautiful," she said, tracing the lines of the illustration, even more colorful and vibrant than the first manuscript she'd admired. It was one of the most artfully crafted scenes she'd ever seen. Cadmium yellow and crimson wove around gold leaf in a naval battle scene. Knights in one ship raised their swords against Saracens in the other. So stunning was the scene, she hardly even noticed the perfectly formed words.

"The romance of Gillion of Trazegnies," she murmured.

Toren reached out for her from behind and grazed her hand as he traced the initial at the opening of the text. And Juliette, who normally would have been too enamored with the craftsmanship of the text to pay any attention to her companion, could think of nothing other than the man who stood behind her.

"Aye." He guided her hand to the bottom of the manuscript and turned the page with her. "This is where Gillion is stripped to the waist and tied to the column where he'll be saved."

The memory of Toren stripped to the waist, fighting to be the champion, surfaced in her mind, though in truth those edges and ridges of muscle were never far from her mind.

"By Gracienne." She knew the tale well, though had never seen it illustrated.

Toren encircled her waist and pulled her closer to him.

"The Sultan's daughter," he murmured in her ear.

She shivered.

When he pulled her hair to one side, Juliette was powerless to stop him. The brush of his lips on her neck forced her eyes closed. A pool of desire flooded her as his lips moved upwards.

As much as she wanted to stand there, to turn the page and continue to relish this moment that melded the two things she held most dear, she needed to speak with him. Juliette closed the manuscript, stepped away from him to replace it, and finally faced him.

"Their story did not end well," she started. "And I fear ours will not either. Unless you begin to trust me."

Toren's jaw clenched.

"Tell me what holds you back. Why you left as you did." Juliette warmed to her topic. "Should I leave now that the message has been delivered?"

He didn't answer at first. Finally, he ran his hands through his hair and tipped his head back.

She couldn't take it any longer.

"What is it, Toren? Tell me!"

He looked directly at her, his expression unreadable.

"I don't want you to leave."

After making that declaration, he made no move toward her. It was what she'd wished to hear, but it wasn't enough.

"What do you want then?"

He moved so quickly she hardly had time to react.

"I want you."

He brought his lips down on hers, and she had to fight to retain any semblance of thought. And that was the effect of one mere kiss.

She allowed herself much more. His lips moved expertly across her own, his tongue dueling with hers until she finally relented and wrapped her arms around him. He pressed their bodies together, and Juliette now understood the need that drove him. That drove them both. She relished in the feel of him against her until she finally remembered her purpose.

"Nay," she said, pushing against him. "I need answers, Toren."

The look on his face told her he was at war with himself.

Juliette could only wonder at the cause. She nearly told him that she loved him. But that look on his face stopped her. It dawned on her again—the certainty that he was keeping something important from her.

"I'd give them to you."

"But?"

"I can't."

"Can't or won't?" She backed away from him. "You say you want me. And mayhap even care for me. And yet you do not trust me. . . even though I've done nothing to earn such treatment. I gave myself to you, Toren. Do you understand what that meant for me?"

"You're not being fair," he said.

"Fair?" She couldn't help but raise her voice. "You're right. I gave myself to you with no expectations for the future. Knowing you were unable, unwilling. . ." She couldn't continue. What more could she say? If he didn't love her enough to be fully honest with her, however difficult the truth, what was she fighting for?

She tried to walk around him, but he grabbed her arm.

"You don't understand."

"Of course I don't," she agreed. "Am I supposed to?"

The look on his face made her heart weep. He looked so. . . vulnerable.

"*Stay*. For a few days. I promise to explain everything. But I need more time."

"Time for what, Toren? What are you waiting for?"

She could tell he still wasn't going to tell her.

"My father will be looking for me. Hedford—"

"I will take care of Hedford. Please, Jules."

Juliette wanted to say she'd be returning home immediately. That if he didn't trust her enough to explain himself now, immediately, he wasn't the man she'd hoped for anyway.

But something Christina had said at the end of their stay at Condren stopped her. She'd asked her friend if she'd come to love Lord Hedford, and her response had been most curious.

"'Tis hard to love a man I've known for such a short while," she'd said. "But I do love that which he's shown me. When I know all of him, I can answer your question more honestly."

It was an interesting point. She fancied herself in love with Toren because he made her feel things no other man had ever made her feel before, and she'd had plenty of suitors. But could she fully love a man she didn't know completely? Mayhap the only way to know for sure how she truly felt about him, and him about her, was to wait. To wait and find out what he'd been hiding from her.

"You will tell me everything in a few days?" Jules asked him now.

He didn't flinch. "Aye, I will."

They stood there like that for a while, silent and staring at each other, when the door suddenly swung open.

"Oh, pardon," Catrina said, more flustered than Jules had ever seen her. "I didn't realize you were here, Toren."

Before Catrina could close the door she'd opened, Juliette called her back.

"He was just leaving," she said.

Except he made no move to leave. His eyes had not shifted one inch from hers.

Finally, she nodded. As long as all was revealed at the end of it, she could wait a few days.

So why did that thought leave her so unsettled?

19

The clergyman would live.

Catrina had made that spectacular announcement yesterday eve at the start of the meal. None were happier than Juliette, for she knew the implications for her father were substantial.

She hadn't been able to stop thinking about the poor, innocent men who had been so brutally attacked. The villains who'd used her father's name as a shield still had not been found, and Juliette feared that the arrest might not be the end of the matter.

She hadn't see Toren since the conclusion of that meal.

"Something troubles you?"

She ignored the question. So much troubled her, she hardly knew where to begin.

It was the following afternoon, and she was walking arm in arm with the lady of the manor, who'd promised to take her for a "most spectacular view." Juliette had been reading when Catrina had shown up to fetch her. Christina and Hedford had left that morning to visit Bristol's village. She had declined their offer to accompany them, wishing to give the couple some time alone.

Catrina led her into what appeared to be an unused bedchamber. Though it appeared modest, Bristol housed an impressive number of rooms.

"A bedchamber?" she asked in confusion.

"Not just any bedchamber," Catrina said with a wink. She led the way to a small window, its wooden shutters already open. Curious, Juliette peered over the other woman's shoulder.

The scene below that offered exactly what Catrina had promised.

A most spectacular view.

She smiled as her hostess moved to the side, allowing for her to get a better look.

"That isn't... typical."

Granted, the training yard back home was quite a distance from the main keep, and she hardly visited the place regularly. But she was sure that most men trained with at least light armor.

"Nay, not in England at least. Back home Toren and his men regularly train this way, and I suspect my husband is doing it simply to prove he can."

They weren't the only shirtless men on the training field, but they were certainly the two who attracted the most attention. The sight of Toren's naked chest, the muscles responding to his every move, was enough to draw her even closer. It only just occurred to her that she should be embarrassed to stare so brazenly at her companion's brother.

"I. . ." She began to back away, stopping only when Catrina pulled her back.

"Do not be embarrassed. My brother is quite fit, nearly as much as Bryce."

"Nearly as much?" She stopped, realizing she'd been goaded.

Juliette watched as Toren struck a wooden pell from every angle. She marveled at how easily he wielded his training sword. Most often these were twice the weight of a regular broadsword, making even experienced knights look slow and clumsy in training.

Not so with Toren. He attacked the stake as if it were the enemy, applying himself with such vigor that some of the other men actually stopped to watch.

"Like two boys," Catrina said. Juliette hadn't noticed Bryce performing a similar 'dance' on a different pell. She smiled now, realizing that they were indeed treating it as a competition.

"It must be difficult for them. . ." Juliette stopped herself.

"'Tis very much so," Catrina answered unselfconsciously. "I told Bryce once that there was only one man more stubborn than he: my brother. A five-year-old feud is not so easily buried."

Juliette's heart fluttered when Toren stopped and looked directly up at her. How long had he noticed them watching?

His body glistened with sweat, the sunny day unrelenting, she imagined, for such rigorous training. Even from this distance, she could see each of his muscles clearly.

"He loves you."

Juliette froze.

"I know my brother well and have never once seen him look at a woman the way he looks at you."

Tearing her gaze from the training yard, Juliette looked at Catrina. Her eyes, the exact shade of her brother's, were intelligent. Unwavering.

"Did he tell you that?" Though she intended to sound confident, Juliette could hear the uncertainly in her own voice.

"Nay," she admitted. "He would not. As I said, Toren is stubborn, and he's said in the past that marrying was for us, for his siblings. That his job was simply to keep us safe."

She walked toward the bed, its covering a pure white embroidered with pink flowers. Sitting, she gestured for Juliette to join her. With a final glance below—Toren was no longer looking up—she lifted her blue gown, one of her favorites for its simple cut and bright color, and sat next to the lady of the house.

"St. Mary help him." Catrina twisted her lips in apparent frustration and began again. "My apologies. I haven't quite become accustomed to not swearing. Although—" her face lit up, "—that was my first slip of the day!"

Juliette had never met a woman who took holy names in vain. She'd heard plenty of men do so, but never a woman. And while Sister Heloise would no doubt be appalled, she herself found it quite refreshing.

"Toren has been both brother and parent to us, as he likely told you."

Juliette nodded.

"He has made some difficult decisions for the sake of his family and clan." Catrina frowned. "And I fear he'll be forced to make the most difficult one of all soon."

"I don't understand."

Juliette recognized Catrina's expression, for she had seen the exact same expression on her brother's face the previous day.

"You will."

She stood and Juliette followed suit. "Please be patient with him," Catrina rushed to add. "I know he's not been completely forthright, and it's not for me to tell you what he has not. But when he *does* tell you. . ." Her shoulders slumped. "Please remember that he loves you, Juliette. Of that I am sure."

Juliette's stomach sank, and it felt as if she'd just eaten something rotten. Not for the first time, she wondered if it might have been easier not to have found love at all. To have joined the convent and been done with it. For whatever Toren wasn't telling her was increasingly becoming something she dreaded to hear.

"Toren, you need to tell her. For God's sake, you're going to lose her. Is that what you want?"

He had avoided being alone with Catrina after their last discussion, which had ended much like this one seemed doomed to end. For someone who was always accusing him of being stubborn, his sister could be so as well.

"You've had my answer. And I'll ask you not to interfere in this."

He had asked Juliette to stay nearly two days past, and he knew he could not keep her here for much longer, especially not without telling her all. She wanted answers, and though she deserved to get them, he had none to offer. Until he heard from Douglas, he could do nothing more than attempt to mollify everyone around him. Juliette. His sister. Hedford and his wife.

"What happens if you're relieved of your mission? What will you do then? Do you plan to tell her, 'Oh happy days, we can be together. Let's be off so I may obtain your father's permission for us to marry?' Will you really leave it at that?"

His eyes narrowed. "I never said—"

"You didn't have to, Toren. You asked her to stay for a reason. 'Tis obvious to anyone with eyes, or at least to anyone who knows you well, that you love her. Just admit it, you stubborn fool."

He already had. To himself.

"What does it matter? The only thing that matters now is Douglas's decision."

"Ugh." Catrina paced restlessly in the solar chamber. She'd pulled him in there after the evening meal. "You're even more thick-headed than I thought, brother. Even if Douglas calls off the mission, Juliette must know your true purpose. You can't begin a life based on lies."

"And if he doesn't?"

He'd thought of nothing else these past two days—it had haunted him while he was in the training yard, when he was dining across the table from her, when he was trying to sleep at night. He could not kill her father. And yet, if he was ordered to do so and didn't, he'd put his clan at risk. Endangering his family and kinsmen was not something he'd do willingly. It would put him in an impossible situation.

"Tell her."

He'd heard that refrain too many times.

"Enough." Fists clenched, he marched toward the door, which he pulled open with so much force Waryn nearly fell on top of him from the other side.

He shoved past his brother-in-law, pausing only to glare at him, and made his way to his own bedchamber. After pacing there for what seemed like hours, he left in search of the timid maid. After he found her, nearly scaring the poor girl witless with his rumbled request, Toren retreated to his chamber once again and waited until she brought him a flagon of ale.

Then he drank.

Kicking into the fire with his boot, he rearranged the logs and drank some more. Though the day had been warm, the night was as cold as it always was here.

Angry at everyone, most of all himself, Toren was prepared to refill his mug when the sound of a soft knock at the door stayed his hand.

He opened it, prepared to tell Elise he did indeed require more ale.

"Your timing is impeccable. I—"

It was not Elise.

"Were you expecting someone?"

"Jules."

She was a vision in blue, standing in the threshold of his chamber, awaiting his answer. It was as if she were desire given human form. He grabbed her and pulled her into the room, shutting the door behind her.

Without any preliminaries, he kissed her, hard. She responded by wrapping her hands around his neck.

"Ah God, I've wanted this so much." He kissed her neck, pulled down the thick robe and shift under it, and then kissed her shoulder.

"Who were you—"

"The maid," he murmured against her soft, creamy skin.

He then realized how that must have sounded.

"Nay," he said. "For more ale. Not for..."

He groaned, looking down at her exposed skin dotted with wisps of hair that had escaped onto her shoulders.

"Not for this."

He opened the cream robe wider and reached beneath it for the hem of her shift. Lifting it, Toren gently backed her against the stone wall for support and glided his hand up to the treasure he sought.

He held her gaze while he explored her with his fingers, intent on easing some of the pain he'd caused by leaving Condren so abruptly. By avoiding her these past days.

She watched him as he began to ease his fingers in and out, slowly at first. Touching her, bringing her toward her release, made his own arousal grow, but he never took his eyes from hers. Jules swallowed hard, her lids hooded and her head tipped back, and he knew she was close. Her expression was one he'd never forget.

It was one of complete trust.

She'd given herself to him completely, and his heart lurched with the knowledge that he still could not do the same. But he'd bring her pleasure, at least for this moment. He thrust his fingers inside her tight, wet sheath and moved his thumb to the place he knew would make her cry out.

And it did. Closing her eyes, she parted her lips just enough to show him the tip of her tongue. As much as he wanted to press his mouth to hers, Toren wanted to see her expression more.

"Toren."

He knew what she needed.

And he gave it to her, stroking and caressing. He felt the wetness beneath his fingers as the deep, sensual sound escaped from her soft, supple lips. He did capture them then, moving his mouth across their sweet softness as she melted beneath his fingers.

Lifting his head again, Toren smiled as his proper English lady slowly came back to him.

Perhaps proper wasn't accurate. Sensual. Smart.

"Beautiful." He hadn't meant to say that aloud.

He half expected her to argue the point. Instead, she simply said, "Thank you." Most women did not accept compliments well, but Jules was not most women.

"I want to please you, Toren."

He'd withdrawn his hand and began to draw away from her, knowing their joining could not be repeated before the present uncertainty was settled. Even now she could be carrying his babe —in the lake, he'd not had the presence of mind to withdraw from her before his release.

"Nay," he choked out. He did move away then. He was uncomfortably hard, but that was no matter.

"Toren," she reached for his arm and stayed him.

"Jules, do you understand what you're asking?"

Was she so innocent that she did not?

"When a man and a woman come together. . ." He couldn't believe he was saying this. "There are ways to prevent it, but I didn't. . . I took no precautions at the lake. I can't continue to put you at risk that way."

She didn't understand.

"A bairn," he blurted out.

Jules shook her head, smirking. "I may not have much experience," she said. "But even I know 'tis not possible to grow with child from what you just did to me."

Oh God. No.

"You are not—"

"Let me please you, Toren. I—"

"Nay. I don't. . ."

He was about to say he didn't deserve it. And he didn't. Which was why he hadn't gone to her before now.

She reached out so quickly he didn't have the chance to stop her. Dammed if the woman didn't actually lay her hand on his extremely hard cock.

"Show me. Give me the same power you have over me."

Although it was beneath the fabric of his low-hanging shirt and breeks—he'd not been prepared for visitors—he could feel her touch so intensely Toren was afraid he would spill his seed even now.

"Jules—"

"Mayhap I will not ask." The saucy woman lifted his shirt and loosened the ties that would ensure there was no turning back.

"You do not have—"

Dear lord, she pulled down the only remaining barrier between them. Moving the material aside, she actually put her hand on him —and the intensity of the pleasure he felt confirmed what he'd already suspected: their connection was both unusual and special.

He'd dreamed of this. Imagined her hand, and more, on him so many times that he was powerless to stop her.

The room had grown uncomfortably warm even without him attending to the fire. He shifted so that he could brace himself against the stone wall with one hand, for something told him he'd need the support.

Her feather-light touch teased him beyond measure, and when he could take it no more, Toren covered her hand with his own, wrapping both of their fingers around his swollen member. After just a few strokes, she needed no guidance.

"'Tis like you did to me."

She began to move her hand even faster.

"It feels so hard. But soft here." She stopped pumping him to circle his tip with her thumb, exploring the skin with a light caress. He could not do this.

The urge to be inside her was so strong, he simply could not resist it.

He envisioned pushing her against the wall and entering her, thrusting so hard there was no doubt he'd spill his seed inside her.

He never had the chance.

Jules wrapped her delicate fingers around him once more and moved so expertly he could do nothing other than clench his buttocks and lose himself to her.

"Oh Jules."

He'd surely die of pleasure, the pulsing sensation so strong he clenched and released a thousand times in that brief moment.

Not even aware he'd shut his eyes until he opened them to find her watching him, Toren stared at her in wonder.

"How did you—"

She smiled so broadly he couldn't help but do the same.

He moved away then, reaching for the cloth near the wash basin the maid had left earlier. He quickly cleaned himself, fastened his breeks lest he be tempted again, and made his way back to the blonde goddess who had just given him the most powerful release of his life, rivaled only by their lovemaking in the lake.

"I'm not sure. But I quite liked it."

Liked it. For him, those words were too small to belong in any description of his Juliette, let alone the pleasure of being with her.

He pulled her to him then, and they stayed in each other's arms for so long the fire at the other end of the chamber began to smother itself.

He wanted her to stay with him. Tonight. Every night.

"You should go."

His voice was harsher than he'd intended.

"Aye."

Without another word, Jules slipped out the door. She glanced back once and was then gone as quickly as she had come.

Though she was staying in the room next to his own—by

design, if he'd correctly divined his sister's intentions—the void she left was so complete Toren nearly called her back to him.

A chill that had nothing to do with the dying fire ran up his back at precisely the same moment the candle by his bed snuffed out.

Luckily, he did not believe in omens.

20

Finally.

Although it had only been three days since Jules and her party had arrived, it had felt like the longest three days of his life. When one of the knights Catrina had sent to Douglas as messenger walked into the hall, Toren wanted to embrace him.

The man nodded to him from the entranceway of the hall where they sat eating a rather subdued meal, and Toren tried to ignore the glances from those gathered around him. Especially from *her*. Did Jules suspect this was the message that would determine their future?

The day before, Lord Hedford had warned him that Juliette's father would not be put off much longer. He'd sent a message to the man in his capacity as Juliette's guardian, explaining that they had been delayed, but it would not buy them much time. Hedford had gone hunting with Waryn, and though they'd asked for him to join them, the prospect of spending an afternoon with his brother-in-law made him yearn for home. To be back among his brothers and clansmen.

But Jules is not in Brockburg.

Toren had waylaid Hedford in the stables and decided to be blunt.

"I know that you are an English spy."

The man's gaze had not wavered.

"And that you're likely retired due to an injury that sent you home and to the altar."

Although Hedford had not validated his observations, neither had he denied them.

"Though I'm unsure as to why you're still here. Or why you agreed to come in the first place."

Though not as tall or broad as he, the Englishman was nevertheless a large man, one who must have been formidable before the injury that had given him a near constant limp.

"I told you—"

"That you want peace. That's not an answer."

Hedford frowned, a remarkable occurrence for a man who showed expression as rarely as Catrina's husband did.

"My wife." Lord Hedford didn't look happy to admit such a thing.

That was *not* the answer Toren had expected.

"My wife pleaded with me, and she can be quite persuasive."

He could imagine, her visit to the tent city still fresh in his mind.

"She and Juliette are more akin to sisters than friends. And Juliette... she cares for you. As you are surely aware."

He had never been more intensely aware of anything.

Hedford shrugged. "Hallington will not be pleased. But the man never is. Perhaps that's why we're here."

He would have liked to ask the man about Jules's father, but their conversation had been cut short by Alfred's arrival. He'd not seen much of the lad since their arrival at Bristol even though he'd sought him out on more than one occasion.

Now, standing at the back of Bristol's hall, Toren carefully avoided a serving maid who smiled suggestively.

"What news?" he asked as he pulled the messenger into an alcove which afforded them some modicum of privacy.

The trusted messenger was a young, scarcely bearded Scottish knight, one of the few who had remained when Waryn took back Bristol. He had ridden across the border and back more swiftly than most, though not quickly enough for Toren, for the message he'd brought was of utmost importance.

The knight looked over his shoulder, presumably to ensure their conversation was indeed private, and then said, "Douglas knows of the arrest and says to carry out your mission."

No. Please God, no.

"What else?" he growled.

"That was all he said."

Toren had both feared and suspected such an answer. It didn't matter that Hallington himself was innocent. The incident with the clergymen had reminded him as much. The rumors had resulted in a loss of faith so grievous, it would be near impossible to come back from it.

The king wished to eliminate the threat to the tenuous peace, no matter who was truly at fault. Had he not been personally involved in the situation, he might have agreed with him, and with Douglas.

The messenger looked over his shoulder, then nodded to him and walked away.

"Brother," a soft voice said behind him.

Catrina slipped her small hand into his, and he let her guide him to the garden, where the sun's dwindling light cast an eerie glow. They sat on a bench surrounded by flowers, and neither said a word for a long while.

"What will you do?" she finally asked.

Hell if he knew. He'd thought of nothing else for days, but he still struggled to form an answer.

"Talk to her. Tell her."

He glanced at Catrina's profile, pretending to consider her suggestion.

"Trust her, Toren. She loves you."

"And I love her."

It was almost impossible to say such a thing aloud, but the words slipped from him easily.

"I know."

"If I refuse, our clan will pay for that decision."

"You don't know that," she said, shifting on the hard stone bench. "Douglas may understand."

He gave Catrina a hard look. "Understand that I fell in love with the daughter of the man I was sent to kill? And even if he does, what then? I stand by and allow him to send someone to kill a man who could be my father-in-law? If she'd even have me now. And if he accepted such a match. The man could very likely refuse my suit—"

"Toren, quiet!"

He had not intended to raise his voice.

"So don't tell her. Don't tell Douglas. Don't ask Hallington for her hand. Trust no one, as always. If that's what you want, Toren, then by all means, continue down the same path you've followed since Mother left."

She leaped to her feet and began to walk away before turning back toward him.

"I would never betray your trust, brother. But know this. If you don't tell her, you'll lose her either way. Though the outcome is doubtful, Bryce and I will help you to the utmost of our ability. Always. But if you're determined to be a horse's arse, then you can do so alone."

Dear lord. Had he really helped to raise such a woman?

He smiled. Though her words were harsh, they were also full of love. And he was so incredibly proud of the woman she had become. Of the men his brothers had become.

He had to protect his family.

"What do you mean, you don't know?

Juliette closed her eyes as Christina pulled the ivory comb through her hair. They'd often done this growing up, and it always comforted her.

"I haven't seen him since he left the hall. I had hoped..."

She closed her eyes and attempted to enjoy the soft pull on her hair. But Christina would not let her.

"We cannot stay here forever," her friend said, telling her what she knew to be true.

After Toren had gone off with the messenger last eve, she'd expected him to return and explain everything. Instead, Catrina had left the hall after him, only to come back looking extremely vexed.

Juliette had then assumed Toren would come to her bedchamber to explain the evening's events, and to give her the answers he'd promised her, so she had lain awake for hours, waiting.

He had not come.

She heaved out a sigh. "If I ever decide to trawl through the English countryside again, looking for love, please advise me otherwise."

Christina chuckled behind her.

"I don't believe your father will allow you to trawl anywhere after this ill-fated excursion."

"I do believe you're right." She kept any other musing on her future to herself.

"Christina, I wanted to speak to you about your husband."

Her hand paused momentarily before resuming its ministrations.

"What do you know about his background precisely?" she ventured.

She couldn't see her friend's face but knew her well enough to read the long pause.

"You know," Christina finally stated.

"Aye, and Toren confirmed my suspicions. How long have you known?

"Since just before we left Condren. When I asked that we accompany you here. It took some convincing, but much less than expected. Which is when he finally opened up about his past, his role in the English government—"

"As a spy."

"Aye, as a spy. A good one, I assume, as I only surmised then he knew all along of your father's plans concerning Henry Rode. He knows your father better than either of us assumed."

"I've guessed as much. Why do you think he has all but assisted Toren and I?"

"I do believe he—"

"Pardon, Lady Juliette?"

She hadn't heard the door open. She turned to see a familiar maid standing at the entrance.

"Yes, Elise?"

"Your presence is requested in the hall, my lady."

Toren! He would not come away unscathed from—

"You've a visitor."

Juliette looked at Christina, who appeared as confused as she felt.

"A visitor?" she repeated.

The chambermaid simply nodded, but her worried expression was Juliette's first indication there was a problem. Her second indication did not take long to manifest itself, for as she and Christina followed Elise down the stairs to the hall below, she could hear a raised voice she recognized all too well.

Dread pooled in her stomach. How had he found them so quickly?

With one final glance at her friend, who looked desperately

uncomfortable, Juliette took a deep breath and rounded the corner.

His back was to her, which gave Juliette an extra moment to prepare for the wrath that was sure to be unleashed on her.

"Good day, Father."

It appeared they'd waited to summon her last, for everyone else was already gathered in the hall. Including Toren. He stood near the entrance, his face as expressionless as that of Catrina's husband, who stood next to him. Their close proximity caught her off-guard. Juliette couldn't recall ever having seen them stand so close.

"Juliette." Her father was mad, aye, but relieved as well. He surprised everyone gathered, including her, when he took several strides toward her and embraced her openly. It wasn't that her father had never hugged her before, but she could not remember him doing so publicly. He was a warrior in every way.

She took a deep breath, smelling dirt and sweat and. . . home. At that moment, she wanted nothing more than to go back to Chauncy Manor and forget the uncertainty and heartbreak of the days since she'd left. To take the well-worn path to the abbey each day, be ordered about by the abbess, who put her to work under the guise of 'instruction.' To see her brother, whom she missed dearly, read to the ladies, and wait for the rare moments when her mother appeared more happy than forlorn.

The velvet of his surcoat brushed against her cheek, and as he released her, Juliette received the type of greeting she'd expected.

"What the hell are you doing here?" he asked, so loudly that others may have mistaken it for yelling. She knew otherwise. This was her father's brusque way of speaking. When he truly raised his voice, all would know it.

When he pulled back, she realized with a shock that her father, who was normally quite regal-looking, seemed rather disheveled. Stewart Hallington's blond hair, a shade darker than hers, fell to his shoulders. His beard appeared more grown than usual, as if he'd not bothered to trim it.

Lord Hedford stepped forward.

"As I was saying, my lord—"

With one pointed glance from her father, the sharp and typically commanding Lord Hedford was completely silenced.

"Juliette?"

She was not afraid of him—at least not exactly. But she was also not very comfortable at the present moment.

"I trust you've attended to your business, Father?"

She laced her voice with the same sweetness she'd needed throughout her childhood when circumstances dictated.

His eyes narrowed.

Juliette's smile reached her eyes. "We must speak in private," she whispered. Turning to face the crowd of onlookers, which now included more than one curious servant, she said, "My father and I will retire to the garden. I trust it's been a long journey. Lady Catrina—"

"I'm happy to look after your father's men," her hostess responded. Juliette smiled her gratitude.

"Come, Father."

She began to lead him out of the hall, but not before catching the strange look Toren was giving her father. By anyone else's standards, it would be judged as mere curiosity. But Juliette had begun to learn her Scotsman's mood and expressions. There was something more there. . .

And then the fool man stepped forward.

Her father had just begun to follow her when Toren made it clear he intended to come with them.

Afraid of what might happen if she didn't first speak with her father alone, she shifted her gaze to Toren and said, "It appears as if we've taken you from your training. Please, do continue."

Without waiting for a response, she continued to lead her father down the stone corridor, its walls lit by iron lanterns.

Before she stepped outside, Juliette turned to face her father and found that he alone was following her. She clenched and released her fists, not surprised her hands shook slightly.

He didn't wait long to address her.

"You will explain what the hell you're doing here, Juliette. Something tells me you planned this little excursion, and I'll know immediately how you convinced Lord Hedford to leave the—"

"Forgive me, Father—"

As always, it felt as if she were confessing her sins to the priest. She'd asked for her father's forgiveness more times than she could count, but he never quite seemed to give it. She was not the biddable daughter she knew he wished her to be.

"—you are correct." Denying the truth would not work. Her father always knew, well, everything.

"When we learned about Rode's involvement—"

"We?"

She'd become so accustomed to Toren's willingness to discuss such matters with her—with one notable exception—that she forgot, for just a moment, that her father believed there was no place for a woman in discussions of a political nature.

"I overheard a conversation I should not have." She lowered her gaze. "But I'd met the Scottish chief and knew he was hoping for an audience with you. He'd been sent by his king to gauge the truth of the rumors. I suppose Hedford—"

Her father raised his bushy brows.

"Lord Hedford must have also heard of the man's interest in you. He knew the Scottish chief had left the tourney and was only a few days' ride away. We agreed it would be expedient to your cause to bring the message in person. You are innocent of any wrongdoing, Father! I knew it. And everyone else must know it as well. What if—"

He raised his hand, and Juliette immediately fell silent. She hated that hand.

"'Twas none of your concern, Juliette. These are dangerous times. Traveling this close to the border. . ."

He shook his head, disappointed with her. As always.

If he only knew.

"I'll speak to this chief myself. In the future, you're not to involve yourself in such dealings. You need a husband to control you, as I've most certainly failed at doing so."

It was no wonder her father and Sister Heloise could not tolerate each other. He'd threatened many times to bring a tutor to Chauncy to "save" her from the sister's corrupting influence, but the convenience of the abbey's location and, she suspected, her mother's interference, had always stopped him.

Sister Heloise had made her believe and trust in her own judgment. Unfortunately, the sentiment that women *lacked* judgment was shared by most men. But not by her tutor.

Or Toren.

"Yes, Father."

She suddenly envisioned herself entangled in a conversation like this with Lord Wytham, continuing to offer false deference for the remainder of her days.

She would not do it. Either she would wed Toren or join the sisters. She couldn't continue to pretend to be this woman.

To be her mother.

Shaking his head, her father spun away and left, presumably to berate Hedford. Or Toren. Or perhaps both.

Juliette sat on a nearby bench and attempted to calm her beating heart before she went back inside. At least her father's unexpected appearance meant Toren would be forced to share the contents of his message. Forced to share his mysterious reason for leaving the tournament and for asking her to stay in Bristol.

Forced to decide their future.

So *this* was the man he'd been sent to kill.

Toren had come back to the keep from an early morning ride, one that had cleared his head and firmed his resolve, only to find that Hallington and his retinue of English knights had beaten him to the hall.

The man's proud stance was the only quality he seemed to share with his daughter. Hallington's face was scarred and battle-hardened behind his beard, and his stature was large and likely intimidating to most—exactly what Toren would expect of a man chosen to keep peace between borderers who cared little for the law and even less for each other.

The shock of their visitor's identity had quickly turned to fury. He abhorred the way the man spoke to Jules. That she clearly loved him, despite the shameful disregard he showed her, had only slightly tempered his anger. He did not like that his love became a different, more timid woman in her father's presence.

His brother-in-law had held him back from following Jules and her father, and Waryn pulled him down the hall and into the solar.

"Did you intend to protect her? From her own father?"

"Had that been Catrina—" he yelled, not caring who overheard them.

Waryn closed the door of the solar.

"Toren, I did not stand out there with you because Catrina asked me to, but because I'm trying."

Toren startled. His brother-in-law had never before called him by his given name.

"I've forgiven you for taking my home and for everything that happened on that fateful day. I've offered my counsel, and you refuse to accept it. What must I do to earn your trust, you stubborn Scottish bastard?"

His words were measured, his tone even. As always. But Toren had begun to know him well enough to read his moods. The man was furious. And rightly so.

"You're right, Bryce." It was the first time he had ever called *him* by his given name either.

"Do you not—" Bryce stopped talking, his eyes wide.

Toren didn't deserve the man's forgiveness, but he had been given it. Should he not offer him the same consideration? Had he not allowed bitterness to cloud his judgment for too long?

He held out his hand and Bryce took it, shaking it firmly. It felt like his first step toward redemption.

"I nearly completed my mission for Douglas then and there when Jules looked down at her feet so demurely. That bastard has no right to speak to her in such a. . ." Toren said.

Letting go of his hand, Bryce disagreed. "He is her father and could treat her more harshly if he so pleased."

Toren vowed never to treat his daughters thus—if he were lucky enough for Juliette to forgive him and give him children one day.

"He'll be coming for you," Bryce warned.

"Aye, he will," Toren agreed. "But I have a plan. . . I could use your help."

Bryce did not flinch.

"Tell me."

And so he did. As he explained himself, his brother-in-law's normally expressionless face turn from interest to curiosity and finally shock. They discussed the matter further, and Toren was surprised by how grateful he was to have an ally in this. These last days, he'd stewed by himself, trying to find a solution without help, and now he was no longer alone.

Moments later, when the man in question burst through the solar door with Bristol's steward not far behind, waiting, presumably, for a fight, Toren was ready for him.

"Men," he said before Juliette's father could utter a word. "We're going hunting."

21

They'd been gone all afternoon.

Although a hunting trip was a common enough pursuit, the sky had begun to darken, and Juliette could tell even Catrina had begun to worry.

Christina and her husband, along with two of her father's men, had left earlier that day. Unneeded as a guardian, Hedford had been anxious to return home. While Juliette sorely missed her friend, she was thankful to have made another. She adored Lady Catrina, and even though she was a mite intimidated by her knowledge and beauty, the woman was simply too nice for someone to remain in awe of for long. She felt as if they'd been friends for years.

They waited together in her chamber—Catrina in the chair, Juliette pacing back and forth restlessly. When she caught her hostess frowning, Juliette began to panic in earnest.

"They should have returned," she said, not for the first time.

"Aye," Catrina admitted. Again.

Though hunting deer par force was a favorite pastime of her father's, a fact she had mentioned to Toren, she still found it odd he'd agree to such a venture with a man who had so infuriated him. Juliette was more inclined to believe her father would challenge Toren than hunt with him.

"Come to the kitchen. Cook can make you—"

"Nay, thank you." The evening meal was being served in the hall, but Juliette's stomach turned and twisted. She couldn't think about food. Something was seriously amiss.

"I must check on your father's retinue, but I will—"

"Please tell me when they return," she finished, impatient to know all was well.

With a nod, her hostess left the room, now completely darkened save for the glow of the fireplace and the candles beside her bed.

After having most of the day to dwell on recent events—namely the arrival of her father—Juliette had come to a decision and was impatient to speak with Toren.

She would tell him the truth.

The thought of saying, 'I love you,' to a man who'd offered her no promises was terrifying. But watching the interactions between the Lord and Lady of Bristol, Juliette had been convinced of something very important.

Love was *not* bound in books. She'd seen it. It was unmistakable in the way Catrina looked at her husband, and he at her. Christina and Hedford looked at each other much the same way. They'd obviously grown closer, learned more about each other, and though she may not know it yet, her friend was surely in love.

She did not need to know any more. It was how she felt for Toren, and she would tell him.

As soon as she had the chance. *If* she had the chance.

Where are they?

She could wait no longer.

Grabbing a nearby candle, Juliette made her way through the hall and down the stairs.

Remnants of the evening meal sat on the tables. The servants had begun to clear the hall, but some guests still lingered over their ale.

There was no sign of Toren or her father. Or Catrina, for that matter.

As she walked toward the solar, a figure appeared around the corner, nearly slamming into her.

"Pardon, my lady," the small voice said.

Alfred. He, or rather she, attempted to brush past her, but Juliette stayed her hand.

"Tell me, Alfred, why do you disguise yourself so?"

The look of utter terror on her smudged face made Juliette instantly regret she'd said anything.

"How..."

"Your movements. I thought, at first, you were just a small boy. But when you struggled to lift the lance... How you did so at all I will never know. And your eyes. The long lashes you show no one, out of fear?"

She guessed correctly.

"You never have to fear anything from me. I must tell Toren—"

"Please, my lady..."

She nearly did relent, but he should know. And though this girl did not, Juliette trusted him to keep her secret. He would never willingly harm her.

"He will help you. Tell him... what is your name?"

The squire blinked, her light brown eyes troubled.

"Never mind. Just please, tell him. Trust him. He does not see women the way many men do. He values my opinion, even in important matters. You can trust him. Will you do that?"

Though she nodded, Juliette was not convinced she'd do so. She would have to consider whether or not to tell Toren herself.

As the squire ran past her, Juliette heard a raised voice coming from the solar, the private room adjacent to the hall. She was sure it was Catrina. She made her way to the solar door, which was opened just a crack, and the raised voices inside drew her closer. That was when she heard another familiar voice.

Toren.

"How could you?" Catrina wailed.

"Lower your voice," Toren said.

Juliette knew she should not be listening to a private conversation between brother and sister—nevertheless, she could not pull herself away.

"I never thought you'd do such a thing. I understand your motives, but I thought you loved her. *Why*?"

Her hostess was clearly infuriated.

"What exactly do you think I've done?"

Juliette heard two voices approach from farther down the hallway. Not wishing to be observed eavesdropping, she began to walk away. The passersby went in another direction, though, and she slowly made her way back toward the door.

Toren laughed, which seemed strange given how angry Catrina sounded.

"You think I killed Hallington."

Juliette didn't move. She didn't breathe.

"But the blood. And you've been gone all day. You were expected *hours* ago. Where is he?"

"He and his men went straight to the kitchen. The blood is from our prey, a spectacular hart of ten that—"

"I don't want to hear about the hunt! Tell me of Juliette's father."

"As I said, the man is fine. They're likely filling their stomachs as I stand here arguing with you. I came straightaway to speak with Jules."

What was happening? Toren? Kill her father?

"So you didn't kill him." Her voice calmer now, Catrina said something Juliette could not hear. Though she suspected it was a sentiment of which Sister Heloise would not approve. "When you didn't return. . . I just thought. Your mission. . . You never told me—"

"Can we speak of this later? I want to find Jules."

That nickname had seemed endearing before. Intimate. Now it sounded cruel and hollow to her ears.

Toren had not been sent to England to speak to her father. He had been sent to kill him.

She ran, not caring where she went. Juliette raced out of the hall and into the courtyard and hid herself in a small crevice in the wall of the manor. The candle she'd grabbed from one of the tables gave off hardly any light, but she didn't care. Juliette knelt onto the ground and clenched her stomach. Tears had begun to form even before she left the manor, and they spilled freely down her cheeks. Her chest hurt. Her hands shook.

She stayed that way for so long, it was a wonder no one came to look for her. Eventually, once her tears began to dry, Juliette allowed herself to more fully consider the conversation she'd overheard.

The Scots bastard. That devil's offspring had been sent to kill her father, and Catrina had worried he'd done so during the hunt. Which meant he'd considered carrying out the mission up until this morning. He had held her, kissed her, and made love to her, all while planning to murder her father.

Who else knows?

Catrina clearly did, which meant Waryn did too. Did Lord Hedford know? Christina? Nay, her friend would never betray her so. Unlike that swine who had pretended to love her while refusing to answer any of her questions. And she'd allowed it. Her father's would-be murderer.

She wanted to kill him.

But unlike him, she was more civilized than that.

She would simply leave. And never return. For she wanted nothing to do with that man. And to think she had nearly told him she loved him.

Ha!

Love *was* a fantasy, and she was finished with fantasies. And dreams. And books.

And most especially finished with Toren.

Juliette stood, wiped the dried tears from her cheeks, and smoothed the front of her ruined gown.

She had to find her father. It was time to go home.

She was gone.

After leaving his sister, Toren had searched the whole manor for Jules. He was happier than he'd been in a long time. The day had gone much better than expected. Hallington was as curt and hardened as he had expected, but Toren had learned from Jules that hunting, especially this kind of hunt, was one of the man's most treasured activities. Toren had used the skills his father had taught him to ensure they felled two handsome harts. This particular type of deer was hallowed as a more prestigious kill, and he'd correctly guessed a successful hunt would put Hallington in a more agreeable mood.

That had seemed incredibly unlikely at the outset of the hunt. Indeed, he had started to think he might have to kill the man after all. But slowly, throughout the day, he'd explained his role and the plan he'd formulated for them both.

Toren was elated that Hallington had finally agreed.

And now the woman whose troth he'd just secured from her father had disappeared into the night.

He hadn't managed to find her anywhere in or around the manor, so he'd looked instead for her father. He'd quickly learned from the groom that both Jules and her father had left, accompanied by the small retinue of men from Chauncy.

In her haste, she hadn't even taken her trunk of belongings.

Now he and Catrina sat in the chamber she'd occupied, Toren holding a discarded garment she'd left behind.

"Why?"

"I don't know."

As they sat in silence, Toren's chest tightened. He couldn't help but remember his search for another woman he had loved.

"Do you remember the morning our mother left?" he asked softly, still looking down at the cloth in his hands. He couldn't quite make himself release it.

Catrina simply looked at him.

He'd never wanted to talk about that day before. Although he'd comforted his younger siblings, as the new chief he'd thought it his duty to show strength, not weakness.

"Aye," she said finally. "Very well. It could have been yesterday rather than eight years ago."

"I was worried most about you," he said.

Catrina moved closer to him and laid her head on his shoulder. She'd done so many times during their childhood, but not very often in recent years.

"I love you, brother."

He took her hand, his eyes blurry.

"And I love you."

Of course he did, but why had he not said those words more often? Why didn't he tell her all the time?

"She's not Mother."

No, she was not.

"I told her father. Everything."

Her head lifted abruptly from his shoulder.

"Everything?"

Toren had wanted the man to know his original purpose for being sent to England before the hunt. Had Hallington chosen to abandon the hunt, leave Bristol, and take Jules with him, Toren would not have blamed him. But the older man had chosen differently. He explained all to his sister.

"He admitted to having skipped the tournament for that very reason—he'd suspected his life would be forfeit to protect the peace. The man's only curiosity was why I'd chosen to share such information."

Catrina waited patiently for him to continue.

"I may not have been forthright about some details. . ."

"Such as taking Juliette's maidenhood?"

It was his turn to be surprised.

"I'm no longer an innocent myself, Toren. And if I had not guessed, I did come upon you at the falls."

The large, black-haired Englishman who looked as if he would devour his sister at any moment was all the evidence he needed to attest to the truth of her words.

"But we did not—" He stopped. They had not been together that day. But they would have if Catrina had not come. It hardly mattered either way.

"Even if I was myself a maid—" she shrugged, "—the looks that passed between you were hard to ignore."

Unwilling to discuss the topic further with his sister, Toren continued, "But once I explained my plan, he was not only in agreement with it, but it was *he* who suggested a union between Jules and I. How anyone could have thought Hallington would have undermined his position, I will never know. Before I could even ask for his daughter's hand in marriage, he was already offering her to me as a 'sign of friendship and peace.' That he was willing to 'sacrifice her to a Scotsman' was evidence, he said, of his devotion to his duty to the borderers."

As he spoke, Catrina's eyes widened.

"You asked him to marry her?"

"Were you not listening? *He* asked *me,* if you can believe such a thing."

"But. . . you were going to ask his permission. To marry? Juliette?"

Catrina was typically quite quick-witted.

"You are surprised?"

"Aye. Nay. Damn, Toren. You were going to marry her."

"What does it matter? She's gone," he said, throwing the garment onto the floor.

"But you have to go after her! She—"

"Nay," he stood. "Never."

He would carry out his plan to placate Douglas without having to actually kill the English warden. But only because it was the right thing to do. The man, though not quite likable, was innocent. He didn't deserve to die—and he wouldn't meet that fate at Toren's hands.

But Toren had effectively sabotaged any chance he'd had with his daughter.

"Toren—"

He narrowed his eyes, and though Catrina likely could not see his expression in the darkened chamber, she must have understood there would be no discussion on this.

She had left him. The reason hardly mattered. Had her father told her by now of their conversation? If so, it had not compelled her to return.

Either way, she wasn't coming back.

And he'd bloody well be damned if he'd look for a woman who didn't want to be found.

22

Juliette had been desperate to leave Bristol immediately, but she hadn't felt up to explaining the truth to her father—not in the same manor where Toren and Catrina and the others were up and about. And a part of her didn't want to... even now.

So she had simply walked into the stable, told the groom that she and her father would need their horses prepared, begged the maid Elise to give her father a message, and left. No one had stopped her even though the hour was late. It turned out that getting into a castle was much more difficult than escaping one.

She jumped at every noise and whipped her head around at every movement, even more scared than the evening she'd made her way to Toren's tent alone. Surely she would emerge unscathed now, just as she had done then. Her father and his men would come.

After what felt like an entire night had passed, Juliette heard the unmistakable sound of horses behind her. Then, finally, men's voices. Taking a deep breath, she stopped and waited for what promised to be a most difficult confrontation.

"Jules?"

Her father never called her that. Only Kelvin and Toren used that name for her. And while his shout was laced with fear, it would surely change to fury soon.

"Aye, Father. I'm here," she called.

Bits of light swayed through the night as the men finally approached her, their lanterns flickering in the dark air. Her father rode ahead of his men. All looked as if they were prepared to do battle.

"What in the name of our Lord and heaven above are you doing out here?"

He was more than a little angry.

"Did you not receive my message?"

The moonlight, though it had aided her on the journey, cast a foreboding glow on the man she'd always slightly feared. Her father appeared every inch the warrior now. His sword drawn, black shadows falling around him, he swayed with the horse who danced impatiently below him.

Quick for such a large man, her father sheathed his sword, dismounted, and pulled her off her own mount before she could formulate another thought.

"What is the meaning of this, Juliette?"

He held her by both arms as one of the men led their horses away.

"Father—"

"Do you know how frightened I was? Riding alone at night, here..."

"I'm sorry, Father. I—"

"What is wrong with you, girl?"

How to answer that particular question?

"I wanted to leave and didn't know another way. As I said in my message, I will marry Lord Wytham and do as you please." Although she would do no such thing. But one shock was enough for the night. "We just could not—"

"Marry Lord Wytham? You are to marry the Scots chief."

Nothing her father could have said would have surprised her more.

"Marry Toren?"

Cold seeped up the back of her neck despite the warm summer night.

"I've given my permission. He led me to believe you would be agreeable. Juliette, I demand to know—"

"He asked for your permission to marry me?"

It made no sense.

"Father, the man was sent to kill you." She hadn't planned on telling her father that, but the turn of events had dictated she must. Especially if he entertained the idea of actually marrying her off to that bastard Scotsman.

"Yet I am still well enough to chase you into the night on this fool's errand, am I not?"

"You're not surprised?" Juliette asked, struggling to understand.

"He told me everything."

Likely not *everything*. But there were some things she'd not say aloud to her father. That she'd given the man her virginity was another fact she'd keep to herself.

"Then you know we met under false pretenses," she said. "I learned just this eve when I overheard a conversation between the chief and his sister. I never knew. Father, I—"

"Juliette."

She hated that tears welled in her eyes and though she willed them back, they would not obey. And for the second time that night, her father wrapped his arms around her. The mail on his chest scratched her cheek, but she didn't care. It was all so confusing. So very heavy.

"Hush."

His tone softened. It hardly sounded like her father at all.

"Daughter." He pulled away and took her hands in his gloved ones. "I have been harsh, mayhap too harsh. But everything I've done has been to keep you and your brother safe. You know your grandfather was a landless baron, and I've fought to earn Chauncy Manor, given my life in dedication to the king to earn his respect and this position. But I fear I may have done so at the expense of your happiness."

"Nay, Father, I know—"

"I don't agree with those nuns often, but they've taught you well. I'm proud of the woman you've become, though I wish you'd bend to my will just once, Juliette. I'm tired of fighting. . . everyone."

She never would have believed it, but the moonlight clearly illuminated a gleam in her father's eyes. He was not perfect, but he was her father. He cared about her, despite his bluster, and she would do anything for him.

But this.

"I cannot marry him, Father. He deceived me."

He didn't say a word. Had she pushed too far?

"He loves you, daughter," he finally said.

"You've never had any use for love in marriage, Father."

She could not believe she said such a thing aloud, but it was true. Before he could respond, she pressed on. "And even if it's true, he does not trust me. The man trusts no one save his family and his clan. I cannot marry a man who doesn't trust me."

She wanted to ask her father so much more. What had Toren told him? What was his plan? For surely he must have one. If he married the daughter of the man he'd been sent to kill, how would he explain his actions? And to whom must he explain them? Who had sent him on such a mission?

Most importantly, why had her father agreed to their marriage?

But if she asked, it would be akin to admitting she cared.

And she most certainly did not.

Toren was dead to her. Every moment they'd been together was a lie.

Without another word, her father turned to the men waiting in the shadows. "Find a clearing off the main road. We make camp here tonight."

He turned to her.

"We will talk in the morning. Come."

He helped her mount once again, and Juliette let out a sigh of relief.

At least they would not be returning to Bristol. For now.

With Catrina's assistance, Toren finished the last of his missives and sat back in the cushioned oak chair that had once belonged to him.

"You've done the right thing here. I'll have these sent right away."

He wasn't so sure.

Catrina's smile encouraged him, but when Toren shifted in his seat, she left him to his discomfort.

He despised asking for help, and they both knew it. He had never expected to rule any differently than his father, who had been notorious for his purposeful lack of allies.

Except that he was different.

And these were different times. It was no longer possible for them to isolate themselves. As a border lord, in order to keep peace, he needed to work together with his neighbors. Including those across the border to the south.

"Toren."

Including this man.

"Bryce."

His brother-in-law sat across from him, extending his legs and crossing his arms as if he expected Toren to speak first.

He would not do it.

They sat in silence for a few moments, but then he remembered the impassioned speech he'd made to his sister. He'd promised he would learn to ask for help. Make allies. And not be quite so stubborn. It was time to prove it.

"So, what do you want?"

Bryce raised his eyebrows. "I must have misunderstood, Kerr." Without smiling, he added, "Catrina mentioned something about you being more open to allies."

"Ones who do not kidnap my sister, aye."

Though he said the words, it was a rote response—there was no malice behind them.

"If you'd not dropped her while making your escape, she would not have been kidnapped."

"I didn't drop—"

Bryce actually had a smile on his face. Of sorts.

"Do you think it will work?" Bryce asked.

"I don't know," he admitted. "MacDuff and Campbell will not be a problem. deSowlis will balk but will likely agree."

"And Douglas?"

"He will be the most difficult to convince. But if the others accept my pledge of loyalty in exchange for their support on this matter, Douglas will be forced to relent."

"And you think he can convince the king to reconsider his plan."

Toren didn't hesitate. "I know he can. If the others agree to rally their kin around Hallington as an innocent victim, he will have no other choice."

"And a pledge of loyalty from Clan Kerr is that important to them?"

"Aye."

Bryce shook his head. "*Sero sed serio.*"

Surprised he knew their clan motto, Toren smiled. "Late but in earnest."

The men fell silent again.

"And the girl?"

"I told your wife—"

"Catrina said nothing to me about Juliette."

Toren didn't believe him.

"I'm keeping Hallington alive because he's innocent. Juliette left of her own accord."

He tried not to think about her. After learning about the message she'd sent to her father through the maid Elise, something Catrina had tried to keep from him, Toren was even more angry. She planned to marry Lord Wytham? After he'd thrown himself on her father's mercy...

He refused to think about it. Standing, he bid Bryce a good day and left to find Catrina to ensure she sent the messenger. With another Day of Truce approaching, swift action was necessary.

But as he walked through the hall, a familiar face greeted him. Or rather, tried to run from him.

"Alfred, wait!"

He caught up to the squire, who appeared quite terrified.

"Please, I—" Alfred whispered.

Without a choice, the boy followed him down the dimly lit hallway. Even though it approached midday, this part of the manor was only lit by the flickering of candles positioned along the walls.

"You've been avoiding me."

He felt neglectful of the lad who he'd promised to keep safe. Although he'd never said those exact words, it was more out of pity than need that he'd asked him to return to Scotland. But if he were going to serve in their household, be trained by Alex and perhaps squire for him, Toren needed to know more.

"No, no, I—"

"Look at me."

Gulping, Alfred finally lifted his head.

"I stand by my decision. You're competent and—" he realized what was likely distressing him, "—and welcome in my household."

The fear in his eyes sliced into him. He'd never intended to scare him.

"Truly. Of course you may come to Brockburg. Though I will need to know more of your background before presenting you to the others."

He began to say something and then snapped his mouth shut.

"In good time, lad. Not today." For some reason, he was scared. Of him. Of revealing anything. There was no need to press the matter.

He nodded and turned to leave. Clearly he was anxious to escape him, so Toren was surprised when he turned back around and blurted out, "She told me you were different. That you valued what she said where others did not. That I could trust you."

It took a moment for Toren to understand what he was saying.

"When did she tell you that?"

Alfred bowed his head once more. "The night she left. I passed by her as you spoke to your sister in the solar."

With that, he did turn around. And run.

He considered running after him, but the lad had been through enough that day. And longer, if his suspicions were correct.

He moved to a bench at the end of the dark hall and sat. Had she overheard Catrina's accusations after the hunt? Toren tried to remember exactly what he'd said to her. He leaned against the cold stone wall and closed his eyes.

She knew. And that was why she had left. And he'd done the exact same thing as her father by not trusting her. But it was not like that. She could have handled the truth. Catrina had been right.

Bollocks!

He'd been a fool not to tell her. Not to trust her. And now she hated him.

But not as much as he hated himself.

23

"Stay here," her father commanded.

Juliette's backside ached, and her head hurt. Virtually every part of her screamed for a rest, but she'd not complained all day. They were going home, and that's what mattered. A stable hand took their horses, and while her father's men circled around the inn, presumably looking for evildoers and other such threats, only one knight remained, though he didn't appear inclined to speak with her.

Her father tended to recruit men like himself—serious, hardworking, and a bit ruthless. She'd become used to them over the years, so it didn't insult her that his man stood just a few feet from her, arms crossed, looking from side to side but never at her.

Dusting off her riding gown—how she wished she could have worn Catrina's breeches, though her father would never have allowed such a thing—she began to walk toward the inn. An arm shot out in front of her, and remembering she had been told to wait, Juliette backed up obediently.

Until she remembered she was a woman grown and not a young girl to be ordered about.

Looking up at the dark-haired knight, she touched her hand to his arm, lowered it, and began to walk toward the entrance once more.

"My lord—"

"Is not here," she said in her most authoritative voice. If Anna Comnena could write a fifteen-volume history in Greek, certainly she could inspect a building without permission.

Holding her head high, she marched forward unencumbered and peered inside the window of the moderately-sized stone building. Apparently this was a popular destination for travelers, for male laughter and calls for more ale filtered through the small window. She could see a barmaid and at least twenty men, some of questionable origins.

"Why must you disobey even the simplest of orders?"

She spun around at the sound of her father's voice. The sun had just begun to set, and since her clothing had never quite dried after being drenched by a light morning rain, she truly hoped they had finished traveling for the day.

"Are we staying here for the night?"

Her father frowned. "Aye, unfortunately."

With no other dwellings on this part of the journey, Juliette knew it was a choice between the inn and staying outdoors. They'd taken a different route from Chauncy to Condren, but there were few options this far north. The inn was located at the crossing of two important and well-worn roads, her father had said. As such, it was nearly as lucrative, though not as well-reputed, as The Wild Boar, the only other inn where she'd lodged in her lifetime.

"I've made arrangements for a room. Unfortunately, they've only one available. The men and I will sleep in the stables. The innkeeper and his wife have assured me you'll be quite safe as long as you stay in your room."

Grateful for a bed, she agreed.

"You will enter through a back door and supper will be

brought to you. Do not venture into the great room. Do you understand?"

"Aye, Father."

And she did. This was not the sort of place one wandered about.

"Lock your door and do not open it for anyone save me or the innkeeper's wife."

She supposed she was meant to follow him, so Juliette did just that. Walking around the building to the back, where the stables were located, she spotted a plump but pretty woman not much older than herself.

The woman wiped her hands on a dirty apron and waved to them.

"Hurry then," she called, her voice deep. She was holding the door open.

With a final glance at her father, who nodded, Juliette entered the inn and nearly gagged at the smell.

"Tallow," the innkeeper's wife said.

Juliette was sorry she'd seen her face. "I meant no disrespect—"

Leading her up a creaking set of stairs, she called back, "I thank you for sayin' so. But I agree with mi'lady. Have been askin' my husband for beeswax candles for years."

She stopped at the end of a hall and opened a door.

"Yer father worries for your safety, but this is safe enough. The other rooms here are used for storage. Just lock yer door anyway. I'll bring yer dinner myself."

The innkeeper's wife stepped aside and allowed her to pass. Juliette hadn't been expecting much, but the room was surprisingly well appointed. Clean though sparse, the bed was much larger than average. Likely it had been inherited. Beds were taken quite seriously, and this was obviously a well-established inn. Some innkeepers were very wealthy, and Juliette guessed the owner was either a merchant himself or a descendent of one who had made a good living despite the hard conditions here in the north. The door closed behind her, and she hurried to lock it.

Hours later, after changing, washing, and eating, Juliette turned around and around in bed, ignoring the noise below. Most of all, she tried not to think of *him*. Because her every thought led back to the one man she refused to consider.

There was one small window, but she had closed the wooden shutters for the evening. It was now completely dark outside, and the only light came from a single candle that cast a flickering glow. She was watching the candlelight, mesmerized, when the innkeeper's wife knocked on her door once again. The woman had returned twice—once with porridge, bread, and cheese, and another with a washbowl which Juliette had relished after two long days on the road.

Juliette discarded the outer bedding, its squirrel fur lining a further clue as to the owner's wealth, and made her way to the door. Her hand on the lock, she waited for the woman to call her name. But there was only silence. Had she imagined the knock?

"Jules, open the door."

Nay! It could not be.

Her hand froze and began to tremble. How was it possible? What was Toren doing here?

He knocked again, and she finally found her voice.

"I have nothing to say to you."

"Then say nothing, but please open the door before I'm caught out here."

What did she care if the traitor were caught outside her door? It would serve him right to be apprehended by her father's men. Although she'd seen him in a swordfight. If someone ended up dead, chances were it would not be her chief.

"Jules. . ."

It was the voice of the man who had come to her at Condren.

That seemed so long ago, but in truth it was not. It was simply that so much had happened since then. Juliette was no longer that naïve girl. She was no longer a maiden.

She unlocked the door.

He must have heard the click of the iron lock because the door flew open and Toren pushed his way inside, immediately closing the door behind him.

"Jules—"

"Nay, Toren, you will not speak first." If she were to endure the presence of this man she'd hoped to never see again, she'd at least say all of the things she'd been thinking these past two days.

He looked quite disheveled, which somehow made him look even more handsome. When he reached up to tame his tousled hair, Juliette became momentarily distracted.

Though she knew this hallway was deserted save for this sole room, Juliette nevertheless scolded him in a hushed tone

"You lied to me. From the first time you admitted to being at Condren to 'speak' with my father to the day you took the most precious gift I had to offer. I risked everything to bring you word of the arrest. My father's knowledge of our relationship, my reputation. . . everything. Aye, you told me we couldn't be together, but I gave myself to you willingly. Do you know why, you despicable man? Because I loved you. Well, if this is love, I want no part of it. No part of you."

She turned, unable to look at him. Luckily, she could not see his face. They were too far away from the solitary candle, something for which Juliette was grateful. She had only to breathe in the scent that was uniquely Toren's to be reminded that this man was her greatest weakness. Even though she wanted to rail at him some more, hate him even, part of her also wished for him to take her in his arms.

She hated that part of her.

He didn't respond. Good! There was nothing more to say.

She could sense his presence behind her. For a moment she thought he'd reach out for her, but he did not.

"You have every reason to hate me, lass," he started. She opened her mouth to tell him to stop, but the part of her that still wanted him demanded that she listen.

"I was wrong. I should have trusted you with the truth sooner. When I learned your identity—you'll remember your family's 'aversion' to using titles—it was too late."

She had forgotten about that. Juliette forced herself not to smile at the memory of her ridiculous statement.

"I was already drawn to you. When I learned you were Hallington's daughter, I did try to stay away. But I couldn't. You are the strongest, kindest, and most beautiful woman I've ever met. And it was as if there was a higher power that kept forcing us together. I was too weak to fight it. But my mission, the reason I was at that tournament. . ."

She didn't want to hear this.

"The king knew of my reputation. No suspicions would be raised by sending his 'champion' to fight. The Scottish warden was an ally of my father's, one of a very small number, and he trusted me. They believed that peace was no longer possible with your father in power. Men were killed because English reivers believed they could bribe their way out of justice."

"And they were right. You saw what happened at Bristol—"

She did turn then.

"My father did not accept bribes."

"It didn't matter whether he accepted them or not."

She attempted to calm her breathing, but Toren stood so close. She could feel him even though they were not touching. The pull toward him was just as he described—it was as if something larger than them were pushing them together.

"Do you not remember the conversation we had on the dance floor after I learned you were at Condren to speak with my father?" she asked.

"I do," he said. "But please hear me out. I've spent every day since my father died trying to protect my family and my clan. To shield them from pain and keep them safe. I trusted no one. Until I met you. I'd never met someone so willing to be themselves in a world that cares more for political alliance than courtly love. You were open and honest, even if it put you at risk of being hurt."

He took her hand, and she let him.

"I realized how much I loved you the night you gave yourself to me, wanting to experience something beautiful even if it would cause you pain. I love you, Jules, and if you can find it in yourself to forgive me, I promise never to utter another lie to you again."

I love you. The words she had wanted to hear more than any other for as long as she could remember. She pulled her hand from his.

"Love is not enough, Toren. I thought it was so important, but 'tis nothing without trust."

He would not be dissuaded, and this time he took both of her hands.

"You're right. Which is why I informed every clan that has ever attempted to ally with Kerr about the situation and asked for their assistance. Begging them to support your father, a man I know to be innocent, in exchange for our help when it's needed."

"That doesn't sound like you, Toren." Indeed, she could hardly believe he'd do such a thing.

"I thought being strong meant not needing help, but I was wrong. You showed me that strength comes from allowing others to see you for who you truly are. Trusting others isn't a sign of weakness, but of strength."

"Trusting others sometimes leads to pain, Toren."

"Oh God, Juliette, I never wanted to hurt you. I promised Christina I'd never do so, but perhaps it was uttered too hastily. I should have said I'd never deliberately hurt you, and I make that same promise now."

She wanted so badly to believe him.

"How did you convince my father that we should wed?" She couldn't help but ask that question.

"I did nothing save tell him the truth. Well, most of the truth. I shared my plan to rally the border clans, making it nigh impossible for the order of his execution to be carried out. I told him that I'd developed an 'affinity' for you, and I believed you felt the same way. It was his idea to align our families. The man really does want to bring peace to the border region."

That, she had already known well enough. "He suggested it?" He'd chosen a Scottish clan chief over the son of one of the most influential English barons in the region? Could he have learned about their relationship? Would he care? But her father had no use for love between a husband and wife, something he'd shown on many occasions.

"And is that why you agreed?" she pressed.

She could feel herself softening. She'd known the moment his hand touched hers that it would be impossible to stay angry at this man she loved with all her heart. But she really needed to know that he meant what he said. That he trusted her.

"What do you think?"

Nay, Toren may have been forced to dabble in border politics by those around him, but that was not what drove him. Love for his family, and for his clan, was what drove this man. And he wanted to make her a part of that family.

Or did he?

"I think you never asked my opinion on the matter," she said.

He pulled her into his arms, tilted her head up, and kissed her softly on the lips. A benediction.

"Lady Juliette Hallington, the only woman I've ever loved, would you do me the honor of becoming my wife?"

"Will you answer one question first?"

"Of course."

"Would you have killed my father had he been at the tournament?"

She could feel his muscles tighten under her fingertips.

"I don't know. I've lain awake many nights since we met trying to answer that very question. With each meeting between us, the answer was less clear. I knew disobeying the king's order would put my clan at risk. But destroying the family of the Englishwoman I'd come to love and adore above all others. Juliette. . . I don't know."

"Thank you for being honest."

She breathed in the scent of him, hardly able to believe he was here. But how had he even found her? Or reached her so quickly?

"Toren, how—"

"I believe you owe me an answer, lass."

She smiled to herself, excited to wield her newfound power and satisfied to be in the arms of the man she loved.

And I plan to give you one.

Toren couldn't believe it.

She pulled him down to her, touching her tongue to his without hesitation, and pressed against him in a manner that could only suggest one thing.

This was her answer.

She had forgiven him! Not only that, his future wife was seducing him.

He didn't stop her from removing every piece of his clothing, and indeed, he divested her of hers just as quickly. Shifting her closer to the candlelight, he looked down at the luscious curves that would be his forever and ran his hands from her shoulders, down her arms, and rested them on her hips.

Toren was fully primed, but he somehow held himself back. He wanted to look at her more, enjoy the sight that was his very own English maiden.

"You're incredible," he said honestly.

Jules smiled, her soft features angelic in the candlelight.

"You aren't difficult to look at yourself," she teased.

He took a step closer, though not so close that they were touching. She sighed when he cupped both breasts in his hands.

"I planned to join the convent."

He laughed, more loudly than he should have. But the thought was absurd.

"If ever a woman were not made for such a calling, it's you." Running his thumbs over the tips that quickly hardened under his touch, he smirked. "As you can see."

He dropped one of his hands to her core, entering her easily, and his smile stretched even wider. "You're wet and ready for me with just that simple touch." He pressed and she swallowed. "You'd not have lasted long under such a vow, Jules."

He moved his fingers in and out, pressing his palm against her as he worked.

"It was the vow of obedience I was most worried about," she said on a gasp.

Toren moved his hand even faster, vastly amused at the idea.

"Then you feared the wrong one."

Quicker still, he moved, willing her to come apart under his fingers.

"I didn't think to see you again." Her voice was barely a whisper.

That thought, along with the need that had been building since they'd last lain together, drove him to pull his hand away and nudge Jules toward the bed. He moved over her and poised himself to claim the woman he loved.

Until he realized she still had not answered him with words.

"Will you have me, Jules?"

She didn't hesitate. "Always."

He did slip inside her then. She was tight and wet. Her hips circled, and he understood her need. He couldn't get close enough, deep enough. By the sounds she made, Toren knew she felt only pleasure, so he let himself go completely. They moved as one, the bed creaking under them.

He lifted himself up and covered her breasts with both hands. Tipping her head back, Jules gave herself to him completely. The sight of her sprawled beneath him, her hips moving in perfect harmony with his own, filled him with peace and joy.

Finally, she was his. And he belonged to her, now and forever.

He thrust into her, his buttocks clenching as she cried out.

With that, he let himself go completely and spilled his seed deep within her. Shuddering, he collapsed, shaken by the intensity of their lovemaking.

"A maiden no more," he said, lifting himself from her.

"Nay," she pulled him back down. He rolled to the side and took her with him, smoothing her hair into place behind her.

"Nay? So you are a virgin still?"

He ran his finger along her smooth white cheek, the candle-light dancing on her perfect face.

"Of course not! I meant nay, don't get up."

"Ahhh. . ."

"But I was not a maiden before this night, as you well know."

"And if you carried my child? How would your Sister Heloise have felt about that, I wonder?"

"Don't you dare laugh at me! It was my decision, and a good one."

He tried not to smile.

"Or it seemed like a good one. Would you have had me marry Wytham instead?"

He shuddered. "I'd have you marry me and none other. For maiden or no, you are mine."

And he was a better man for it.

EPILOGUE

"What do you mean, he's missing?"

Toren and Juliette had stopped at Bristol on their way to Brockburg, and after an overnight stay, they now stood in the courtyard preparing to leave once again. But he refused to leave without Alfred. After being away from home for so long, he was anxious to return.

Toren had never intended to be away so long—the tournament, their first visit to Bristol and then the wedding... Jules's mother had wanted him to return home to put his affairs in order to give them more time to plan a "proper wedding," but he'd respectfully declined.

His bride, more apt every day to voice the thoughts she'd previously kept to herself—although never with him, of course—had a more direct response: "Either we arrange it quickly or your daughter will be the scandal of the north when she runs away to Scotland unwed."

Neither he nor Christina, who had visited them days after their arrival at Chauncy Manor, had been surprised by such a statement. This was the woman he'd fallen in love with. But not the one, it seemed, she'd presented to her family. With the exception of her younger brother, Jules acted much more subdued around her parents and many of the servants.

He'd been eager to get her away from there.

After a quick announcement and mere days of planning, the woman who'd fallen into his arms while running from an ardent admirer at Condren Castle had become his wife.

Toren couldn't be happier.

"We cannot leave without the squire," he said.

"The squire?" His wife walked up from behind them and slipped her hand in his. Toren squeezed it.

"The squire. You know, the one from the tournament. The young lad I planned to bring to Brockburg."

"Nay, young girl," Juliette clarified.

Toren simply stared at her. "Girl?"

Was it possible? A flood of memories came back to him. Her struggle to lift the lance. Her refusal to look him in the eyes. Her modesty as they traveled. Of course.

"But how—?"

Juliette simply smiled. "Although I did wonder how she could have been strong enough to assist with your equipment."

"Apparently women are quite good at some things."

As if to prove him correct, his saucy wife rubbed the palm of his hand in a most suggestive manner.

Perhaps they didn't need to leave just yet.

He'd asked Bryce to search for her and was genuinely concerned she'd not yet been found.

"'Tis not your fault," Jules said.

"What's not your fault?" Bryce asked, joining them.

"The girl," Juliette answered.

Bryce frowned. "I looked for her everywhere. None of the servants have seen her. I searched the village as well."

"Thank you," Toren said. And when Bryce reached out his hand, Toren, though reluctant to release his wife for even a moment, shook it with sincerity. "And thank you for your help with Juliette's father."

Because of Toren's efforts and Bryce's influence, they had received word the day before the wedding that his mission had officially been called off. And though he didn't look forward to a meeting with Douglas, at least an innocent man would live and he and Jules could be together without jeopardizing his clan.

"If you find her, please let me know."

He turned to Jules, who looked at him with a glint in her eye. Suddenly, he was glad he'd traveled to England without a retinue. It would be an interesting journey indeed.

"In the meantime," he said to his sister and her husband, "my wife and I are going home."

ALSO BY CECELIA MECCA

The Ward's Bride: Prequel Novella

English knight Sir Adam Dayne, to keep peace along the border, must accept a betrothal to the Scottish Marcher warden's beautiful daughter. Lady Cora Maxwell hates everything English. When Adam proposes a unique challenge, Cora is forced to face her greatest fears and the burgeoning desire he has awakened.

The Thief's Countess: Book 1

The son of a baron, Sir Geoffrey has been reduced to stealing the resources he needs to reclaim his family legacy. Lady Sara is distraction he resents. With her betrothed coming to claim her hand in marriage and a distant cousin intent on usurping her earldom, the countess feels beset by controlling, unwanted men including the reiver sent to protect her. As the threats continue to mount, Sara must decide what's more important—her duty or her heart.

The Lord's Captive: Book 2

After reclaiming his brother's inheritance, Sir Bryce is faced with an unwanted distraction—the sister of his greatest enemy. Divided loyalties pull the English knight and his Scottish captive, Lady Cora, apart even as passion ignites between the unlikely pair.

BECOME AN INSIDER

The absolute best part of writing is building a relationship with readers. The CM Insider is filled with new release information including exclusive cover reveals and giveaways. Insiders also receive 'Border Bonuses' with behind the scenes chapter upgrades, extended previews of all Border Series books and a copy of *Historical Heartbeats: A Collection of Historical Romance Excerpts* from various authors.

CeceliaMecca.com/Insider

ABOUT THE AUTHOR

Cecelia Mecca is the author of medieval romance, including the Border Series, and sometimes wishes she could be transported back in time to the days of knights and castles. Although the former English teacher's actual home is in Northeast Pennsylvania where she lives with her husband and two children, her online home can be found at CeceliaMecca.com. She would love to hear from you.

Stay in touch:

info@ceceliamecca.com

Made in the USA
Middletown, DE
01 February 2023